A
LONESOME
BLOOD-RED
SUN

A LONESOME BLOOD-RED SUN

A BONE DETECTIVE NOVEL

DAVID PUTNAM

LEVEL
BEST BOOKS

Praise for The Bone Detective Series

A Fearsome Moonlight Black

"A cop's life, whether a rookie or a seasoned detective, is jammed with encounters that are often routine, sometimes disturbing, and all too often life-threateningly dangerous, a grind that takes its toll on personal relationships. *A Fearsome Moonlight Black* pulls back the curtain and takes the reader into that world with in-your-face clarity."—DP Lyle, awardwinning author of the Jake Longly and Cain/Harper thriller series

"In this lean, fast-moving cop-novel, you're riding shotgun as Dave Beckett goes from a raw, idealistic young newbie deputy to a cynical, world-weary veteran homicide detective…in a compelling case that spans a decade. You can't fake the realism that underscores every word and scene in this book. Want to know what it's like to be a trainee deputy on patrol in 1979? Then read this book. You will live it…right alongside Dave Beckett, who discovers what it truly means to wear, and embody, the badge. He craves high adventure but discovers the grit, heart-ache and horror of the streets instead. Joseph Wambaugh said you don't work the job, the job works you…and Beckett makes the hard discovery himself, and you're there with him…every grueling step of the way. You may not have graduated from the sheriff's academy, or patrolled a beat in a squad car, but you'll believe you have after riding the mean streets of San Bernardino County with Dave Beckett."—Lee Goldberg, bestselling author of the Eve Ronin series

"Nobody writes cop stories like David Putnam! He lived the job. Read

A Fearsome Moonlight Black and so will you."—Matt Coyle, author of the bestselling Rick Cahill Crime stories

I

Book 1

Chapter One

Southern California, 1984

The wind muffled the sirens' sorrowful call. In the rearview, back a couple miles, red and blue rotating lights caught my attention. I'd just left the sheriff's station at the end of my shift, headed home. The conga line of cops came from the direction of the station. I pulled to the curb and waited. I was off duty, wearing a sweaty white tee shirt and a pair of hundred-percent-wool uniform pants. My off-duty weapon, a .38 S&W Chief, was stuck in my waistband.

Ahead the dying sun, normally a faded orange egg yolk, now sat on the horizon, blood-red from the season's constant dirt and sand blown up by the wind. The low-level light and forlorn sound made the desert a lonesome place.

On either side of the street clear to the freeway the mixed-use zoning had houses converted into businesses; attorneys, real estate, and construction offices. The result of a town that grew too fast and out-paced the zoning planners. Between the buildings, the open fields were filled with sage and Joshua trees.

The unidentified cop cars grew larger in the rearview and came on at low speed. I rolled down the window to my uninspired Toyota Tercel. I'd bought it used with a hundred and twenty-six thousand miles on the clock. The blue paint pitted in some places, and in others, bare metal gleamed from the blow-sand.

The sirens drew closer.

In another mile the low-speed pursuit came into focus, a dark blue classic Ford Mustang being pursued by three black and white California Highway patrol cars. The driver of the Tang, obviously drunk, couldn't stay in the two westbound lanes. He suddenly drifted over to the far right, rode up on the small dirt berm, and knocked over two mailboxes on wooden posts.

I sat in his path with nowhere to go. *He rear-ends me. I'd at least get a nice insurance settlement. A nicer car. Along with a broken neck.*

The Tang grew larger in the rearview. I turned back in the seat, put my head firmly against the headrest, and held on to the steering wheel.

With only a microsecond to spare, the driver yanked on the wheel and pulled out of a direct hit. He banged off the side, a solid sideswipe. Screeching from the tearing metal filled the air. In the brief moment when both cars joined, the driver looked over and caught my eye.

"Ah, shit."

The moment of impact expanded. Ben Siderites, another off-duty deputy who worked at the same station. He'd worked the shift before mine. He couldn't hold his head upright, his eyelids at half-mast. His smile, cool, calm, a little crooked. He didn't recognize me. No way did Ben know CHP was on his ass. Alcohol had him so anesthetized he wouldn't have cared in any case.

"Ah, man, Ben."

Time caught up to speed. His car continued on. The three CHP cars passed, all the drivers visually checking to see the dumbass sitting in the Tercel. A dumbass who wasn't smart enough to get out of harm's way.

I half-knew one of the cops—sort of—Ken Miller, the others were too new to the highway patrol desert district.

I pulled my car into gear and fell in behind the last CHP. My left front fender rattled and dragged on the tire. I wouldn't make it far.

Ben was headed in the opposite direction to his home. He'd gotten off graveyard shift and sat in The Desert Fox for eight hours nursing double Jacks, neat.

When he crashed into the Tercel, he snapped out of his alcohol-fogged state and made a quick left down an abandoned street. Made the turn in front of an eastbound car on Main that skidded to avoid him. The cops followed with me right on their tail.

He drove another fifty yards and started to make a Y turn to head back the way he came. The highway patrol cut him off front and back, blocking him in. Since he had failed to yield to their red lights, he qualified for a felony car stop. The cops had their doors open, guns drawn, pointed at poor Ben.

The alpha male in the group, a sandy-haired thirty-year-old with green aviator sunglasses, called out the commands. "Turn your car off and toss the keys out the window." Wind buffeted all of us. Sand speckled our skin and stung our faces. Clawed at our eyes.

"Huh?" Ben said, "Hey, Dave, is that you, Dave?"

He didn't care that cops pointed guns at him. He lived in that world where guns were merely tools, like a hammer to a carpenter.

He'd seen me. I had gotten out and moved up behind the CHP officer, making the tactical calls. "I'm a deputy with the SO. He's also a deputy. Come on, ease off him. He's harmless."

"Doesn't matter now. We have to do this by the book."

"Don't be a dick."

"Deputy, take a step back and stay out of this, or you'll find your ass in the can cooling your heels."

Ben got out, staggered, used the car for support. He carried his off-duty pistol in his front waistband in plain view.

Two CHP officers at the same time yelled. "Gun!"

"Hold it. Hold it." I yelled.

I stepped around the officer behind his car door and into the line of fire. I held up my hands. "No one shoot. Sweet Jesus, no one shoot. He's a cop. He's just a drunk cop. Put your guns away."

"Is that you, Dave?" He staggered the rest of the way over, almost falling down. I grabbed the gun in his front waistband.

Once I had the gun, the CHP officers swarmed us. Two grabbed Ben, threw him to the ground, and cuffed him. I tried to intervene, and the guy with "Williams" on his nameplate threw a wristlock on me, cranked it up until pain roiled up my shoulder into my neck.

Ben wore expensive ostrich skin cowboy boots, an older pair he'd worked hard to keep nice. Now, they were scratched and marred from the takedown. Ruined. He wouldn't notice until tomorrow or even the next day. Then he'd wonder how it happened. His face and arms were nut-brown from working in the intense desert sun too long. He'd converted fully to a desert rat, never planning to leave. The desert sun had aged him beyond his thirty-two years. He looked forty or forty-five.

He was a great street cop, fearless. He'd just seen too much his mind couldn't comprehend. Most recently, an ugly murder-suicide that involved three dead cops. A love triangle gone wrong. Ben took the call and was first on scene. I couldn't imagine what that must've looked like. What he thought when he walked in on that ugly blood-filled room. Dead friends on the floor.

The department hadn't done Ben any favors. His mental injury should've been treated the same as a physical one. This was 1984, after all. Law enforcement had progressed from the primitive, one-two-buckle-my-shoe era. Instead, the department pretended like nothing happened. The department had enough problems navigating the bad press with three of their cops killed. A huge public relations black eye.

The two CHP officers dragged Ben over to the lead patrol car, stuffed him in the back, and slammed the door.

I got up into William's face. "You don't wanna do this?"

"It's done."

"You let him go right now, or I swear you'll regret it." I tried to tamp down the anger that continued to rise.

"You interfere anymore, deputy, and I'll take you in for PC 148. It'll end your career."

I pointed over to the cop car. "Let him out, now."

"Or what? What do you think you're gonna do?"

"I'll tell you what I'm gonna do. Your station is situated in the middle of our city. I'll set up in front of your office. I'll ticket every one of you. You want a war, you got it."

"No way would you do that. You'd find yourself in a big jackpot with your brass."

Ken Miller walked over to back down the both of us. He suddenly recognized me. "Ah, shit."

"What?" Williams said.

"It's Dave Beckett."

Williams, his face bloated with red, caught Miller's tone, turned, and looked at him. "I don't care who it is."

Miller folded his arms across his chest. "I would strongly recommend you rethink this. He'll do exactly what he promises to do, and be damned. He doesn't give a shit about what the brass think."

Not true. I cared about my career. It just took a backseat to doing what was right. All I wanted out of my career, what I'd always wanted, was to get to homicide and put the real bad guys in prison. I needed to break out of the patrol rut I was stuck in and get promoted to a station detective job. Then work my way into homicide. A jurisdictional battle would put all that on hold.

I took a deep breath and stepped back. "Hey, Miller, how's it going? Sorry. I didn't mean to make an ass of myself." I lowered my voice to a conspiratorial tone. "Hey, come on, Siderites needs a break. He was first in on that murder-suicide."

Williams's head whipped around to look at me.

I nodded, "Yeah, no shit."

"God damnit. Get that asshole out of the car. Take the cuffs off him." He turned back to me. "You gotta handle the crash involving your car and the mailboxes. I don't want any blowback on any of this."

"I understand, I'll take full responsibility." I stuck out my hand. "You just made a friend. If you ever need anything, and I mean anything, you call me."

Chapter Two

Two days later, after the new shift rotation started, I sat window to window in our sheriff's patrol cars with Ben Siderites. We'd parked in an unnatural dirt turnout at the far edge of the station patrol area. The night's blackness, along with the desert's stillness, had a smothering effect and allowed every little sound to travel a greater distance. The patrol car engines ticked as they cooled. Siderites smoked a Marlboro, one from a two-box-a-day habit. You dressed him right, he could easily be the Marlboro Man. White smoke hung in the cool desert air.

Except during the summer monsoons, it rarely rained in the desert. But a storm had gone through and dumped buckets of moisture. The desert, as dry as it was, still couldn't absorb that much water. Not all at once. In a flash, the arroyos would fill to the brim and rage in a muddy roil. Then, go dry just as quickly as if nothing had happened. The air smelled wonderful, one of the few selling points of working in the high desert. Every rock, Joshua Tree, and sage scrubbed clean and ready for a fresh start.

Neither of us had said a thing since we turned off the cars. Sometimes it wasn't necessary. Brother officers could draw solace just from close proximity. Brothers and sisters in a fraternal order few civilians understood.

Siderites looked almost normal. Sober anyway. The sorrow and emotional pain of what he'd walked into last month, the three dead deputies, hung on him like a silent partner. One that would never leave. He'd take those images to his grave. No job paid enough to deal with that kind of horror, that kind of grief that claimed a chunk of your soul and could leave you an emotional cripple.

Since swing shift started, the radio that dispatched calls non-stop had finally turned quiet. In the vast patrol area, travel to a call sometimes took forty minutes or more. Houses perched in the middle of nowhere on dirt roads that were more trails than thoroughfares made travel difficult with ruts, rocks, and obscured tracks. No street signs or streetlights to guide you. Just your headlights and razor-sharp nerve to keep driving deeper into the dark, hoping you don't get stuck in a drift of blow sand that hadn't been there the last time.

Along with the call, dispatch sometimes gave out unique directions: "Drive six miles and exactly four tenths, turn right, or north. It doesn't look like a road, but turn anyway. Then drive to the tall Joshua Tree that looks like Moses holding up the Ten Commandments, and make a left turn. Then drive to the big rock...."

Many times, halfway through the shift, I'd have to run back to the station and refuel. Then refuel again at EOW, end of watch, so the on-coming deputy had a full tank to start his shift.

The Ford Crown Victoria patrol cars rode like buckboards from the 1800s, the suspension shot. The cars ran twenty-four hours a day under brutal conditions and should have been traded out at eighty thousand miles. Instead, the department has squeezed out every budgetary dollar they could and took the cars to a hundred and fifty thousand, usually more. They kept them until the repair bills surpassed the price of a new car. The decision has nothing to do with deputy safety. Or, God forbid, their comfort. In the end, the broken-down wrecks are not worth the cost to junk them.

The department also still held firm on the antiquated doctrine, "One riot, one deputy." A deputy fights his steering wheel and the elements to get to a call. When he or she gets there, they're alone to deal with the problem. If it turns to shit, backup can be an hour away. All of these factors make a single dispatched call a true adventure. Hot summer nights when the temperature hovers at a hundred at midnight and the constituents have imbibed all day, the excitement ramps up even more.

Siderites finally spoke. "How do you keep up with all the reports? You hand write everything, right? Never understood that with you. I dictate all of mine and I have a hard time keeping the sergeant off my ass for late paper."

"I take them home and turn them in the next day. I hand-write 'em because I'm a control freak. I need to know every word that goes into the report is mine."

"You really don't have a life, do you?"

We sat just off Ranchero Road east of Mariposa at a higher elevation. Down in the valley, the lights from Victorville and Hesperia glittered, a blanket of diamonds in the brisk air purified by the rain.

He said. "I can't take my paper home. I work on my house after shift and on days off." He tossed a cigarette butt out the window and lit another.

"And you say I don't have a life?"

I'd been over to his house. He was over-building for the area in Hesperia. He'd never get comps to support the mansion he was erecting. Doing it all on his own, stick by stick, tile by tile. In decades past, people built sailboats in their backyards, took years doing it, with a recreational retirement in mind. Siderites worked on his house, a fully upgraded mansion, more a hobby to keep his hands busy than a house to flip for a profit. Every bit of his paycheck and overtime went for building supplies. He took his time. It looked beautiful. But at the rate he built, it would be another four years to finish it.

"Hey?" He said. "I…ah…I wanna thank you for what you did for me. I'm gonna pay for the damage to your car."

"Forget it. Those dents give my little Toyota character it didn't have. Like a black eye, a badge of courage."

Headlights came blasting south on Mariposa and took the corner wide, sliding on the black asphalt still wet from the rain. The car almost hit us before the driver got it under control. He shot eastbound on Ranchero Road.

I only caught a glimpse, a blur. The car had unbelievable acceleration, a candy apple red Nissan 300ZX.

Siderites tossed out his freshly lit cigarette, started up his patrol car, and yelled as he stuck it in gear. "I took paper on that car. It was carjacked at gunpoint in front of The Desert Fox." His patrol car slewed sideways. His rear end banged into my rear end.

Perfect. How would we explain that one?

The crooks in the stolen car had brought it down to Ranchero Road to open it up to see what it had under the hood.

I whipped a U-turn and jumped into the chase. Ben called out the pursuit. Our backup was at least thirty minutes away, rolling hot.

Ranchero is a straight shot eastbound clear to Summit Valley Road, fifteen miles away. The beat-up and tired patrol cars took a long stretch before we gained on them. We might not have if the criminal driving it knew how to handle that much power. At a hundred and ten miles an hour, the old Crown Vics shook and rattled. On the edge of total breakdown. The thrill of the chase jacked up my adrenaline and made my eyes pulsate in time with my heartbeat.

Cops were always outgunned and under-equipped. It was a wonder we caught anyone.

The Nissan driver lost control when he drifted to the curb-less asphalt edge. He over-corrected, shot across to the other side, and went off the road into the dirt. The mud shifted his coefficient of friction—the drag factor—and slowed him down twenty or thirty miles per hour. He hit the mailboxes at a hundred mph. He knocked them down like picket fence slats even though the houses sat on two-and-a-half acre lots.

Ben spoke on the radio cool and calm, purely professional, calling out the pursuit.

Until seven miles into the chase, when the Nissan 300ZX again over-corrected and, this time, hit the other side of the road, a muddy berm. The front of the Nissan dug in. The car flipped end over end. Over and over. Three-four times. The spectacular crash spewed car parts and chunks of mud in every direction. The headlights, a kaleidoscope on a stick.

Ben had keyed the mic to talk when the crash occurred and said into the radio, "Shit!" Then, "1181. 1181, single car rollover. Roll paramedics. We're seven miles east of Mariposa on Ranchero Road."

We skidded up and jumped out of our patrol cars, not thinking about a felony car stop but to render aid to the injured driver and passenger.

The car ended its dance sitting upright. The T-sunroof had peeled away, and each time the car tumbled, it gouged mud up into the car. Filled the interior to the window sills. The front and back ends were crunched beyond recognition.

Siderites stood close, both of us stunned.

The car was empty of criminals.

Siderites said, "Fahrvergnugen." An obnoxious automotive ad from television.

His careless statement brought me back to reality, and I realized we stood in the headlights of our patrol cars. Sitting ducks. Perfect silhouette targets. I stepped out of the halo and into the shadows, grabbed onto Ben's arm, and pulled him with me.

I held my flashlight away from my body and checked around the car west of the POR, point of rest, and found two tracks to two suspects who'd somehow not only survived the horrendous crash, but got up, brushed themselves off, and took off running. The only explanation for their escape, they must not have been wearing seat belts and were thrown clear on the first tumble. Catapulted in the air and landing to the side. Had they worn seat belts, the crash would've been fatal for both.

Siderites came up beside me, his light also on the foot impressions. "It's true what they say about stone-cold criminals. In order to kill 'em, you gotta cut their heads off and bury them ten feet from the body. Come on, let's get after 'em."

Chapter Three

I advised dispatch to cancel paramedics and that we were tracking the two suspects across the desert. I also asked that the first responding unit tow the totaled Nissan 300ZX.

The owner, the victim of the carjacking, wasn't going to be happy with the outcome. The car had once been a real beauty with sleek lines. It had a stock paint job to die for and was a feat of engineering. Now, it was nothing more than a beast. A lump of metal and rubber.

Without a moon, our flashlights made a perfect target if the crooks wanted to lie in wait and pick us off.

I said. "I'll track. You stay out of the light halo on the right flank and cover."

"Kiss my ass, Beckett, I'm a better tracker, and you know it. Cover the damn flank."

I turned off my flashlight but stayed right next to Ben. I kept one eye closed to retain my night vision in case they did try to ambush us. We walked, then jogged when the tracks said they were running.

Somewhere in the night, we crossed the invisible line from the county area called Oak Hills into the city of Hesperia. The south part of the city had few houses, and we never got close to one. The tracks led straight north as if these two knew the area.

Every fifteen minutes, dispatch asked for a safety check. The lovely voice of our guardian angel, too loud on the lowest setting. She startled me each time she asked. We crossed empty dirt roads that ran perpendicular to the tracks, and still, the suspects kept going due north.

I wished I'd pulled a 12 gauge from the rack before I left the unit. The longer we tracked, the greater likelihood we'd run into them and encounter a violent confrontation. They had the advantage of picking their killing ground.

Two hours passed. Up ahead, far in the distance, headlights from cars on Main Street zipped along, traveling east and west.

Ben said, "They're going to carjack someone else."

He wasn't wrong. But just after he said it, the tracks veered north, northeast. These guys really did know where they were going. They had to be local and not from one of the gangs in LA who had come to the desert to caper. Those gang members believed the county hick cops acted like Barney Fifes and were not professional enough to catch them. The 15 freeway to Vegas gave them quick off-and-on escape routes. Some stopped to rob and pillage on their way to the vice capital of the world, a faux oasis in another desert.

Fifteen more minutes passed. Ben squatted, turned off his flashlight, and lit a Marlboro.

"What's up?"

He pointed in the dark, my one open eye trying to adjust to the sudden darkness. "They split up right here." He went to hands and knees, then stretched out prone in the dirt. "Look, there they are." He was using the light from the artificial horizon created by the street lights on Main to skyline the crooks. I got down with him. He was right; they had split up. These two were good.

Ben let out a long exhalation of white smoke that smelled sweet after breathing too much clean desert air. He said, "I'll take the one on the left. You go for the one on the right. They're running full out now. We gotta take 'em before they reach Main Street."

"No, we stick together, follow our training. They used a gun in the carjacking, which means they're armed. We stick together, no argument."

He stood, flicked his cigarette into the darkness, and took off running. I stayed with him until his smoker's lungs started to flag his progress. Then I poured it on, leaving him behind.

He yelled, "You asshole."

I ran long distance four days a week, not to stay in shape but to help me sleep. If I didn't, the little girl visited me.

She asked why I let her die. Asked how I ended up in the same slit trench as she did. Eye to eye with plastic over her head. Her cold body against mine, her blue lips parted in an eternal scream, showing teeth and purple tongue. Maybe that was why I had lately bonded so well with Siderites. We'd both experienced freakish emotional sideshows that tried their best to rip loose our souls from muscle and bone.

The lights on Main Street grew larger. I ran without seeing the rabbit.

All of a sudden, he popped into view. He was there all along, but darkness had concealed him. I wouldn't catch up before he made it to the commercial area on the south side of Main, a couple of strip centers separated by a narrow street. Some of the stores were still open, filled with people, cars ripe for the taking, victims who had no idea what was headed their way. An evil we herded right toward them.

I ran full out until my heart pounded, threatening to burst through my chest. Logic dictated that I get on the radio and call in the patrol cars to cut the crook off. To get them set up on Main in those two strip centers, but I hesitated. A hunter of man never wants to give up the take-down, especially after he's tracked for better than five miles in the dark across barren desert. The entire time, dealing with the possibility of an ambush.

Far behind me, Siderites, out of breath, spoke on the radio, doing the right thing, calling in support. Or maybe he was just mad I'd left him in the dust. Left him out of the take-down.

I hadn't left him with any malice. I just didn't want the punk to get away. Sure, that's what it was.

I wore boots, long underwear, body armor, and twenty-seven pounds of gun belt, gun, handcuffs, extra rounds, radio, baton. It was a wonder we ever caught anyone in foot pursuits. My energy flagged as I cut his lead to fifty yards. His running figure still just a shadow.

I yelled, "Hold it, asshole, or I'll shoot."

The suspect's legs leapt forward, not from the threat, but because he didn't know, I'd closed the gap between us.

Behind me, Siderites yelled. "Go get 'em, Dave. You're right on his ass."

I gave it the last bit of gas in the tank and cut his lead down to thirty yards. Just as he made it to the closest strip center. He ran between the anchor, a Kentucky Fried Chicken restaurant that supported lesser stores. The backup units were still three to four minutes out.

I hit the asphalt, my feet grateful for the break from the loose desert soil, and stopped at the building's edge. I drew my gun and jumped around the corner, ready for a confrontation.

Nothing.

Empty space between the two buildings.

I ran to the front, looked up and down the street, and in front of the stores. Breath came so hard, little lights sparkled in my vision. I bent at the waist and put my hands on my knees.

We lost him. How could we have lost him? I didn't even know what he looked like. I couldn't pick a shadow out of a lineup. Damn.

My only hope had been to spot a guy who looked sweat-soaked and breathing hard.

All that stress and strain for what? I chuckled and put my gun away. "For the thrill of the hunt, Dave. What other job would give you that kind of thrill, that kind of chase?"

Now I was talking to myself.

I walked between the buildings to the back. Just as Siderites caught up. His words came out stressed. He didn't have enough air to both talk and remain upright.

"Don't...tell...Me...Please...don't tell me—" He bent at the knees. He put his gun back in his holster. "You let the bastard get away?"

I smiled and shrugged. "You know how it is...You win some, you lose some."

"Son of a bitch, Dave...you gotta be kiddin' me. I saw you. You were right on his ass. You had him."

"Yeah, that's what I thought too. But I turned that corner right there and...and he was gone. Poof."

16

Both of our eyes tracked at the same time to the KFC trash dumpster in between both of the buildings. We simultaneously drew our guns.

Partners who work together didn't have to verbally communicate. We separated and aimed at the steel trash dumpster. I yelled. "We know you're in the dumpster. Come out with your hands up. Show us your hands."

A backup patrol car arrived, headlights filling the space between the buildings, lighting us up. The deputy saw us with our guns drawn, stepped from the patrol car, and racked a shotgun. Her voice came over the air on my belt radio. "Seven Paul One is ten-ninety-seven. We have a suspect at gunpoint."

It'd turn embarrassing if we'd guessed wrong and the dumpster was empty. Siderites yelled, "I'm holding a .357 magnum with hot loads. You don't come out by the count of five. I start pumping rounds into the dumpster. One."

The blond deputy with a pageboy haircut moved up close to me, pointing the shotgun at the trash can, and whispered. "He's not really going to shoot, is he?"

She smelled nice. Perfume on a deputy did something to my libido. I didn't look directly at her and maintained my focus on the task at hand. "Of course, he will. Hesperia deputies don't make spurious claims."

Spurious? I couldn't believe I just used that word.

"Two."

She said to me. "You're Dave Beckett, aren't you?"

"No, his twin brother. Focus here, okay?"

"You don't really think someone is in there, do you?"

"Three."

From inside the dumpster came a muffled yell. "Okay. Okay. Don't shoot. I'm coming out."

The deputy next to me whispered. "Oh, my God, he is in there. You tracked him for two hours and—"

Everyone on the radio had been listening to our progress across the desert, like some kind of 1930s crime program. *The Shadow Knows.*

The metal flap of the dumpster opened a crack.

Siderites yelled. "Hands. Let's see those hands."

The crook, a Hispanic male about thirty-five with tattoos on his face and neck, slowly stood on the trash, lifting the top with his head, his hands out in front of him. He had tattooed teardrops next to his eye, one for every poor victim he'd killed for his gang.

Siderites shoved his gun in his holster and approached, violating protocol. He grabbed the crook by the shirt and jerked him out. He launched into the air and thunked hard on the ground. Siderites kicked him with long, hard strokes, trying to empty a soul that bulged with grief and suppressed feelings.

I re-holstered and grabbed Siderites, pulling him away from the suspect, who writhed on the ground, holding his arm while curled in a ball.

The patrol sergeant appeared out of nowhere. As they tended to do. He yanked the shotgun from the female deputy and said, "Get him cuffed." He got on the radio and asked for medical aid.

I pinned Siderites' arms to his side and whispered. "We had him. Why'd you go off on him? Man, we had him cold. Now you're in the shit again."

Chapter Four

Paramedics strapped the injured crook to the gurney after immobilizing his arm. He knew when to run his mouth. When it was safe. When uninvolved witnesses stood close by to hear. A small crowd had gathered from the businesses still open. "Did anyone see that?" he yelled. "Police brutality. I had my hands in the air. They kicked me. My arm's broken. Someone get their names. Get their God damn badge numbers."

Siderites smiled at that one, said in a half-whisper, "We don't need no stinking badges." A quote from the movie *The Treasure of Sierra Madre*.

"Siderites!" The patrol sergeant yelled.

Siderites said, "Uh oh, time to pay the piper for doing good police work." He hurried over to the sergeant, who pulled him aside and dressed him down.

Afterward, Siderites hurried off with another deputy to shuttle our abandoned cop cars down from Ranchero Road up to Main. Siderites had really done it this time and was in the grease.

The patrol sergeant, Carl Jessup, a long-time narc who'd worked undercover and had recently been promoted, came over and stood next to me, smoking a Mores, a long brown cigarette. They smelled like burning horse shit. He had light brown hair with interspersed gray. He'd made it known that he only wanted to do his time on patrol and get back to working dope. This time, instead of working undercover, he'd be in charge of a whole team. That was if he survived patrol without any major boners from the likes of me and Siderites. He said, "He's your partner. You should've stopped him."

19

I should've protested, said that Siderites jumped the guy before I had the time *to* stop him, but that would be me trying to cover my own ass. When I really needed to help Siderites outta the crack he just stepped into.

I said nothing. I tried to think our way out of this mess.

Jessup said, "Looks like the guy broke his arm when he got tossed out of the trash bin. He's got a black eye, a cut lip, and some teeth missing. He'll look worse tomorrow with all the bruising."

"Sarge, come on, you know Ben. He's a good guy. He's going through a tough time right now."

Jessup took a long pull on his narrow brown piece of horse shit and blew out white smoke. Firemen wear oxygen masks because of smoke inhalation while going into a fire. Cops smoked cigarettes, purposely forcing smoke into their lungs. On a crusade to see who got cancer first. It didn't make sense.

Jessup said, "I heard about what happened the other day with CHP. At some point, Siderites pulls his head outta his ass, or he sinks. You don't want to be on the Titanic when it goes down. The undertow will take you with it. You can bet I'll still be left standing."

"Did you go by the crash down on Ranchero? The G-ride flipped over and over. We were right on his ass, we saw it. That car is trashed." I pointed to the paramedics loading the obstreperous crook into the ambulance fifty feet away. "That guy sustained all of those injuries in the crash. You show anyone photos of that crash and they'll say the guy got off lucky."

"You're a real piece of work, Beckett." He looked around as he thought about it. "Okay. This is the last time. If I put my ass on the line, you have to get Siderites into rehab. And I mean tomorrow."

"Okay. Yeah, sure. I can do that. Sarge, you won't regret this."

"Jimmie Poe was here too. She saw the whole thing. You also gotta square it with her. If you do those two things, then, *I didn't see a thing. This time only.* Siderites screws up again. I'll rack him up." He turned and walked away as he yelled. "Poe?"

"Yeah, Sarge?" She'd been standing by the ambulance and hurried over. Jessup kept walking and hooked his thumb over his shoulder, "Beckett needs to talk to you about something." He got in his sergeant's car, a brand-new Crown Victoria with smooth cushy suspension, and drove off.

"What's up?" Deputy Poe said as she sauntered over. Her thumbs were hooked in her gun belt like some kind of veteran dep. She couldn't have that much time on the streets, or I would've heard of her. But deputies came and went with not too much fanfare. Or maybe I was just too busy doing my own thing to pay attention.

Poe was assigned out of the Victor Valley station in Victorville, and I worked Hesperia station. Even so, our paths should've crossed while booking in the jail or at training. I would've remembered her. After thinking about it, I did remember hearing her voice on the radio and wondering who it belonged to.

Poe had an almost casual beauty. Nothing that stood out. She did have a quiet kind of feminine presence.

She stood two feet away, a little close, and smiled. Her entire persona transformed her into someone you wanted to like. Someone you wanted to hang around with. She had a couple of killer dimples and brown eyes like my Beth's. Dimples that pleaded for more attention.

"Hey, ah—"

"What?" She lost her smile.

Words tangled and fought to get out. "My pal Ben's in the grease—"

"Yeah? If he is, I sure didn't see anything that would cause it."

I let out a long sigh. "You're all right, Poe. Is your name really Jimmie?"

She squirmed a little, looked around as if about to reveal a big secret. She lowered her voice. "I don't like it to get around. Some people know. Not many. My real name is Judith. Can you imagine a patrol deputy named Judith?"

I smiled, couldn't help it. "You mean like, 'Hey, Jude?' in the Beatles song?"

She shoved me. "Exactly. I thought you were different. I go and tell you a deep, dark secret, and you immediately take it out for a walk and laugh at me."

"My lips are sealed. And for the record, I didn't laugh. That was a smirk."

"No. It's still not fair. You have to tell me your worst secret. Then we'll be even."

I lost my smile as a dark cloud blew in, shading the already dark night. Even if it was only in my mind. The image of the little girl in the slit trench, me lying next to her, our faces inches apart. While the suspect tossed dirt on top of us. I shuddered and shook it off.

I needed a pint of Old Granddad whiskey to tamp down that horrible feeling. It was going to be a bad night. The bad nights came further and further apart. I was healing emotionally. My brain was taking its sweet time about it. Adrenaline-fueled nights tended to bring them back.

She was joking. Some unlucky cops carried around enough baggage to sink Jessup's Titanic. And maybe she'd been lucky enough to avoid walking in on scenes with three dead deputies who lay slaughtered on the floor. Or little dead girls in slit trenches.

She put her warm hand on my arm. She'd read my expression. "I'm sorry, I didn't mean anything by it."

"It's okay."

I yearned for the touch of a woman more than I realized. She took her hand away too soon. After my brutal divorce, I hadn't ventured out into the dating world. I loved my wife too much. Being a romantic fool, I thought she might eventually cool off. That she'd let me come around again. Maybe work my way back. If I started dating, somehow, that felt like a betrayal. I understood why Beth had left. Under the circumstances, who wouldn't?

"Hey...ah...you want to get a drink after shift?" The words had slipped out before I could pull them back.

"I'm sorry, I have a personal policy. I don't date the people I work with."

"I understand. That's a good personal policy." And I did understand. How could you have an emotional relationship and do the job on the street without getting someone killed?

Of course, she was right.

But the smartassed Beckett shoved the disciplined and conscientious Beckett out of the way. The Beckett that was always there standing in the wings, ready with a quip to toss on the fire like gasoline. "I can fix that."

"You can do what?" Her nose crinkled in the cutest way when she said it.

"Sure. I'll write a memo on department letterhead and resign. I'll sign it, and you can hold it until we're done having that drink."

Her mouth dropped open. I gave her my biggest smile. The moment hung, fat and sassy between us. At least, I thought it did.

She turned and walked away, shaking her head.

I could track an armed and dangerous crook five miles across the desert on a moonless night, but for the life of me, I couldn't figure out how to talk to women without stepping on my tongue.

Chapter Five

A week later, Dad jabbed me with his spit-shined shoe. I rolled over on the cot in his back room where he stored all his dry goods supplies for The Hobo Cafe.

"Wakey. Wakey."

"Come on." I kicked at his shoe, which smelled like road kill from standing on the diner's duckboards. No matter how hard he cleaned and polished them, they still smelled until he'd break down and order new ones. He wore the same black shoes every morning while he cooked breakfast, and though he kept everything spic and span, fry grease permeated his shoe leather and turned rancid. Yuck.

"I said not to wake me before ten. I get off late, Dad."

He stood next to my cot, smoking an unfiltered Camel. He always pinched the end where he held it. He'd rolled his own Bugle Boy tobacco while in the joint and couldn't get out of the habit. He wore white pants and a shirt with a full-length red apron covered with smears of lard, flour, and bits of potato. His hair had long ago gone past gray and was now stark white. But was still thick, almost lush in a military flattop. Old ink navy tattoos littered his arms. A salacious woman wearing a one-piece swimsuit, hands on hips, hip cocked. An anchor. And "Subic Bay" and "Guam." In his youth, he was a cook on the USS Delbert D.

He held a thick-bladed butcher knife and waved it. "I know that Junior G-man, but your station called and said you're needed in there, A…S…A…P. Back in the day, we called it PEE…DEE…Q." He put the hand with the knife up to his mouth as he let loose a long coughing jag. Lucky he didn't cut his

24

nose off. His eyes turned bloodshot and watery. He said, "Now get your ass up, you're sleeping your life away."

He didn't need much sleep. How did he do it? He got up at three-thirty in the morning seven days a week to start his breakfast prep. He opened at five and worked his ass off as a short-order cook until noon. He had one dishwasher and two wait staff. Then he closed up and cleaned while a case of Old Milwaukee beer sat chilling in the large stainless-steel ice maker. At four o'clock on the dot, he started drinking. He didn't stop until the entire case of empty cans sat, willy-nilly, on the table in the red vinyl booth. He always sat in the same booth, smoking his hand-rolled Bugle Boy cigarette, drinking Old Milwaukee, and doing the crossword puzzle. He'd look up to watch the cars bathed in moonlight go by on Foothill Boulevard, the old Route 66. He stared out the window as if in deep contemplation about world problems and how to solve them. We never talked at length. While I was growing up, he was a fifteen-year resident of The Q for a crime of violence. I only recently reconnected with him.

Around eleven every night, he curled up in the booth and slept. He always got up without an alarm. His routine only varied when he had to venture into the world to take care of business, banking, and the like. After fifteen years locked up in a six by eight cell, he couldn't adjust to his freedom and preferred the enclosure The Hobo afforded.

He drove a 1973 Ford Pinto that no longer had a reverse gear. To back up the Pinto, Dad stuck his left leg out the car door and pushed. The small car was more like a kid's go-cart.

In his morning routine, the first thing he started with was a washcloth bath. He'd stand at the same sink the dishes were washed and wipe himself down. Head to toe. Said that was the way they did it on the USS Delbert D. I truly wanted to believe him, but my cop instinct wouldn't allow it. A better explanation was that he didn't want to shower with Gen Pop during his stint in San Quintin and instead cleaned up in his cell sink.

On those mornings at the sink, he wore just his tidy-whitie underwear. Something a son should never have to see. The first time I saw him like this, I noticed how much bigger his left leg was in comparison to the emaciated right. At first, I thought him infirm. I was about to say something but realized it was due to the Ford Pinto's broken reverse gear.

I said, "Did they say why they want me in early?"

He was walking back to his stove, his grill piled high with diced potatoes, eggs, pancakes, sizzling sausages—patty and link—and strip beef steaks. Breakfast already in full swing at the Hobo.

"None of my business. Didn't ask 'em."

"Thanks, Dad." And I meant it. He let me crash in his café. I gave more of my salary than the judge ordered to my wife, Beth, and our daughter. I didn't want them to go without. And by no stretch of the imagination was Beth a spendthrift. Sure, I was bitter about the situation, but that didn't mean my daughter needed to suffer over our failed relationship.

He raised his hand over his head, walking away, and waved the knife. "No problem."

No way did I want to drag my tired ass into work early to find that the summons was no big deal. I'd then have to sit around without pay and wait for my shift to start. I already dedicated too much of my life to the cause.

I used to work at Central Station down in the Valley, but I couldn't keep my mouth to myself. Sometimes, I thought maybe it had a mind of its own. The way it tended to blurt out at the most inopportune times. Mostly my fault, but the brass carried some of that load as well. I caught a midnight transfer to the desert in what was called "Freeway Therapy." Instead of a fifteen-minute drive to Central, I now had an hour drive to Hesperia. That was without traffic.

Dad didn't want to pay for a phone line in The Hobo, so he had a payphone installed. I struggled to my feet, hair mussed, sleep in my eyes, and shuffle-stepped to the restaurant seating area. I still wore my uniform pants and tee shirt from the day before.

Darla, the waitress, a friendly old crone with too many wrinkles and bright red lipstick, truly a nice gal, said, "Hey, Dave?"

"Morning, Darla."

Some of the Hobo regulars said, "Hi." I nodded and waved. I picked up the receiver to the payphone, dropped in the last quarter I had in my pocket, and dialed the Eagle's Nest. The nickname for the high desert dispatch center. I asked for the supervisor and got Sam, a call intake gal who said the lieutenant from the Victor Valley station was looking for me. She quoted Lieutenant Wes Cordova, "Call Beckett and tell him to get his sorry ass in here now."

I thanked Sam and hung up. I stood staring at the wall for a long moment. My lieutenant from Hesperia station could order me in. But could a lieutenant from another station? And what could he possibly want with me? Cordova wasn't one of my favorite people. I worked for him when he was a sergeant in the jail. We by no means saw eye to eye. He never yielded on policy, and I liked to play it fast and loose if it meant everyone got along and nobody got hurt. You treat a crook decent, like a human, and the jail ran a lot better. To Cordova, the inmates were nothing more than cattle. His full name was Wesley, "Wes." He was Caucasian. His stepfather adopted him, giving him the surname Cordova.

I looked around, shrugged and sat down in a recently vacated spot at the counter. Darla poured me a cup of Black Joe. That's what Dad insisted we call it. Navy coffee brewed strong with eggshells to take away the acrid aftertaste. He frowned when anyone ruined it with sugar and cream. "You want graham crackers to go with that sissy concoction?" That's why we tried to keep him corralled in the back, supervising no one but his grill.

I had to admit a cup of Black Joe in the morning got me off to a good start. Dad came over and set a platter in front of me: four runny eggs, rye toast, sausages, and sausage patties, two wheat pancakes, and a large dollop of grits. The thought of food caused my stomach to roil. I stifled a Black Joe burp. If I walked away without eating, I'd hear about it for a week and a half, the length of his memory. I'd tested it before just to see.

I rolled the eggs into the pancakes, dumped some syrup on the pile, and mashed it up with the grits. He wouldn't be able to see how much I ate. Twenty-eight years old, and I still had to act like a child in front of Dad.

Three uniformed Sheriff's deputies from Rancho Cucamonga station came in to eat. Dad didn't like cops. Cops put him in San Q. for fifteen years. He admitted to the crime because that was the way he was wired. He just didn't like the beast that bit him. The bureaucracy that enforced societal rules, that said he couldn't defend himself with a knife. He put up with the deps because I insisted. I also insisted that they ate not just HO, half-off, but entirely on the cuff. Darla loved it because they always left big tips.

All three of them walked by the counter on the way to the booth. All three patted me on the shoulder, "Hey, Dave." I was a minor celebrity over the OIS, officer-involved shooting. The one where six years earlier, I was in the slit trench next to the little girl, with the suspect throwing dirt on top of us. I came to after being hit in the face with a shovel. And while being buried alive, I pulled my backup ankle-carry pistol and shot the suspect five times.

I didn't consider myself a hero.

The crook got away and was still on the loose. Because of my failed marksmanship, the little girl continued to follow me around in my nightmares, asking me, "Why?" The department shrink said the girl would continue to harangue me until I found closure with what had happened. Closure? I asked. "Like finding and shooting dead the asshole who'd perpetrated the heinous crime."

That's why I worked so hard to get to homicide. I wanted to reopen the case that had gone cold, track the bastard down.

I shoved the platter away. I got up, went to the back. I picked up my gym bag and drove to the gym to push some weights around and take a shower.

Cordova could wait.

Chapter Six

Three hours after Dad woke me to say the department called, I parked in the Victor Valley County station parking lot dressed in civilian attire. I trailed a uniformed deputy in the backdoor. I didn't have a card key entry. The deputy didn't follow protocol to "confront and inquire." Maybe he knew me, and I didn't know him. Not likely. Deputies tended to act according to their leadership.

I walked down the hall past the empty captain's secretary's desk and the captain's office. His door stood open. He sat at his desk, his feet up reading the Los Angeles Times. Tough job. He was a good Joe, though. He had been the DI at my academy class and had since been promoted three times while I still stood at the starting gate.

I continued on down to the Lieutenant's office and knocked on the door frame. Wes Cordova sat behind his desk working on shift schedules, the bane of all lieutenants. Lieutenants had to work around everyone's special requests and the department mandate that all deputies work one full three-month rotation on every shift in a one-year period. Which meant everyone took a turn at the hated graveyard shift. Grumblings on the department grapevine were that when it came to scheduling, Cordova was an asshole. He ignored all special requests and strictly plugged the deputies into slots according to the mandate. This cut his difficulty in half. He chose to make his job easier rather than put the work in and make, or at least try to make, the deputies who worked for him happy.

The bars on his collar weighed him down and over-inflated his head, the worst kind of leader and dangerous to deal with.

I again knocked on the door frame, louder this time. He looked up, his expression neutral until he recognized me and scowled. "Beckett, get in here and close the door." His tone dripped with antipathy. I closed the door, came in, and sat in one of the two chairs in front of his desk. He had the smallest office in the station.

He glared at me, trying to heat up the space between us. I didn't squirm. I wasn't afraid of him and should've been.

He wasn't my lieutenant.

"I didn't say you could sit."

I continued to glare at him and remained seated. I wasn't violating policy other than following a direct order. No way could he bring me up before a board for not standing when ordered. He'd look like a buffoon. And my guess was the Office of The Sheriff already had Cordova's number when it came to his buffoonery.

Cordova had a long face and a narrow chin. He wore his brown manicured mustache an inch below his upper lip, a half inch out of policy. Was he trying for reckless and bold? Not likely.

His right ear was pierced sans any accoutrement. A leftover from his time working narcotics. He kept his hair short, no sideburns.

Rumor had it that he had a tattoo of his wife's name on his chest with a kiss in red lipstick.

He, too, continued to glare, waiting for me to stand. I needed some damage control.

"I apologize if I did something to upset you, Lieutenant." Still nothing. "I really don't know why I'm here."

His jaw muscle worked as he ground his teeth. I'd somehow gotten on his bad side and didn't know how. I worked for another station, so what did it matter?

He finally broke his calculated attempt to make me squirm. Even though I understood his game, to some degree, he still accomplished his goal. I wanted into homicide, and he could load up my jacket with "Ah, shits."

"The reason you're here right now committing insubordination by sitting instead of standing in front of my desk is based on our involvement with

Deputy Ben Siderites."

I muttered under my breath, but not low enough. "Ah, shit."

I said out loud, "That guy sustained all his injuries in the crash. The car rolled multiple times. Go look at it in the impound yard."

"What? Who?"

I'd violated the first rule of interrogation: never volunteer information. "I'm sorry, what?"

"What are *you* talking about?"

I shrugged and kept mum.

He waited again to see if I'd compound my error. Now, I did start to squirm. That pursuit had started in the county area, which was Cordova's station jurisdiction. He had every right to look into it even though it involved two Hesperia deps.

He knew about Siderites.

He got up from his chair, came around his desk, and leaned against it. Far too close to me for comfort. Another calculated move.

I recognized his Calvin Klein cologne that he'd over-doused himself with. My daughter, via her mother, had given me some for Christmas. I threw away the cologne and, for the rest of my life, would cherish the hand-drawn Christmas card in Crayola depicting a Christmas tree covered in multi-colored bulbs and me in uniform with a large yellow star on my chest, holding my daughter's hand.

Cordova finally said, "You interceded in the arrest of Deputy Siderites for hit and run and drunk driving."

I let out a long sigh. Cordova couldn't get either one of us on that incident. Everything had been smoothed over. The mailboxes were replaced. And Siderites' blood alcohol would have had to have been taken at the time of the crash. Cordova had nothing except rumor.

"Why are you interested in something that happened in Hesperia? You're the county lieutenant.?"

"Don't you dare tell me what I can and cannot do. We are all deputies under the sheriff. And you have no authority whatsoever to question my inquiries." He turned on a tape recorder. "Now tell me what happened when you interceded in the CHP pursuit. Saturday last at fifteen thirty-eight in the afternoon."

"Sure, no problem." *Saturday last*, the pompous ass. He knew his interview would be read by the office of the sheriff. He was trying to show off. But doing it to the detriment of a good deputy.

He grinned at my sudden acquiescence.

"I don't know about any pursuit. But I *was* driving home from work and spotted a car pulled to the side of the road. Being a good deputy, I stopped to render assistance and found Deputy Siderites out of gas."

Cordova jumped forward and switched off the tape recorder. His jaw muscle had gone back to knitting. His overt anger tell. He'd never worked homicide or even any detective bureau, for that matter. He came up through administration jobs in the office of the sheriff. After a short stint working patrol at Yucaipa, a Sleepy Hollow station, he was transferred to narcotics for his Spanish-speaking capabilities and value in undercover work. He stayed there too many years. Then, he started his meteoric rise in the department. He was transferred from narcotics to headquarters, where he worked the Bureau of Administration, Public Relations, Internal Affairs and then was promoted to work as a supervisor in dispatch. He had no idea what it was like working the field and hence didn't know how to interview, or worse, interrogate.

Everyone knew his history. The rumors flew when he first transferred to the desert station. A copy of his career history floated around. A disgruntled deputy had made copies and put them in everyone's mailbox. Rumor was that Cordova had been sent to Victor Valley station for some "station time" before being promoted to captain and given his own command.

After Cordova had time to think about his strategy, he turned the tape recorder back on. "Deputy Beckett, I'm ordering you to tell me what happened when you intervened in the CHP investigation."

"Oh, I see."

He sat back, smug.

"You're right, CHP did stop to see if we had a problem. But I told them I could handle it—you know, putting gas in Ben's car—and they left.

32

Lieutenant Cordo*ba*, are you headhunting deputy Siderites? Because I really can't see any reason why you'd want to know about such a harmless incident that occurred off-duty outside your station area. It just doesn't make sense."

He boiled over, his face turning red. "It's Lieutenant Cordova, 'va,' not Cordo*ba*. And you will not speak down to me unless you want to be working graveyard in the desert for the rest of your career.

I stood to leave. "Beckett's spelled with two t's."

I turned and left.

I girded myself for him to call me back. Yell an order through his open door for all to hear and witness. He didn't. He probably figured out I was holding all the cards. This time.

This time.

He'd be all over me now, watching and waiting. Without any evidence or witnesses to Ben's hit and run and drunk driving, his only hope had been to flip me. Get me to spill my guts over what had happened. I had to find out why he was gunning for Siderites.

And now me.

Chapter Seven

C ordova going after Ben and now me was like putting a pot on the stove and watching a long, slow boil, the bubbles starting out small and growing larger and larger by the minute. I walked along the corridor headed to the officer's counter, intent on calling Ben and telling him what happened. Warn him about what was coming his way. But by the time I got there, anger had taken over and now controlled the ship headed for the rocks. Uncontrolled anger, another one of my shortcomings I'd been trying to work on. Only it was like an unsated sweet tooth that had to be fed five chocolate bars. I sat down at a computer CRT assigned for the field deputies to use. The system was common in every station. I took out my wallet and withdrew a crumpled business card from deputy Ross Clark who'd left the department after getting his degree in accounting and going to work for the FBI. Lucky him.

On the back of the business card, he'd left me his password and department ID number to get in the system. He told me to use it. "Wreak havoc in all the wrong places."

He knew me too well. I didn't want to use my own password for this felony. I was saving the card for something special, and this little dust-up fit the criteria.

I switched to a Department of Motor Vehicles computer mask and typed in Lieutenant Cordova's name and date of birth. I held my breath. One day soon the IT department would find their error and shut down the defunct Ross Clark account.

The machine burped out Cordova's driver's license number. I memorized it, not wanting to put it to paper. I shut the machine down.

I got up and casually looked around to see if anyone had noticed me. I was a Hesperia dep, after all.

Next, I made my way to the officers' counter, and next to it the wall with myriad boxes containing all the report forms. Sixty-six at last count. Forms deputies used in their everyday travels to keep the streets safe from those who would cause deceit and tyranny and injury. Do it for no better reason than to fulfill some misplaced primal urge. The six percent of the populace that should be segregated from the socially acceptable. What I had in mind would yet again lump me into that very same six percent.

I stood at the officers' counter filling out a D-1035 DMV form, the one that deputies used to order a driver too old or infirm to continue driving safely on the public streets. Ordered the driver back to the DMV for reevaluation and a physical driver's test.

I'd worked the streets long enough and had investigated enough forgery cases to know how to circumvent the system, and filled the form out, writing left-handed. I purposely misspelled Cordova's name, spelled it Cordoba so he'd know who had done him wrong. He had to learn you don't poke the bear without consequences. I used Ross Clark's name and ID number at the bottom of the report where I signed under threat of perjury. I wasn't afraid of fingerprints. The form was going to the DMV, they would keep it. I folded the form, put it in an envelope, addressed and mailed it. You'd think I'd have hesitated before dropping it in the mail basket.

I didn't.

You don't go after my pal Ben and not expect repercussions from his partner. That was the way of the jungle.

When I finished, I looked around and realized my visit had happened just the way I suspected it might. Now, I had dead time until the patrol shift started. Idle hands are the devil's workshop.

I decided to drive down to Hesperia station, put my uniform on, and go out early to hunt criminals. That way I wouldn't be chained to calls for service. I wasn't getting paid for the extra time.

I walked out the backdoor and headed across the parking lot. An old beat-up patrol car, an all-white Crown Vic with a blue slash next to the gold sheriff's star on the door, pulled up and stopped.

Jimmie Poe.

The friendly blond from the other night behind the KFC who had a policy about not dating fellow deps.

Her window was down, her elbow casually protruding. I walked up. "Hey?"

"What are you doing at my station?"

"Getting chewed out by your lieutenant. I guess he doesn't have enough of his own deputies to pick on. He has to call in Hesperia guys to fill his quota."

She didn't chuckle or even smirk.

I came closer. "You okay?"

Her skin was creamy, soft, and unblemished. If she stayed in the desert much longer, that would change. She'd quickly age beyond her years.

"It's nothing. I just caught a bad case. No big deal. It happens."

I squatted in front of her window, so she could look down instead into the sun. "What kinda case?"

"A rape."

I cringed. The only two cases I hated to take were rapes and anything to do with children. I couldn't handle those investigations. They were soul-crushing and then when I did have a suspect in the interview room, I couldn't talk to them. All I wanted to do was bash in their heads.

The department policy was that whenever possible, a female deputy was to investigate rape calls. I understood why, but it still wasn't fair. The women deps caught the worst calls because of it.

"Can I help?"

"Really?" She stuck the car in park right there on the thoroughfare to the parking lot and got out. "You really don't want to get involved in this one, it's a stinker. I mean, a real stinker. I was just on my way in to brief the lieutenant and the detectives."

"Cordoba?"

"It's Cordova. Don't let him hear you make that mistake. You'll make an enemy for life."

"Oh, really?"

"Yeah, no kidding."

"Tell me about the case."

"This one's a code 20, for sure, a sensational crime the press will get ahold of, and it might even go national. No, it will go national. I'd really, really like to catch this asshole, Nico Sumter."

"You have a named suspect?"

"Yeah, and like I said, I wanna be the one to put the hooks on him."

She paused. "Besides this guy being a grade-A asshole and needing to be thrown in the joint for life, I'm trying to get promoted to the detective bureau, and this is one of those career-making cases."

"Yeah, don't we all. I'm trying to get in the detective bureau at my station. That name, for some reason, sounds familiar."

Another patrol car came into the thoroughfare and honked, wanting to get around Jimmie Poe's car.

She pointed to the dirt field that adjoined the sheriff's parking area. "Meet me over there." She didn't wait for an answer, jumped in her cop car, and took off. I turned and headed to the dirt field.

Chapter Eight

The back of the sheriff's station sat right up against the 15 freeway to the west. The large empty dirt field to the north was a space in between the station and the Roy Rogers Museum, an old-time TV and movie cowboy popular in the fifties and sixties. The museum put on display all his old memorabilia, including his clothes, all his guns, and his stuffed horse Trigger. On the other side of the museum, out of view of the station, there stood a sculptured mock-up of the same horse. Only this horse was up on his hind legs pawing the air with his front hooves, a depiction of a proud, valiant steed that could be seen from the southbound 15 freeway traffic and an ad for the museum.

Under Trigger was also where the county deps drank after swing shift. If that stupid rearing horse could talk, he'd tell some great stories of debauchery, drunken mischievous acts, and, of course, sex. Lots of sex. The horse could also tell of ADs, accidental discharges, both kinds, one being with duty weapons.

The field in between the station and museum had been there forever and had its own stories to tell. One night, according to legend, a deputy brought into the station an old World War II pineapple hand grenade. The question was its authenticity. The watch sergeant, a crusty old throw-back from the Korean War, didn't freak out like most would have nowadays. He also didn't call Arson/Bomb. Instead, he took the grenade from the deputy, stepped into the back parking lot, pulled the pin, and tossed it into the open vacant field. The grenade wasn't so old after all and exploded, peppering the cars and the station with rocks and bits of sand. Luckily, no one was hit by shrapnel. The sergeant, laughing, looked at the deputy who brought it in, "*God Damn*, that was really something, wasn't it?"

The deputy nodded. "But now, what am I going to do for my case? You just blew up my evidence. I got a suspect back in the jail for possession of an explosive device."

* * *

Jimmie Poe pulled into the dirt field, stopped, got out, crossed her arms, and leaned against her cop car while she waited for me to catch up.

I wore an old long-sleeved flannel shirt and denim pants. Comfortable clothes, and now I wished I'd worn something better. Not that I had any nicer clothes.

I stopped in front of her. She'd put on a 10-30 (the code for out-of-policy radio traffic used in every instance of out-of-policy activity) ball cap with the sheriff's shoulder patch sewn on the front. Some station commanders turned a blind eye to the caps because the only department-approved hat was the military green campaign hat that looked ridiculous. Made everyone who wore it look like a park ranger out chasing down Yogi Bear and Boo Boo for stealing picnic baskets.

Jimmie Poe had pulled her ponytail through the back loop; it did something to her personality. In some way, it made her playful.

Or that might've just been me.

I said, "Tell me."

"You know the name Nico Sumter because four years ago he stalked and then raped Jessica Purdue, who was a high school senior at the time. Sumter was convicted, got fifteen years. He hired a high-dollar mouthpiece who got his sentence reduced to six years. He was released early last week for "good and work time." Can you believe it. I can't. We've got a broken system."

She talked like a veteran cop, and she couldn't have more than a year on the street.

"I'm guessing another state penal rehabilitation success story."

Jimmie Poe eyed me, then kept talking. "Today, someone wearing a black ski mask grabbed Jessica Purdue, pulled her into a van and raped her. He kept her for three hours and raped her again. I can't imagine a worse nightmare. It makes me sick to think about it. The woman is ruined emotionally. It'll stay with her forever. That bastard needs to be drug out to a scaffold and hung in public."

"Take it easy. I don't disagree, but you need to go by the book, or the whole case will get tossed out."

"I'm supposed to turn this over to the detectives. They're waiting for me right now to brief them. I do that, and I'm out of it. And our detectives couldn't clear a case if their lives depended on it."

She was right about that. One of the detectives at the station had been involved in the murder-suicide. The county detective bureau had yet to recover. The department needed to transfer everyone, get them away from the bad memories, and start all over with a new crew. Otherwise, the bureau would continue to be a dysfunctional mess.

"When you interviewed her, was there anything she said that points to this Nico Sumter?"

"Nothing, not one damn thing. He didn't speak or show any skin. She couldn't even tell me his race. He wore long sleeves and gloves. He's going to get away with it. He planned it too well. She's a mess. She can't remember any details."

"Yeah, you're right about the code twenty. This will go national for sure. And the department's going to get slapped with a big fat lawsuit for failure to protect. The state will get hit for not notifying the victim that the suspect was getting out. This is a helluva mess. An arrest will go a long way to quell the newsies and the severity of the department's black eye."

She shrugged. "I know Nico did it. He's obsessed with Jessica. That came out in the first trial. The evidence is circumstantial, if that. There's only the coincidence that Nico has been out a week. If we can search his house, we might get lucky and recover his clothes or even the black ski mask. Jessica clawed his back. She's sure she drew blood through his shirt before he got her hands taped behind her and tape over her eyes. But we need a court order to check Nico for injuries and a search warrant to search his house. He's living with his mother right now. We have no probable cause whatsoever. Can you think of anything? Am I missing something?"

I shrugged. "Yeah, I can think of something. Let's go talk to him." I turned to retrieve my badge and gun from the Tercel. She grabbed my arm. "Are you crazy? That'll put us both in the grease with the detective bureau sergeant. It'll go right up the line to Cordova and the captain. They'll send us both back in the jail to finish out our careers. I don't know about you, but I hate working the jail. It smells like ass."

"You mean Cordo*ba*." I shot her an evil grin.

She pointed a finger in my face. "The rumors are true, you are crazy." She shook her head. "No. I won't do it. You can forget it."

"I'm not crazy. Seriously. But I do live by the adage nothing ventured, nothing gained. I'm going. Are you in?"

Chapter Nine

I grabbed the equipment needed to confront a rapist and jumped in Jimmie's patrol unit. She drove the car hard and fast. She was under a time constraint. The detectives already expected her back at the station to brief them on the crime. The entire station would be under the microscope on this one. She put on a pair of expensive Ray Ban sunglasses. I couldn't see her eyes or read her expressions.

I asked, "So, where did you grow up?"

She said nothing, turned her head to look at me. I'd overstepped, trying for cool and debonair, and failed miserably, stupid words tripping over each other. *So, where did you grow up?* What kind of opening line was that?

She looked out the windshield and stopped for a red signal at Greentree Avenue. She said, "I grew up in Etiwanda back before it incorporated with Cucamonga and Alta Loma to become Rancho Cucamonga. I have a baby sister who at times passes as my twin even though I'm two years older. Both my parents are dead. My favorite color is red, and I'm heterosexual...At least most of the time." She pulled down her sunglasses and looked at me to be sure I caught the inference. The taunt.

"Oh...my." My bold response to her intimate reply came out in a stutter. I wanted to hit myself in the forehead. How was it I could talk a crook out of telling me where he hid his dope and gun in a car, but I couldn't talk to the fairer sex?

In one of the late nights drinking Old Milwaukee in a red vinyl booth at The Hobo, Dad had said, "Women were put on this earth for no other reason than to confound and taunt men. They were given the key to life that men

42

are constantly chasing. If man didn't have that mandate to pursue, think of the things that would be accomplished. The wars we wouldn't fight. We'd be living on Mars."

She said, "You think we can talk about what we're going to do and say to this shitbird?"

She was scared about screwing up her career.

She moved her sunglasses back in place and hit the gas hard when the light turned green.

"My dad owns and runs The Hobo Café on Foothill, you know it?"

"Are you dodging the question on purpose?"

"Are *you*?"

Her mouth sagged open. "This isn't going to work. I should take you back to the station and turn this whole mess over to the guys who know what they're doing."

"That's fine. I'm only here to help you." I tried for aloof, but internally, I was willing to beg in order to stay in the car a little longer and talk with her. There was something about a woman in uniform. Especially one capable and ambitious. It made her even more of an enigma.

She didn't turn the car around and kept going on a direct path. "Of course, I know The Hobo. I used to eat there all the time. Wait, is your dad that crotchety old man, the short order cook, who calls his coffee Black Joe and gets on everyone's case who adulterates it with sugar and cream?"

"Guilty on all counts."

"He's great. He could be in the movies with some of his dialogue. You oughta get him to write a book. He looks like he took life by the tail and shook out all the kinks. That's what my mom used to say about a 'well-traveled man.'"

"I don't know him that well, not yet anyway. He wasn't around so much when I was growing up. We're just now getting to know each other."

"You're lucky."

"Yeah, maybe."

"His pancakes are so big they lap over the plates and taste great. That café is always packed."

"You don't look like you eat a whole lot of pancakes. He puts in a lot of vanilla extract and some other secret ingredient he won't tell anyone, not even me." Not that cooking is high on my list.

"I run a lot."

"Hey, I do too." I held back, saying that I ran to keep the demons at bay.

All too soon, she pulled over on the dirt shoulder and shut the car off. Did it just as the dispatcher asked for her status and her eta back to the station. The detectives were looking for her.

She picked up the mic and looked at me. She didn't like being on the high wire about to lose her balance and fall, snuffing out a promising career before it even started.

"Come on, let's get this done." I opened the door before she could change her mind.

She said into the mic, "Seven Paul Two, I'll be on a follow-up at Catawba and Sage." She hung up the mic, got out, and closed the door. I didn't know which address and followed her lead. She walked down two houses and turned up a concrete walk to the front door. She didn't park in front of the house, adhering to strict officer survival protocol.

The front yard was all dirt with dead weeds. The house had been baby blue at one time with white trim, but harsh desert weather worked hard at erasing the structure. One front window screen was torn and partially hung from the frame.

I stood off to one side of the door, she the other. She raised her hand to knock and froze. "What the hell are we doing here? This is a really bad idea." She pulled her hand down without knocking, turned, and took a couple of steps in full retreat.

I knocked loudly on the door.

She jumped back into position and socked me in the shoulder.

"Ouch."

"I didn't hurt you." She said through clenched teeth.

I stayed focused on the door's peephole. A shaded peephole meant someone was close, a felon. Just on the other side of the door. My heart rate increased being so close to the prey.

44

The door opened to a man in his late thirties, early forties with a shaved head and no facial hair. Eyes, hazel with dark circles under them. He wore white tennis shorts and a Rolling Stones tee shirt with Mick Jagger's huge cartoonish tongue. Over the tee, he wore a hoodie sweatshirt.

I waited for Jimmie to say something, the pause long and uncomfortable for all persons involved. But for different reasons for each.

The sleeves of his hoodie were pushed up, exposing jailhouse tats: black ink of women with large breasts in suggestive poses.

Jimmie wasn't going to talk out of fear or out of not knowing how to handle this unique situation.

I said, "Hi, are you Nico Sumter?"

"Maybe, who's asking?"

I shot him my biggest smile, tried hard to make it genuine. "I'm Deputy Dave Beckett." I pointed to the badge clipped to my belt so there'd be no confusion later about my identity. "And this is Deputy Poe." She wore a uniform, so no question there. "If we could, we'd like to talk you about an assault."

I watched his eyes for a reaction. He'd been in the joint, the university for criminals. Only it was a school where he didn't come home with a ton of school loans and no job. Criminals always had jobs.

He stared back. He would be a hard nut to crack. Maybe she was right. This was a really bad idea. Then I remembered what this turd had done to Jessica Purdue, and the thought of it straightened my back, put steel in my resolve.

Another long pause that probably wasn't as long as it felt.

From back inside the house came an older woman's voice, "Nico, who's at the door?"

He half turned his head but still maintained eye contact with me and said, "Ma? There's some cops here who say I raped some girl."

I leapt on him and dragged him out the door onto the porch. I took him to the ground hard and put my knee in his back. He bellowed. "What the hell's the matter with you. I didn't do anything. We were just talkin'. Let me go. Let me go. Ma? Ma?"

Jimmie Poe fell on top of his legs, helping to control him while I struggled to get him in a wristlock. He continued to resist, getting more aggressive. Jimmie said in a harsh whisper. "What the hell just happened? What are you doing? What's going on?"

I got him cuffed and rolled him over. Sat him on his butt. I didn't want him to die from excited delirium. He needed to pay his debt, spend precious years of his life in a concrete box.

I stood and kept my hand on his head, holding him down in a sitting position. "We got him. We got him cold."

She took off her sunglasses, her mouth agape, her brown eyes beautiful. "What are you talking about?" She lowered her tone and in a harsh whisper that Nico could also hear. "Are you crazy?"

Chapter Ten

On the front porch of Nico Sumter's house, we detained him for the brutal kidnap and rape of Jessica Perdue.

I held up my hand. "Just take it easy, he made a spontaneous utterance. We got lucky."

"He did what?"

Nico yelled. "I didn't utterance shit."

Jimmie scrunched up her face, angry. "Explain."

"I told him we wanted to talk to him about an assault. I said nothing about a rape. He yelled to his mom that 'the cops are here, and they said I raped some girl.'"

A smile broke across her face as she started to believe me. Believe in the live capture of a heinous criminal.

Nico yelled. "I said no such thing. You're lying, the both of ya. Ma? Ma? Come out here. Ma's never gonna back up your story. She's gonna tell you exactly what I tell her to say."

"He's right," Jimmie said, "It's going to be their word against ours."

I reached into my shirt pocket, pulled out a micro-recorder, and pushed the button to turn it off.

Jimmie's expression again broke into a huge smile. "We…we got him, didn't we? We got him cold, just like you said."

Nico yelled. "You're both sons of bitches. This is illegal search and seizure. I know it is. It'll be thrown out of court. You wait and see if it isn't. And then I'm going to sue both your asses off. You wait and see if I don't. Ma? Ma?"

I pulled back so Nico couldn't see my expression. "We now have probable cause for a search warrant. Let's get him in the car and secure the house, get mom out."

She nodded. Leaned over and whispered. "I don't know how to write a search warrant."

"I do, it's easy. I'll show you." I'd written a couple of follow-back search warrants after car stops where I found contraband. I wasn't good at it either, but would bluff my way through it.

She smiled again, and I decided I'd do anything to keep her smiling.

I took an arm, and she took the other. We got him up and headed down the walk toward the car. I said, "Since he's in our custody, we're allowed to do what's called an "accelerated booking search." At his back, I pulled up the bottom of his tee and hoodie over his head. He had long claw marks from fingernails. Fresh.

Jimmie froze mid-step. "We got him. We really got him. Son of a bitch."

"Yeah, we do. Let's get him in the car. You tell dispatch you have one in custody for 261."

Her smile grew even bigger. She pulled her handheld and called it out.

Two houses up, I put him in the cop car and closed the door. "We don't have much time. We have to write the affidavit and get a telephonic search warrant before the detectives figure out we just pissed in their Wheaties. You go in there and get Ma, bring her out, and interview her. I'll write out the affidavit. It's a short one. Then I'll show you how to call the judge."

She leaned up and kissed me on the cheek. A chaste peck, but still, the soft contact sent tingles up and down my back. I'd been away from women for too long.

First, I pulled the cop car to the front of the house, then got out and wrote the affidavit on the hood of the car, away from the crook who yelled his lungs out. He knew he was caught and would now be going away for decades. A wolf with his paw caught in a steel trap; his only option was to gnaw off his leg.

* * *

The house phone had a long cord. I pulled it into the living room so we could watch the car and talk to the judge. I got the on-call judge's number from dispatch. I briefed Jimmie what to say and dialed the number. Her confidence had returned. Like a pro who's done this for years she spoke to his honor, reading the affidavit that I'd written. I filled out the booking slip and put her name on the bottom so a chickenshit detective couldn't try and steal the arrest from her.

She affixed the judge's name to the warrant just as the station detectives pulled in front of the Sumter home. I wasn't supposed to be anywhere around the incident, and all I could do was pretend like I knew what I was doing. I whispered to Jimmie as the detectives got out of their cars and put on their suitcoats. "Don't let them hoorah you. Keep control right from the gate. Show 'em the search warrant and assign them rooms to search. We're looking for the things we listed in the search warrant: the duct tape, clothes with blood on them, a ski mask, and gloves."

"I got it."

"I know you do. I'm gonna call in a patrol dep to catch a ride to my station. My shift is about to start. Good job."

"I owe you, Dave Beckett."

"You don't owe me anything." I smiled and left before anyone could ask too many questions about why an off-duty Hesperia dep was in the county at the scene of a sensational arrest.

I didn't know at the time that filling out the simple booking form was something that would echo forward into the future with repercussions that would cause hate and murder. Why was it always the small things I wished I could take back?

Chapter Eleven

I quick-stepped late into the Hesperia briefing fresh from the scene on Sage, where I'd left Jimmie and the rapist Nico Sumter. The watch sergeant, Carl Jessup, stopped speaking as he looked up from the briefing board. He gave me the stink eye without commenting. He wouldn't harass me about being late. I worked harder than anyone at the station. The stats bore out that fact: the most arrests, case numbers drawn, and citations issued. I was a dependable workhorse. I wanted to get to homicide and thought a strong work ethic alone could get me there. I sat, took out my notepad, and wrote down notes given to us that described happenings from the two previous shifts.

Slowly, a dark cloud of despair and depression had blown in to shadow the world. I didn't know why. It usually only happened at the end of the day, at night, just before I drifted to sleep, prepping me for The Reckoning. The little girl coming to call. With each passing month, those horrible nights had finally started to recede, growing farther apart. I was healing. And yet the soul-crushing despair had returned, this time during daylight hours. I could deal with it, but what worried me the most was why.

Briefing over, I grabbed my gear and headed out of the room with everyone else, when the watch sergeant yelled, "Dave?"

I turned as the other shift deps flowed around me, fleeing, not wanting to get caught up in another one of my issues with supervision. When something came up in briefing, I always spoke my mind when I should've remained mum. I was working on this personality defect.

"You got a minute?"

Ah, shit. He found out about what happened on Sage with Nico Sumter. My off-duty antics in the county area. How could he not? Everyone used the same dispatch center. Not only that, but the rumor mill worked faster than the speed of light.

I made my way back into the room that turned vacant and lonely. The dark cloud lording over my world and making the air thick.

Patrol sergeant Carl Jessup sat on the briefing table, put his Wellington boot on a chair, and stared at me while he took out one of those narrow brown cigarettes that smelled like burning horse shit.

I stood in front of him and waited. I was getting tired of being dressed down. Now, twice in one day. I held back the Bad Dave, who stood at the mental door about to kick it in and go off. Rant and rave about how cops not only had to fight the bad guys on the street, but they also had to fight the administration *and* supervision, who were supposed to have our backs. The sergeants were classified as supervision, the liaison between the deputies and the brass.

He finally asked, "How's Siderites doing?"

I shrugged. "Good. I personally dropped him off at rehab. He'll be in for three weeks and then have outpatient counseling for another six months. After that, he'll have to go to meetings."

"Good. In fact, that's great."

He didn't think I could pull it off, that Siderites would buck and fight and refuse to admit he had a problem. He did all of that. We had a physical fight in the rehab parking lot. We both came away with cuts and scratches and torn clothes. Had he not been half in the bag, he would've kicked my ass. He lost the fight and accepted his fate. I should get down there and visit him, reinforce the severity of the problem. But who was I to throw stones? At the moment, the urge to walk away from my shift and find the closest bar was difficult to suppress. And I wasn't sure why. It scared the hell outta me. You corner a scared animal, and you're gonna get bit.

Sergeant Jessup finally got to the crux of the issue. "Cordova from the county station called our Lieutenant Buchanan and complained about your insubordination. I told our lieutenant I'd deal with it. What happened?"

"You want the party line, or do you want the truth?"

He glared at me and puffed his little brown cigarette.

"Cordoba has it in for Siderites."

Jessup shrugged and puffed as if saying, "Who doesn't."

"Cordoba called me in thinking he could get me to rat on Ben for the drunk driver contact with CHP."

Jessup's eyes turned hard. "That's none of his damn business. That happened in our area with our personnel."

Jessup also knew all about what happened.

"Yeah, that's what I told him."

"You did?"

"Well, kinda."

Jessup smiled. "You stepped on your dick, didn't you, Beckett?"

I shrugged again, "Well, kinda. Maybe just a little. It wasn't a full-on stomp, though."

Jessup said, "I'll deal with that pompous ass. Next time he calls you in, you call me first. Our lieutenant has your back. Don't worry. It happens again, our lieutenant will deal with him."

The pregnant pause. I didn't know what else to say. I turned, picked up my war bag, and headed for the door. Had my day not been clouded with my unwanted passenger, grief, and regret, I might've stayed, had a joke or two with Jessup, told each other cop stories. Jessup was like that, and he had some great dope stories.

Again, at the doorway to the hall, he said. "Beckett?"

I turned.

"That was a helluva case you pulled off on Sage. I made sure the lieutenant and captain heard about it."

The rumor mill again.

I could only nod and head out to my patrol car.

Three hours later, dispatch asked me to go to channel three. Jimmie Poe came up on the frequency. "At EOW, (end of watch), Can you 10-87 at Roy's."

She wanted to meet under Trigger, across the field, and in front of the museum for a beer after shift.

I clicked the radio twice to acknowledge but knew I wouldn't attend. Alcohol while under the dark cloud was gasoline on a fire. I had enough problems without getting ensnared with Poe. In the end, I'd only hurt her. She was right about not dating anyone in the department, and I decided to respect her first instinct. After shift, I'd head straight home.

Chapter Twelve

The patrol shift was kind and kept me busy going call to call. It wasn't a myth that when the night sky is filled with a full moon, the weirdos and wackos come out in force and put to work the cops, the fire department, and hospital personnel. I drew eight DRs (deputy report numbers) on calls for service and arrested two for spousal abuse. I couldn't determine who was at fault, so I took them both in after getting them stitched and bandaged. Let the judge figure it out

I had to clear the husband and wife at the hospital, get a doctor's approval before I booked them. I finished up a half hour after swing shift ended at 2330 hours.

I exited the county jail's secure parking lot and drove across the field, the one in the past where the sergeant tossed the grenade. I drove into the parking lot of the museum, around the building to the far side. I was thirty minutes late for the Trigger rendezvous. No way would she still be there.

A warm desert breeze blew across the 15 Freeway, speckling the Hesperia cop car with sand and trash, crumpled napkins, and paper sacks from fast food restaurants.

I came around the corner to find Jimmie sitting alone on the concrete square, the pedestal that Trigger stood on, his front legs high in the air kicking. She'd finished her dayshift, changed, and waited around all through swing to meet me under Trigger.

She was waiting *for me*.

Maybe that wasn't as great as it sounded. Maybe she worked overtime and had just gotten off. Maybe she ventured out to Trigger just to see if I showed up.

In any case, was this really a good idea?

I didn't want to admit it, but I needed a shoulder to lean on. What scared me the most was that I didn't know why the emotions had hit so hard.

She wore denim pants, cowboy boots, a white tee shirt that clung to her, and a huge smile that worked hard to cut through my mood.

A six-pack sat next her, the carton empty. Five empty bottles sat next to her on Trigger's pedestal, the sixth one in her hand. She hopped off and started towards my open cop car window, her gait uneven, the boot clop muffled by the wind. She wouldn't pass a field sobriety test. She had a huge smile for me, a great smile. Her eyes big and brown like my ex-wife Beth Abercrombie. Then I realized she reminded me a lot of Beth. That was the attraction. I still loved my wife.

Jimmie put her hand on my arm, hers warm and soft. She leaned in and tried to hand me the beer bottle, her brown eyes bloodshot, her breath thick with the scent of metabolized alcohol, that filled the car.

I wouldn't take the beer or get out of the car. If I did either one there'd be more trouble than I was prepared to deal with.

"What's the matter, aren't you going to have a drink with me?" Her words came out with a hint of a slur. She was vulnerable, happy, and drunk. And most of all, thankful. Even so much as a step out of the patrol car would be taking advantage of her.

She leaned in, put a hand on my cheek, pulled my head over, and kissed me. Her warm tongue pried my lips apart and ventured in, softly meeting my tongue. I didn't push her away. I liked it. I liked it too much. When she broke the kiss, I chuffed.

She moved her mouth close to my ear and whispered. "Come on, get out. Join me."

"I can't." Two words I had to fight to get past my lips.

She pulled out of the car, frowned, swung her half-empty beer bottle around. "We did good today. Good guys one, bad guys zero. This is what I joined up for. And it's all because of you." She rushed the car again, head coming in the window too fast. She kissed me. This time, it went on too long, overpowering my resolve, my hand creeping to the door handle, ready to pull, jump out, and take her in my arms.

She finished the kiss. I kissed her cheek and whispered. "Okay, let me get out."

This was a big mistake.

She stepped back. I got out. She came into my arms. I couldn't feel her against my chest through the body armor under my uniform and wanted to tear it off. Tear it all off.

I was still on duty until I turned in my cop car and told dispatch I was EOW.

I put my face in her neck and took in her scent. I shivered.

She pushed me up against the cop car, pulled my face from her neck, and kissed me again. I wanted to fight it. I wanted to get back in the car and drive away as fast as I could. And yet I couldn't. I fell deeply into the kiss.

I lost track of the number of policy violations. Lost track of everything except the warm woman in my arms.

She pulled back again and nibbled on my ear, whispered. "We got justice for Jessica Purdue and—"

I shoved Jimmie away and bent at the waist the same as if I'd been punched in the gut.

"What? What's the matter?"

I whispered. "Jessica DeFrank."

"No, Jessica Purdue."

I shook my head. "I'm sorry, I can't do this. Let me give you a ride home. You can't drive, not in your condition."

"Dave, what's going on? What'd I say?"

"It's not you. It's me. Trust me, it's me. Come on, get in. I'll give you a ride." I gently took her arm, escorted her around to the other side, set her in the front seat. "Dave? Dave, wait. What'd I do?"

I came around, got in, and put it in drive. "It's not you. My marriage…I'm separated…Officially, I mean. The divorce decree doesn't come down for another month or two." It wasn't a lie, and it wasn't the truth as to why, either.

Jessica DeFrank was the why.

"Are you kidding me? There's a six-month cooling off period after a divorce decree, and that's what you're worried about? You signed the papers. It's just a formality now."

I said nothing and drove. That wasn't the issue, but it's what I was willing to give her as one. I also knew that deep down, I wasn't ready to give up on Beth, not just yet.

When Jimmie said nothing more, I said, "Where am I taking you?"

Her words came out discouraged and yet fearful that she'd somehow screwed something up. "I'll stay with a friend tonight instead of making you drive me all the way down the hill." Her tone lowered. "Though I have to tell you, I thought there'd be a different outcome." She turned to face me. The darkness inside the car left her in shadow. "I thought we'd be spending the night together."

I nodded. Words clogged in my throat, making me unable to speak. I wanted, in the worst way, to explain it to her, but couldn't. Not yet. I hadn't talked to anyone about it, and that was probably the problem. I needed to get it out, vent the built-up poison.

The girl in the slit trench was named Jessica, and the woman raped today was named Jessica. I had not put it together, but my subconscious had. An unfair coincidence had brought back all the emotional pain. That night two years ago, I'd have rather been gut-shot than have this kind of brain pain that continued to linger on and on.

Deputy Jimmie Poe spoke a couple more times, but I'd withdrawn. Her words couldn't penetrate the deep funk I'd slipped into. I fought the flashback images of that slit trench.

I pulled up to a house out in the middle of nowhere in Baldy Mesa, close to Phelan, not knowing how I got there. The last hundred yards, I'd driven across a little spit of land that led to a hill and a mobile home. The naked yellow light came on, one that hung over the rickety wooden porch attached to the double wide mobile home. A woman who I thought looked familiar peeked out. She opened the door all the way and stepped out. She wore shorts and a yellow tank top without a bra. And she really needed a bra. Her brown hair hung down to her shoulders, and she sported a tattoo of a sun on the inside of her left forearm. She looked like a recovering speed freak.

I came out of my funk long enough to think, "What the hell was Jimmie doing staying way out in the middle of nowhere with an ex-speed freak?"

I didn't have time to tell her this wasn't a good idea. She grabbed the handle, pulled the door open, and got out. I reached a hand out to stop her but was too late. When she leaned to get out, her tee shirt pulled up, revealing a muscular back with a strange tattoo of Merlin, the kind of Merlin from King Arthur stories. A bearded man with a pointed hat covered in stars. Beneath Merlin were a pair of red lips—a kiss. The sight of her perfect naked back returned me to reality and made me realize what a fool I was. The recent memory of her three kisses made me yearn for more. More than yearn. I had to have them.

I got out and stood by the open cop car door. The retired speed freak on the porch spooked and jumped back inside.

I said. "Jimmie?" Calling to her.

She came back toward me, the headlights bright on her face and a white tee shirt.

I said, "Can I call you?"

She shook her head, "No," turned, and fled into the mobile home.

I wasn't just a fool. I was a damn fool.

Chapter Thirteen

I dumped the cop car in the Hesperia sheriff's parking lot, changed from my uniform into civilian clothes, and got into my Toyota Tercel. Jimmie remained heavy on my mind. During the long drive down Cajon Pass, I periodically punched the steering wheel and called myself all kinds of a fool.

What was wrong with me?

The hour and ten-minute drive didn't fly by, but it did sneak under the radar of conscious thought.

I parked next to the only other car in the dirt lot at The Hobo Café, Dad's Ford Pinto with the broken reverse gear. What a couple of dumpy cars, in a dumpy dirt lot, at a dumpy café. Yeah, you could say I made a success of my life. No one could argue I'd hit rock bottom. But after working the streets, I found rock bottom didn't exist.

Unless a person started out of the hole, started ascending, rock bottom could easily turn into a cold dirt nap.

Inside, Dad sat in his usual late-night booth, his eyes glazed over, making love to his case of Old Milwaukee as he watched traffic go by on Foothill Boulevard. Soft moonlight spilling in from the long window lit him like a beacon. I wished I knew what demons plagued him. What a pair to draw to, like father like son.

He looked old beyond his years, wrinkled with dark circles under his eyes. He didn't have a life other than that damn café. Why did he do it? He'd enlisted at seventeen and spent his most formative years in the galley of the USS Delbert D. His life had been indelibly imprinted with a work ethic that kept his hands busy. Now, he did the same thing at The Hobo to keep his mind off some traumatic event he wanted to forget and would not share. For him, The Hobo was his default mode. A safe haven. I needed one of those, at least for a time.

I slid into the booth opposite him. He shoved a fresh beer over to me without looking. I didn't often sit with him and drink. Neither one of us spoke. I drank and took to watching the cars go by, the bitter beer hardly a blip on the sensory radar. I wanted to say something and ask him how his day went. Start a conversation so I could tell him about both Jessica Purdue and Nico Sumter. More importantly, tell him about Jessica DeFrank. The little girl in the slit trench. I didn't even know if he knew about what had happened.

I couldn't put the beers away like dear ol' Dad and eventually slid down on the bench seat. Laid my head down and closed my eyes. I tried to think of Jimmie's wonderful kiss, hoping I wouldn't relive the nightmare. But like Dad said, "If you have hope in one hand and shit in the other, which one you think you'll get a whiff of first."

Fatigue and alcohol caught up to me. I gradually eased my eyes closed.

* * *

I picked my way through the hedge row of tall hundred-year-old eucalyptus trees, came out the other side and found nothing but miles of emptiness. Sandy soil and abandoned vineyards overgrown with weeds. My body armor sweaty under West Valley Police Department's blue uniform soaked my tee shirt that stuck to my chest. Behind me on the other side of the hedge row the cop car radio blurted out words from the other officers on shift.

I came upon a slit trench.

A trench someone had just dug, the dirt freshly piled up on one side, darker than the dirt around it. Orange and yellow sunlight knifed through the hedge of eucalyptus creating shadows, an illusion of sharp shadowy teeth eating at the trench.

A white and pink object stuck up from the end of the hole, clean and new, incongruent. I couldn't take my eyes off it, my feet moving all on their own to get a closer look. I didn't want to go any closer, and yet my feet kept moving. My hand dropped to the stock of my handgun, the lieutenant's handgun, the one he lent me until mine came back from ballistics.

With each step, more of the slit trench came into view. When the eyes don't want to see what they're seeing, mixed messages are sent to the brain that come out jumbled. Clear plastic. Skin. Blue denim. White and pink sneakers.

Long brown hair.

For one interminable moment, I stood at the end of the slit trench, no air getting to my lungs. The world had come to a complete stop, and I wanted to step off.

My mind caught up as my eyes digested the scene. My hand yanked the gun from my holster.

I spun around.

In a fraction of a second, my mind registered the flat side of a shovel that twanged off my face, blinking out all light.

I fell backward slowly.

Falling. Falling. Without ever landing.

I woke to clumps of dirt—shovel loads sliding across my body, the weight already too much to bear, making it difficult to breathe. Smothering. The darkness in the world spun round and round. A concussion.

I opened my eyes. My swollen and bloated nose touched clear plastic. On the other side of which was a girl. I'd recognize her anywhere, from her photo. Jessica DeFrank. The missing girl, no longer missing. A milky film covered her once beautiful eyes. I threw up Coke and peanuts. Choked and gagged on it.

Another clump of dirt landed with a smothering weight. I turned my head. The man stood at the end of the trench, shoveling in the fresh dirt. The last rays of sunlight backlit him, obscuring his features and making him nothing more than a tall, thin shadow with a shovel that looked more like a scythe.

"Stop it," I croaked.

Another clump of dirt.

My arm was pinned to my side with the weight of the dirt.

A clump landed on my face, blocking out the last bit of light. I shook and sputtered and gasped for breath. Dirt fell off. Light returned. I wanted to just close my eyes and go to sleep. Let someone else deal with this problem.

The next clump covered over poor Jessica's face. The dirt rattled the plastic.

Lieutenant Womack's speech whispered in my ear, the one he gave as he stood in briefing, cigar in hand: "If for some reason you screw up out there, God forbid, and you go down, just remember, your fellow officers are going to be driving like hell to assist you. They are going to run blindly into a situation you created. It's your screw-up. You will not roll over and give up. You will fix your screw-up, if it takes your last breath. You understand?"

I took in a long breath and let out a yell. At the same time, I shoved my arm deeper. Down along my leg, the only place I could get my arm to go.

Another clump landed on my face.

"Aaah! Stop it! Stop it!" I choked and gasped. My hand found the .38 Smith had given me, the one in the ankle holster. I yanked it loose and used every ounce of strength I had left, forcing my arm up through the loose, heavy dirt.

My hand broke through; the gun pointed at the shadow not six feet away.

He froze mid-toss.

"Say goodbye, asshole." I fired again, again. The shadow stutter-stepped backward as each round thumped into him. The gun clicked empty. I'd fired all six.

If he's good for one, he's good for all six.

The shadow had moved back six or seven feet but still stood on his feet. He wasn't human. He was the devil. Pure evil that couldn't be killed. My arm went limp. Darkness closed in again.

* * *

I woke a second time to blackness and found it difficult to breathe. It wasn't a nightmare; that would've been too easy. I was still in the slit trench with Jessica. Tears burned my eyes. "Bastard. You bastard." Some strength had returned after my little dirt nap.

I wiggled my shoulder until enough dirt fell away that I could get a full breath. More strength returned. I wiggled and clawed and pulled my way out of the trench. I couldn't stand, not without losing my balance and falling on my ass.

That was the concussion.

The full moon with an odd brightness, blanketed the miles and miles of empty vineyard. Blood, an eerie moonlight black, dripped from my head, and face, and mouth, the sandy ground taking it all in; hungry for it.

I crawled on hands and knees to get away from the trench. The shadow wasn't where he should've been, dead or dying where I shot him.

He'd disappeared.

How could that be?

I reached for my HT.

I'd left it on the dash of the patrol car where I was listening to CLAMRs, California Law Enforcement Mutual Aid Radio, the hunt for Gary Hussey's partner.

I crawled. Rested and crawled some more. Crawled miles and miles, it seemed, when it was only seventy feet to the patrol unit on the other side of the hedge row.

From ground level I reached into the car, pulled the mic and asked for help. I couldn't keep the sobs from slurring my pleas.

This time I knew my location.

Chapter Fourteen

I woke with the moonlight shining through The Hobo Café window, an eerie bright with a tinge of blue. No cars sat in the front parking lot or drove east and west on Foothill Boulevard.

Something that never happened. Across from me sat Jessica DeFrank.

The little girl from the slit trench.

No. No. No. Not again. I wanted to be done with her. Forever done with her.

I never knew what to say, my apologies having run out long ago. Her cheeks were rosy with a false blush over gray sallow skin, her lips bluish, teeth yellow as ancient elephant ivory.

She never smiled. Oh, how I wanted to make her smile.

I sat all the way up, blinking a filmy goop out of my eyes. She sat there real and in the same place, Dad had been seated when I first walked in that night.

I couldn't see all her clothes, her blue dress with the white collar and buttons down the front. The plastic shroud still hung on her and crackled each time she took a breath.

But she couldn't be breathing.

I had attended her funeral, saw her put in the ground. For a second time.

Knew where she now rested. This was my mind unable to heal itself, plaguing me with my major error, not finding the killer before he killed her. That had been my job as a patrolman at West Valley police department, and I had failed.

"What do you want? Why are you here?" She never answered the same questions I always put to her. The white death film over her eyes gave her a lizard-like appearance.

She blinked. That film disappeared. Her skin lost the waxy sallowness and turned human, alive.

That too, had never happened before.

My eyes filled with tears and burned my cheeks. "Please don't—"

I had no right to tell her to stop. She had every right to fill my dreams with night terrors. We were partners in that trench.

Her arm appeared above the table edge.

What was going on? Why now? All the other times, she just sat there, not moving, staring, with vacant eyes that ripped my heart out.

Her hand slowly crept across the table. I watched it mesmerized, unable to take my eyes off her delicate young fingers. The plastic crackled as she leaned further across the table. I couldn't move my hand as hers drew near.

She touched me.

I screamed and sat up, gasping.

Patrons in The Hobo sat in booths and at the counter. They quit eating, laughed, and pointed with fork or knife at the funny adult-kid having a nightmare. Dad had cleaned up his empty beer cans and left me to sleep while he did his morning breakfast prep. Then, as a joke left me there while the café filled to capacity and with people lined out the door waiting their turn. He did it because I'd complained about him waking me before ten. He was a stubborn old cuss.

Darla, the waitress, set a mug of Black Joe down in front of me. Dad looked through from his place in the back, his white chef's hat low over his eyes. I reached for the sugar dispenser while staring him down and poured in a long stream.

The patrons went silent and then oohed. I picked up the creamer and made my Black Joe tan. My childish attempt at defiance.

I needed the sugar and the caffeine jolt.

I'd slept until nine-thirty. How many people had come and gone since he opened at five thirty, how many had laughed at me. Well, he poked the bear, and he'd get his. I'd have to think about an appropriate response, something funny, that would, at the same time, get his goat. A childish game of tit-for-tat. And yet, at the same time, my heart glowed warm that my dad would want to play that kind of game with me.

The Tan Joe did its job, gave me a shot of energy, and woke me up.

…And still, Jessica DeFrank's visit lingered, a shadow I couldn't shake loose, one that would shade the day with a hint of depression.

I needed to do something, break a sensational case and get bumped into an acting detective job. Make myself a viable candidate when the county again opened testing for detective. Then bust my ass to get into homicide. Pursue and catch the worst of the worst criminals who would kill the vulnerable, do it before Jessica drove me over the edge into crazy town.

Darla refilled my cup twice before she set down a plate of waffles with the centers cut out containing a fried egg in each. Dad also put two strawberries for eyes, this made the waffles look like funny clowns with open mouths. He knew I hated his mocked-up food art. He did it to get even for the Tan Joe caper in front of all his regulars. I chuckled, looked up at the kitchen. He pretended to be busy with something on the grill.

I ate the waffles and eggs, drank more coffee, "black like coffee's supposed to be drunk."

I realized the café had become a safe haven for me after all, a place away from the real world, the demarcation line just outside the door. The wonderful scents of rich coffee, vanilla, and maple syrup, the warm congeniality from all the regular customers, and of course, Dad. A dad I had not experienced while growing up and had yet to get to know, to really understand. He was still an enigma. Why did he land in a broken-down café, driving a broken-down car? I understood my reasoning, my bad choices. What happened to him?

I had to know more.

No one owned The Hobo Café. The owner, a woman named Konstantina, who hired Dad, left one day in the middle of a breakfast rush and never returned. Dad took over, thinking she'd be back the next day or the next. Didn't happen. Dad ran the place as if she were still present. He took over ordering from the wholesalers the ingredients needed to make the food *he* wanted to cook. He changed the menu. Turned the place around, making a profit. Not by just *his* words but by testaments from his regular customers.

He paid himself his regular salary and deposited the rest into her account, which had gone untouched since she left three years ago. An account that now boasted close to three hundred and fifty thousand dollars. I'd peeked at Dad's small desk in his small office. Dad, on a number of occasions, asked me to find her, to see if she was all right. Each time, I had turned him down. I didn't want to violate the sheriff's department policy by working as a private detective on the side. I wanted to be a homicide dick.

But that wasn't fair. I violated policy on a regular basis for my own purposes.

I didn't want to find her for two reasons. The biggest one, I didn't want things to change. Second, I didn't want to know what had happened to Konstantina. A person, right outta the blue, didn't just walk away from a business. Leave in the middle of a shift. Her disappearance gave off a faint whiff of criminality, either victim or suspect.

But at the same time, she might not have known The Hobo's potential. Maybe she fled, leaving an as yet unrevealed debt load.

Dad, in one of our rare late-night conversations, said that he questioned Konstantina's legitimacy as the owner. She used to drink with him after the café shut down. She told him a wild story about a man, the old owner, how *he* had disappeared. The tale sounded a little like a Postman Always Rings Twice kinda caper with some added caveats. I thought it a pure fantastical fairy tale, machinations of a wild imagination mixed with too much ouzo.

How could I know for sure, because I had never met the woman? The way Dad talked, his mannerisms when he spoke of her, the look in his eyes, I caught a hint of a crush he had for her. Maybe more than just a hint. He wanted her back for personal reasons as well as one concerning the business. And the burgeoning bank account he didn't know what to do with.

The Hobo Café's structure also had a unique past. On the inside walls, high up, two feet down from the ceiling, a brown wavy line circumnavigated the entire interior. The story goes that during the flood of '69, the café filled with mud and water and had to be shoveled out. One night before

I had reconnected with him, Dad, fueled by Old Milwaukee, had climbed on a teetering chair with a fat black felt tip and drawn an arrow with the words: "High tide mark. Pacific Ocean fifty-six miles that way." Those words became legend in The Hobo Café, and people came in just to see them.

After I finished my breakfast, I got up, walked through the kitchen, and thanked him on my way to the back door, thanked him with just a grunt of satisfaction. A communication used between a father and son that said it all.

He stopped me, waving his spatula. "Son, can I talk to you about something? It's important."

It was always important with him. But this time was different.

He had never called me son before. The endearment caught in my throat as a rising lump.

He always called me Davie, which he knew I hated. "Davie" reminded me too much of the old Claymation-stop-action TV show with a dog named Goliath and his owner named Davie. The dog would always say, "Gosh, Davie." When Dad said, "Davie," my mind automatically added the, "Gosh."

"Sure, Dad, what's up?"

"Not now, later. I got all of this going on right now." He swirled his spatula over his grill, an evil sorcerer conjuring a wicked spell on the food meted out to the unsuspecting.

"Sure. Ah...I'm going to work out at the gym. I'll catch you when I come back, before l leave to cover my shift. How's that?"

He hesitated. "Yeah, I guess that has to work, doesn't it?"

I took a step toward him. "Is something wrong?"

"Nah, just the usual bullshit. I'll get wit ya later. You go on."

"All right."

He wanted to ask me, yet again, to take a run at tracking down Konstantina. I thought I could read his bloodshot, blurry eyes, and once more thought I saw he might have a thing for her, an unrequited desire that needed to be fed. Sometimes hope and desire kept a person going. Kept an old navy man doing the same things week in and week out while waiting for his girl to return.

I exited into the bright sunlight, got in the Tercel, and drove to the gym.

This was another time in my life I wished I would've slowed down and listened, paid more attention to the red flags. Looked into Dad's eyes to see the pain and the issue at hand.

Chapter Fifteen

I got bound up in thoughts about work while writing reports from the day before and forgot all about getting back to Dad.

Five hours after I left The Hobo and headed for the gym, I drove the Hesperia patrol car from call to call on swing shift while in between hunting for crooks. They moved among us no different than regular folk and were easy to spot if you knew what to look for. If you didn't, they blended in like insidious little chameleons, waiting to take advantage of a victim who turned his back for a brief second, left his car door open while gassing his car, left a purse in the grocery buggy while she retraced her steps to pick up a box of Captain Crunch as a treat for the kids.

The harder core of this criminal of the species looked for the lone sheep out on a broader range to commit more vicious crimes: rape, robbery, and murder. These treacherous bastards being the more difficult to spot and the more challenging to capture. Those were the ones I really wanted a piece of—to hunt down.

Toward the latter part of the shift, I slowed long enough to take coffee with a new guy, a rookie named Danny Dyer. Dyer worked out of the county station and did his jail time in the station jail instead of downtown. He'd processed all the criminals I brought in and wanted to know how I did it. Some deps got lucky, but I was the one consistent with arrests.

We 10-87ed, at a corner gas station/market on Main Street close to the 15 freeway. Night had fallen hard, bringing with it brisk air that clouded our breath as we stood outside next to the building and our parked patrol units, sipping the hot brew that didn't equal Dad's in flavor or strength. Not many did. That was the problem with drinking a perfect cup of Joe at The Hobo, all others fell short. Worse, that night, the stuff in my cup barely resembled coffee at all. But it was hot enough to hurt the teeth and warm the bones. And best of all, it was free.

Dyer had made it off training but was headed for a "paper-chasing deputy" reputation, and he knew it. He couldn't quite grasp how to hunt for the crooks who populated a world that overlapped with ours. He wanted to make "reasonable" and "probable" cause arrests. And not just arrests discovered at dispatched calls. He was trying to move up to the next level and couldn't. Sometimes, it wasn't a matter of training. Sometimes, a person wasn't cut out for the hunt. Didn't have the nose—or the eyes—for it. The curiosity.

Maybe it was natural selection. Maybe if Dyer did jump levels, he wouldn't be able to handle the quick-to-violence that occurred when you cornered a heavy weight. Maybe nature kept Dyer from progressing to keep him safe.

Cars on Main Street zipped by, headlights illuminating an otherwise dark street. In the desert, the city didn't pay for streetlights not for the vast open areas. Only in the denser, more populated areas. Cars also came south on Mariposa, most turning west to catch the 15 freeway, a main artery that connected to Los Angeles and Vegas.

Dyer wore his sandy brown hair as long as department policy allowed. His thick prescription glasses kept the crooks from taking him seriously. What made it worse, the glasses kept slipping down his nose, and he continually pushed them back up when they slid down.

He was the one to ask for the coffee break. We'd met before on a number of other occasions to discuss tactics and arrests. I didn't mind at all. I liked him. His eagerness, his ambition.

He sipped his coffee and pushed his glasses up higher. "Why are we standing out here in the cold when it's nice and warm inside?"

I sipped and looked at him, wanting him to figure it out.

He thought about it for a second. "Because nothing's happening inside the store, and everything is happening out here."

I nodded.

He asked. "Tell me how you arrested that guy with the two pounds of meth last week. Two pounds, that was a helluva pop. I heard the narcotics division was even pissed about it. They're jealous."

"Ah, yeah, about that caper. The method I used is not really for public consumption. If you know what I mean." The method wasn't illegal. It was just difficult to two-step around search and seizure.

"I understand. But I'm not the public."

"You want me to give away my trade secrets?" I wasn't sure I wanted to give him the boost to that next level. I didn't want the responsibility or the guilt if something happened to him, especially since that three-way deputy murder-suicide was still so fresh and alive in my thoughts. I'd been off duty at the time and asleep on my cot in back of The Hobo when Siderites had arrived at that horrific and heart-rending scene.

Sergeant Jessup had called the pay phone on the wall of The Hobo and told me. Said he called so I wouldn't hear it on the radio or on the TV. TV that I never watched. I appreciated the sentiment, but his words crushed me, stomped me down until I stood two inches off the floor. My world had swirled round and round with an emotionally damaged equilibrium. What the hell, three deputies, friends, all dead. Never to drink beer with, to laugh with while watching their eyes and their smiles. Just gone. Forever.

I wasn't entirely sure Dyer had ever been in a fistfight. The first time a person gets slugged in the face is a rude awakening.

He smiled. "Tell me, please?"

"I made the arrest in the gas station parking lot at the pump."

"I know, I rolled code three when you called for help."

I rarely called for assistance. That incident was one of the exceptions. I usually evaluated and assessed the crook correctly. In that instance, I grossly underestimated him, his response to my presence. He almost got the better of me. It happened so quickly, his violent reaction took my breath away.

I didn't continue and let it lie, my thoughts going back to those images in freeze frame, reliving the threat, again tasting the adrenaline spiked by memory. My heart raced.

"Come on, tell me what happened. How did you spot him?"

"Okay, look. These criminals don't want to be caught out on their own, away from the herd they use for cover. They stand out too much. They want to blend in with Joe Citizen."

"The sheep."

"That's right. The gas station on Bear Valley Road—Bear Valley Road is a main thoroughfare that's used to traverse from one city to another."

"I get that. We talked about this part before. How they hide among the sheep."

"Right. Bear Valley Road gets you to Apple Valley, so if a crook wants to move under the radar, they don't take Highway 247 to get to Apple Valley. It's got too many cop cars and CHP. They go the back way, blending in with all the other cars, people who live in the area."

Dyer nodded. "That's good. I like that."

"You know the mortuary across the street from the gas station?"

"No."

"Kid, you need to pay attention to the streets, buildings, walls, trees, back alleys. You can't just drive around hoping the crook fairy will drop a big fat criminal in your lap."

I was only four or five years older than his twenty-two or twenty-three, but it felt more like a couple of decades. Law enforcement years were like dog years. You experienced life seven times faster, saw the world unfettered in all its soiled glory. A world where moral decay and violence rules and the good of heart are trod upon.

I'd hurt his feelings with my harsh talk. He wanted, in the worst way, to run with the big dogs.

"Okay look, I sit on the side of the mortuary across the street, blacked out with a small pair of binoculars, and watch the gas station. Crooks have to gas their cars, too. And an even better place is the self-serve car washes late at night. Only tweakers wash their cars after hours.

The guy at the pumps that night looked like a tweaker, his clothes, the way he moved. Agitated, his rumpled and soiled appearance. He was worth talking to, so I did. That's all there was to it. There isn't some big secret. It's just a matter of getting out of the cop and talking to people until you can start to tell the sheep from the wolves."

He smiled, one that quickly tarnished. "Wait, what about probable cause to contact him? He was just parked at the pumps, right?"

"You don't need cause if you make a consensual contact."

"You mean you just walk right up and talk to them?"

"It's America, and we're allowed to talk to people. You build your probable cause from there. In that guy's case—his name was Harold Brock—as soon as I walked up on him—he had his back to me and didn't see me approach— he turned, saw the uniform, and swung. Tried to hit me with a hay-maker. That's all the probable cause I needed. The fight was on. He was bigger and stronger. I almost got my ass handed to me. He had the two pounds of meth in his trunk. I found it when I towed the car in on an inventory search. The incident was entirely legal. I wrote the report just the way it happened."

While I spoke, my eyes continued to scan the environment. Driving among the other cars, a white Toyota Supra came down Mariposa and turned east on Main Street.

"Look," I said, "Why don't you check with your lieutenant, make sure it's okay, then come and ride with me on a few shifts."

"Really? Man, that would be excellent."

Then I remembered his lieutenant was Cordova. He wasn't going to approve a ride, at least not with the likes of me.

"Sure, you clear it with your boss, and I'll clear it with mine. Buchanan's cool. I'm sure it'll be okay on this end." I tossed my coffee onto the asphalt parking lot. The liquid steamed. "It's getting late, and I don't have my felony arrest for this shift."

"You get one every shift? I'm lucky to get two or three a month, and those are on calls."

"It'll come. Just keep trying. Get out and talk to people." I got in the Hesperia patrol car, backed up, and drove through the parking lot.

Just as that same white Supra pulled into the pumps.

A tall, thug-looking predator in a denim jacket and greasy Levi's, got out to pump gas. An alert, that little tingle in the back of my brain went off. I swerved over, blocked the front of the Supra, and jumped out. The thug's eyes went wide. He looked from side to side for an escape route.

He was about to rabbit.

I moved on him, increasing my speed just short of a run. "Don't do it. Don't you do it."

I caught him as he took a giant step to flee. I grabbed the front of his denim jacket and yanked him up short. His jacket came open as he tried to spin out.

In his waistband, he had a blue steel revolver.

With my other hand, I yanked it out and stuck it in his ear as I body-slammed him on the hood of the Honda behind his car at the pump. "Don't you move!"

The woman in the Honda screamed, put the car in reverse, and we ended up on the cold concrete, me on top. The suspect didn't move for fear of being shot in the head with his own gun.

I looked up for Dyer to see if he was coming to help. He stood in the same spot where I'd left him, Styrofoam coffee cup in hand, still steaming, his glasses down his nose, forcing him to pull his head back to see through them. His eyes huge, his mouth in a big "O."

Chapter Sixteen

Danny Dyer tossed his coffee cup, drew his handgun, and ran over to the pump island to help me get the guy cuffed, the suspect I held at bay with his own gun stuck in his ear, who kept saying, "Take it easy. Don't shoot me. Please, God, don't shoot me."

Once cuffed, I got him up, pushed him against the cop car and searched him, found a half ounce of meth in his shirt pocket.

Dyer stood back ran the license plate to the car, and put us out on a car stop. I put Fredrick Johnson in the patrol unit and closed the door. I clipped his driver's license under the ballpoint pen clip in my uniform shirt pocket, breath still coming hard from the dangerous struggle and exertion. Thirty seconds of pure excitement. Teeth-cutting adrenaline. To some, an addicting drug stronger than heroin and nicotine. My hands shook like a junkie in withdrawal.

Dyer came up to me and spoke for the first time since I left him standing forty or fifty feet away in front of the storefront. "Son of a bitch. Tell me what just happened. We were standing right over there," he pointed, "drinking coffee. You said you had to go make a felony arrest. Said it easy as you please. You got in your car." He pointed to my car. "And drove over here where you arrested this guy for—"

Dispatch asked if we were "Ten-thirty-five," asking if we were clear for confidential information. I pulled the radio from my belt, "Affirmative."

She said, "Your car is ten-twenty-nine, Frank. Are you code four?"

"Affirmative, one in custody. Please roll a tow for the recovery."

Dyer said, "Son of a bitch, *and* the damn car is stolen to boot. Come on, tell me what you saw."

"It was just luck and nothing more."

"Bullshit. Tell me."

"Take it easy. Okay, look, while we were talking, I saw the car drive down Mariposa and turn east. A few minutes later, when I got in my car to leave, that same car pulled in to get gas."

"That's it? That's nothing at all. I'm never gonna get this. It's bullshit. That was too subtle. How am I supposed to pick up on something that subtle?"

"Come here." I led him to the back of the cop car and opened the door. "Hey, Fred, tell him why you pulled into the gas station in a stolen car with two cops having coffee?"

"Whatta I get outta of it?"

"What do you want?"

"Let me go?"

"Yeah, that's not gonna happen. What's next on your wish list?"

"I want fifteen minutes on the phone with my girl. I'm going away for a long time on this one."

"Five," I said.

"Ten."

"Deal." He cranked his head back so he could look at Dyer. "I knew I was hot, knew if I stayed on the street after I drove past two cops that they might come after me. I drove in here because you'd never think a stolen car would come in here, not with two cop cars. That's why. I've done it three times before without a hitch."

I closed the cop car door. "He was trying too hard to blend in with the herd. That's what I keyed on."

"Son of a bitch, meth, a gun and a stolen car. I'm gonna ask the lieutenant if I can come ride with you. I'll do it on my own time if he won't approve it."

I smiled. "Take it easy. You'll pick up all this stuff once you have more time on the street."

But I didn't think he would. My old training officer, Johnny Maslow, had told me there were only two kinds of people: victims and predators. The crooks also had the same categories. There were victim crooks just like there were predator crooks who preyed upon their own kind. There were victim cops just like there were predator cops who hunted the predator crooks. Unless something clicked in Danny Dyer, and it clicked soon, he'd forever be a victim cop, someone who only chased calls, a paper-deputy—a paper-chasing deputy.

Dyer said he'd tow the car for me. I left, headed in to book Fred. Took fifteen minutes to get there.

The jail must've had a two-for-one special. The CHP and deputies were lined up just inside the door, waiting for their crooks' turn at the booking window.

The number of report forms needed for each arrest, coupled with the bureaucracy involved, the booking process, and court time, kept me from the hunt and arresting more criminals, chasing my adrenaline addiction.

When I finally exited the jail and retrieved my gun and other tools left in my unit trunk—because they weren't allowed in the jail—two hours had passed. I didn't put my gun in the gun locker by the exterior jail door. I learned that lesson the hard way.

One day early in my life as a rookie, I had fled the jail at a full run to back a deputy requesting immediate assistance. When I got to the scene, I realized I'd left my gun back at the jail in the gun locker and was forced to pull the unit shotgun. I looked the fool carrying a gauge with an empty holster. The other coppers for weeks harangued and threw paper balls, wadded up report forms, at me over that bone-headed move. That road to veteran cop status had been a long and lonely one with lots of chuck holes.

Tonight, I also felt guilty for leaving my beat unattended. My partners had to cover the calls for service while I waited in the booking line.

I pulled up to the tall, automatic gate that led out to the free world and tapped my horn so the deputy in the control booth inside the jail would open it. The gate started to open just as Danny Dyer came over the radio, yelling for help.

"Man with a gun! Man with gun! Code three back. Roll me A-back!"

Dispatch acknowledged the cry for help. "Any unit to clear and respond code three to assist Seven Paul Three, he has a man with gun—"

I held my breath, waiting for the address. Danny Dyer was a county deputy from the County station, a station that handled over two thousand square miles. I'd left him at the gas station two hours ago, left him to tow my stolen/recovered car, the Toyota Supra. He could be anywhere.

Dispatch continued and spouted the numbers and street names ending with "In Lucerne Valley."

"Shit." I slugged the steering wheel. That location was a long haul under the best of circumstances. My mind automatically started going over the possible routes adding in the time of night and traffic conditions. I settled on the back way out to Kiowa and then north up through Apple Valley to Highway 247.

The gate rolled too slowly. I had to wait, my breathing rapid. Behind me in the rearview, I caught sight of deputies and CHP running out the jail's hard door, stopping at the gun locker, their hands moving fast.

And the gate still moved too slowly.

The cops behind me jumped in their cop cars, started up, put them in gear, and squealed their tires, backing out.

The gate now acted like the starting flag at a NASCAR race, but in this contest, a deputy's life was at risk.

Chapter Seventeen

The gate at the jail came open enough to slip through. I jetted out with all the other cars lined up behind me. Engines whining out, tires screeching. The units called out their en route status. Dispatch acknowledged each one.

I remained silent. I was a Hesperia unit obligated under contract to protect the good folks of Hesperia.

But we all wore the tan and green. We were all deputy sheriffs, and in my rule book, "a deputy needs help" trumps all else. Screw the MOU, memorandum of understanding.

I picked up the radio mic and asked dispatch to check on Danny's status.

She said, "Seven Paul Three, update your status."

Nothing.

Dead air.

Other units chimed in, stating they were responding.

Lieutenant Cordova came up on the frequency, "Cancel all units except the two closest. I don't want a pile up on Highway 247."

What the hell was he doing out in the field so late?

"Shit." His order may have made sense if a deputy's life wasn't at risk. He just covered himself, covered his career, wrapped it in a nice warm blanket, and tucked it in. Now if any of us, the unauthorized units still responding, crashed, he could say, "I told them to cancel, it's not my fault."

I didn't slow down and put my foot on the accelerator, blowing through stop signs, only using the red lights and siren as needed. People tended to panic when you came up on them too fast with the siren blaring. Within a couple of miles of the thirty I had left to go, the unit brakes started to heat up and fade. I had to watch them, back off a little, or I'd never make it in one piece. A piled-up unit didn't help Danny.

Dispatch came up and asked for the closest units and then canceled all the others. I had not put myself en route, but Cordova had heard me ask for Paul Three's status update. He came up on the air. "Dispatch, make sure *all* Hesperia units have canceled and are staying in their area."

Dispatch repeated the order. "All Hesperia units, cancel and return to your area."

Now, it was all a matter of record. I was hung out. I hated Cordova even more, what a chickenshit.

Dead air, no radio traffic from Danny. I picked up the mic, screw it. I asked dispatch to again check on Paul Three's status."

She did.

More dead air.

Everyone held their breath.

I juked around another car on a two-lane road going into opposing traffic, heading east as fast as the car would go. Horns blared at the close call.

I didn't see any other units taking the route I chose.

Cordova came up on the radio, trying to go car-to-car with me. I wouldn't answer.

His voice came back angry, "Tell that Hesperia unit to cancel. Make sure he acknowledges." He knew my voice.

Dispatch tried to raise me, calling out my call sign. I didn't answer. Let the bastard fester.

"Seven Paul Three. Shots fired! Shots fired!"

"All responding units, Seven Paul Three reports shots fired. Shots fired at his location."

His panicked voice took my breath away. I stuck my foot into the accelerator, pushed it to the floor.

Lieutenant Buchanan, Hesperia Station's Lieutenant, came up on the frequency. "Have all units continue to respond until we get a code four. I was on my way home to Big Bear, and I'm going ten-ninety-seven in sixty seconds. I'll advise status."

I yelled at nobody. Cheered. "Go get 'em, Buchanan."

Seconds ticked by. Was it a minute? Two.

Three.

I'd driven another seven miles in the time-lapse holding the unit at a hundred miles an hour, over-driving the headlights on a dark rural road plagued with dips and chuck holes. The tired patrol unit rattled and shook and banged.

Four minutes.

Lieutenant Buchanan came up on the radio, "We are tentatively code four. Paul Three is pinned down but safe. Call out SWAT. We have a barricaded suspect with shots still being fired."

"Ten-four. Responding units, Code Four Adam at the call in Lucerne Valley, Paul Three is pinned down but Code Four. SWAT is being advised for a barricaded suspect."

Another Hesperia unit, one of my partners on my shift, popped out of a side street, sliding sideways. I veered to miss him, drove into the dirt shoulder at a hundred-plus miles per hour. My car slewed one way, then the other. I almost piled it up. My heart jumped into my throat.

The radio clicked three times. I switched down to channel three to hear what the crazy bastard had to say for himself as I kept a death grip on the wheel with one hand.

"Hey, Partner, that was a close one. You should be running with lights and sirens."

Siderites.

He didn't have his lights and siren on either.

He was supposed to be in rehab. He must've come late to shift, and the sergeant just let him come back to work. I switched to the main channel to listen for an update, *and* I didn't want my voice on channel three. I was going to get racked up by Lieutenant Cordova when all this was over. I didn't want to supply him with any additional evidence.

Siderites had absconded from rehab and was now headed to a violent confrontation. Terrific.

He fell in behind me, staying way too close, giving me the Blue Angel treatment. He liked to play out on the edge more than I did.

The radio turned silent.

Our two Hesperia patrol cars continuously turned and juked, sped up, and slowed down.

Dispatch came on the air. "Nineteen Lincoln, SWAT has been advised they are en route with an extended ETA."

Two patrol units went on scene.

More silence.

Nineteen Lincoln came up on air, "Roll paramedics and have them stage."

An ominous request.

Once on Highway 247, a smooth and open highway, we made better time. In minutes I slammed on the brakes to keep from over-shooting the location. Siderites, following too close, had to go off-road beside me to keep from plowing into the back of my patrol car. His car rattled and banged, throwing a rooster tail of dirt clouding the air.

Two marked patrol cars, both from Apple Valley station, sat on the side of the road at least thirty feet from the address that contained a double-wide mobile home and another house, a two-story manufactured home. Both on one lot, both huddled in a copse of cottonwood trees with acres and acres of open desert surrounding the place.

I pulled the 12-gauge Ithaca Deerslayer shotgun loaded with double-ought buck and my personal bandolero with extra shells in loops. Twenty-five extra rounds. I jumped out of the unit. Just as rounds went off in the compound in between the two houses, the pops more like small firecrackers.

A small caliber weapon.

I flinched and ducked back behind the patrol unit, went down on one knee. Siderites did the same. He'd come around to my side. We crouched together.

"I thought you were supposed to be in rehab?"

He gave me that lazy smile of his, "Yeah, me too. I guess once I sobered up, I looked around and thought, what the hell am I doing here? Alcoholics Anonymous is for quitters. You know what I mean, Dave? I'm not a quitter."

"Ah, man."

I moved up to the lead cop car, the second one from Apple Valley, not fifty feet from Lieutenant Buchanan, who now crouched behind his plain-colored detective car, a Ford Taurus. His head was craned upward, looking at the second story of the manufactured home, the mobile home at his back.

The suspect had the advantage with the high ground.

"Psst. LT."

He turned, saw us, and smiled. He showed the flat of his hand, indicating he wanted us to stay put. He held a .357 magnum in the other. He pointed up, indicating the threat came from the second floor.

A flight of desiccated wood stairs led up to a narrow wood landing in front of a sliding glass door, all lit by a naked yellow light bulb mounted on the wall. The light gave the shooter the advantage. He stayed back in the living area of the second floor in darkness, while outside, the light lit us up like ducks at a carnival arcade.

I scanned the scene and, at first, couldn't see Danny Dyer and then spotted him. He was lying in the dirt behind some trashcans at the bottom of the stairs, his legs curled up, held by his arms as he tried to stay small and out of the line of fire. He had to be piss-in-your-pants scared. I would've been.

My eyes adjusted to the ambient light. Danny Dyer's county car sat in front of Lieutenant Buchanan's, shot to hell. Small caliber rounds, probably .22, dimpled the metal skin, the window safety glass shattered but intact from little high-velocity bullets.

Buchanan said, "Stay put, we're gonna wait for SWAT."

I nodded. I didn't like it, but I would do what Buchanan ordered. I respected him a great deal even though leaving Danny in that deadly position wasn't the right thing to do. We should be laying down suppression fire so he could extricate himself. But cops didn't use suppression fire, that was a military tactic.

Danny Dyer only had the trash cans as concealment, not cover. Bullets could go right through them, and then it would be like a magic show with the magician probing for the pretty girl in the box with the long swords. Danny wouldn't last if the crook zeroed in on him.

Anxiety rose, making me want to bolt over there, grab him, and pull him back.

I needed to talk, to bleed off the anxiety while we waited for SWAT with their extended ETA. Talk to my partner and friend, and at the same time, I didn't want to raise his sobriety issue while at a high-risk situation. Siderites kept popping his head up above the Apple Valley car for a peek. I pulled on his shoulder to get him down. "What the hell did you do to Cordova over at the county station?"

He gave me that slow, lazy smile, again. "Why?"

I gave him the eye.

"I arrested his nephew for possession of stolen property. Cordova came to me, asked me to dump the case, 'clear it, exceptional means.' Walk away from it."

"And?"

But I knew.

"I told him to kiss my white ass."

I couldn't help but chuckle at the way he said it.

Bullets rained down on us, thudding into the Apple Valley car.

Pop. Pop. Pop. I counted ten in all.

"Shit!"

Siderites laughed, "Guy can't aim for shit, can he? My grandma can shoot better than that limp dick."

The firing let up when the crook's gun went dry. Siderites stood and yelled at the suspect. "You missed me, you dumb asshole." He grabbed the shotgun from my hand and took off running.

"Ben!"

Chapter Eighteen

Siderites racked and fired the shotgun on the move, the booming five times louder than the .22, shattering the quiet desert night.

Siderites let the crook know deputies were on scene, and it was time to give up or suffer severe consequences for his actions.

Go get 'em, Ben.

The shadow who stood just inside the sliding glass door firing a .22 semi-automatic rifle stepped back into cover and concealment to reload. The sliding glass door shattered from the buckshot. Siderites hurried over to Danny Dyer and crouched next to him. "You okay, kid?"

"Yeah."

Buchanan yelled, "Come on, it only takes him a couple of minutes to reload. Move your asses."

I moved up to Buchanan's position. Now, I was more exposed to the suspect than over by the Apple Valley car. Siderites and Dyer met me there, sliding in the dirt behind the Ford Taurus, both giggling like kids. Stress and the threat of dying could do that to you: an outlet, covering suppressed emotions, fear of being gunshot, coupled with the realization you're not invincible after all.

Buchanan said, "Good job. Now, after he comes out again and unloads, we're all going to move back to the street, set a perimeter, and wait for SWAT. The two Apple Valley units are covering the back, so this turd can't escape."

Siderites shook his head but said nothing. I could only imagine what he thought. We'd worked together too long. No one shoots at a sheriff's deputy without paying the price. And that price cannot be exacted by anyone else, especially SWAT. This was now our call to handle. "One deputy, one riot."

Siderites took the bandolero with the twenty-five spare shotgun shells from me and started reloading the Deerslayer.

The crook stuck his barrel out the sliding glass door and opened up on the trash cans where Dyer and Siderites used to be. Shredding them with a full ten-round magazine. The bullets punching right through. Dyer wouldn't have survived.

Silence.

If there had been any question of the suspect's intent, there wasn't any longer. He was trying to ventilate all of us.

Buchanan said, "Come on, let's move to the street." In a crouch, he started to move.

Siderites stood and fired the Deerslayer into the dark, open maw to the living room through the frame of the sliding glass door. Shot as he walked on the move, watching the deadly threat elevated ten feet above us.

"Ben?" I yelled. He didn't turn and kept walking. The shotgun had gone dry. He reloaded on the move with the gun still mounted on his shoulder.

Buchanan returned. He wasn't going to leave his boys exposed and alone. *What would Cordova have done?*

Dyer looked at me, his eyes pleading for me to say something, to tell him what to do. When I didn't, he stood and took off running to catch up to Siderites, who now stood at the steps leading to the narrow wood platform in front of the sliding glass door. Dyer's need to be a big dog won out over an oppressive fear that would've made any Joe Citizen piss in his pants.

Good for you, Danny.

With Danny Dyer, gun in hand, behind Siderites, Siderites mounted the steps and advanced upward.

I sucked in a breath and rose to head over and join them. They weren't going to have all the excitement and leave me a spectator. Buchanan took hold of my shoulder. I turned to look into his eyes. He shook his head. "I need you to go over there to the left." He pointed. "See over there? That's another exit. They're interior stairs. This turd gets flushed by Siderites, he could come down those stairs and ambush us all. I need you over there covering."

I shook my head. I was going up those stairs with my friends.

"That turd *is* going to flush as soon as he sees his situation is untenable. Count on it."

I nodded. He was keeping his head about him and not running off half-cocked like Siderites. I wanted to be on those steps with my partners, but also needed to listen to reason. He slapped my shoulder. "Go. Now."

I moved just as Siderites and Dyer made it to the top.

The suspect again started shooting, this time from deeper inside the house.

Siderites stayed back against the wall, stuck the Deerslayer inside. Using just his hands, only exposing his arms, he fired, racking the shotgun. Firing all four rounds.

The shooting stopped.

Quiet.

Buchanan yelled. "Is everyone okay? Anybody hit?"

"We're good, Lieutenant," Dyer said while Siderites reloaded his gauge from my bandelero.

From my position by the ground entrance to the stairs I could look up and see Siderites and Dyer on that narrow landing. What fools. What stupid, brave fools.

Where I now stood, the interior wooden flight of stairs ended at the top with a small rectangular landing and was lit with another yellow light. This one working against the suspect if he came out. I stood to the side in the shadows, gun down at my side, hoping the suspect tired of his game and tried to escape and come my way. I had priors and knew I could shoot him. I had shot the Market Basket 211 suspect, and the shadow who had tried to bury me and Jessica DeFrank in the slit trench.

Siderites said something to Dyer. Dyer swung his .357 pistol and knocked out the yellow porch light that back-lit them to the suspect.

Darkness fell, turning them to shadows.

A loud scraping noise came from inside the house.

"What's going on up there?" Buchanan asked.

Siderites peeked into the darkness of the living room. "The asshole is sliding the refrigerator out of the kitchen into the living room. It's a barricade. I guess he doesn't like the buckshot coming his way."

Siderites finished reloading and racked the shotgun. He shouldered it and fired four more times into the house. The white gun smoke enveloped him and Dyer.

Siderites' shadow said, "Son of a bitch. I'm buying me a Frigidaire. That appliance just took four rounds like they were nothin' at all." He chuckled. "I bet his morning milk's gonna taste like lead."

The suspect opened up again; his rounds peppered the aluminum door frame, the edge where Siderites hid with Dyer behind him. I again fought the overwhelming urge to leave my post to join them.

Silence.

The .22 magazine empty. He must have a brick of rounds in there.

Buchanan yelled again, "Everyone all right? Anyone hit?"

Siderites yelled into the house. "Nice try, asshole, you missed me." Suddenly, Siderites turned and handed the shotgun to Dyer. Siderites drew his handgun and disappeared into the house.

"Ben!"

But he didn't acknowledge.

Buchanan yelled. "Shit. Siderites?"

Nothing.

Silence.

A minute passed, a slow sweep of the second hand.

A loud boom came from inside. A .357 magnum. An unmistakable magnum round. One shot.

"Siderites?" I yelled again.

Nothing.

Anxiety rose until I grit my teeth. My handgun shook with pent-up adrenaline.

Siderites stepped out of the house onto the landing, his feet crunching the cubed glass left from the shattered slider. He walked by Dyer and down the wooden steps. I didn't want to leave my position, but did. I met him at the front of the lieutenant's Ford Taurus.

Siderites leaned against the hood, his eyes glazed over, his mind gone somewhere else, taking a quick down-and-dirty vacation. He'd had enough crazy for one Friday night.

I took the gun from his hand and stuck it in my waistband. Buchanan stepped over and took it from me.

Up on the landing, Dyer came out of the upstairs living room. "Man, oh, man, you gotta come see this."

I stared at my partner, reached up, and moved his face around until he looked into my eyes. "Hey, Ben." I waved my hand in front of his nose. "You in there?"

He snapped out of it as if just recognizing me, as if we'd been apart for many years.

"You okay, pal?"

"What? Oh, yeah, sure. I couldn't get a shot at him from the door, so I went inside." He stalled in his explanation, his eyes starting to again glaze over.

"Ben?" I shook him.

"What? Oh, yeah."

I took in a deep breath.

He continued. "I got behind the bed and waited for him. He came out of the kitchen with the rifle pointed at you guys down here. And…And I shot him." He raised his hand, shifting his fingers to form a kid's gun with index and thumb, and fired, making a gunshot noise with his mouth.

"But you're okay?"

"Yeah, yeah, I'm good. I said I'm good."

Buchanan said, "Dave, go up there and take a look. I'll stay with Ben." He picked up the radio and told dispatch to roll in the paramedics even though he didn't know the suspect's medical status and to cancel SWAT.

I walked up the stairs, my gun still in my hand, the adrenaline a hard, metallic taste in my mouth. My feet stepped on the expended shotgun shells Siderites had fired. On the landing, my boots crunched on the cubed glass. Burnt cordite hung thick in the air.

I took a deep breath and stepped into the dark living room, now only illuminated by Dyer's flashlight. The room contained a king-size bed that sat on a cheap linoleum floor littered with .22 caliber brass shell casings, at least a hundred of them. They twinkled and rolled underfoot.

The familiar stink of copper filled my nose.

Blood.

I again looked down at my feet. A pool of blood continued to grow, taking in the bright brass shell casings, absorbing them, creating odd abstract art with plenty of symbolism. A descriptive aftermath where a soul had been ripped from a human husk.

My eyes adjusted to the light.

The suspect's form grew more distinct right in front of me.

When the suspect came out with the rifle, Siderites had shot him in the back of the head with the high-powered pistol round. It had exited out his nose, taking the nose with it. The suspect's brain had instantly clicked off. He wilted down, sitting on his heels, his arms loose, down at his sides, his head back, eyes open, vacant, and swollen, bulging from the pressure applied to his skull.

He just sat there. One of the most chilling things I had ever seen. Only because this time, it could've just as easily been one of us dead on the floor or down in the desert dirt.

"Come on?" I said to Dyer, "Get out of here. This is a crime scene for homicide to handle."

He gingerly stepped around the growing red puddle. "Man, did you see—"

I turned and scowled at him. He shut his mouth mid-word.

Out on the landing and walking down the stairs, I understood why Siderites looked the way he did. Stunned. Poleaxed. He'd killed a man from behind. Didn't give him any warning. Couldn't. Not without giving away his position and endangering his own life. A legal shot but, morally, a difficult one to endure.

As I looked at the dead suspect one last time, I realized he had the same expression as Siderites. Even without a nose. The expression, one of shock, one that said life as we knew it no longer applied to either one of them. That murder and tragedy both have rotten, black hearts that stink to high heaven and forever, indelibly imprint the memory of those who survive.

If surviving was what you called it.

Chapter Nineteen

Writing the after-action report, along with the interview after interview from homicide, the roll-out DA, the county risk management officer, coupled with all the hurry-up and wait, I didn't finish until four a.m. We had adjourned from the crime scene to the county station, where Buchanan and Cordova both moved about doing their administrative jobs.

Cordova wouldn't dare jack me up for rolling to Lucerne after being told not to, not with my lieutenant present to watch my back. But Cordova would lie in wait for me and get even when the right time presented itself. I had no doubt. At one point, he said, "Beckett, a word."

I shook my head. "Sorry, LT. I got a lot to do right now, maybe in a few minutes." Said it, trying hard to keep the snark out of my tone.

When the adrenaline finally wore off, I was left shaking and exhausted. All I wanted was to drive to Hesperia station, change into street clothes, and then drive home to The Hobo. Maybe stop at an all-night liquor store, pick up a sixteen-ounce Miller Highlife for the drive. I'd have to speak nice to the liquor store clerk. The refrigerators with the alcohol would be locked until six a.m. when the drinking day started for all the drunks. The law stopped the sale at two a.m. and restarted at six as if that made any difference to anyone.

Detective Herrera from homicide came into the small interview room where I'd finally been sequestered and told me I was free to go, said it just like that, as if he were doing me a favor and I was lucky I wasn't escorted into the back to be booked. Thanks for nothing, pal.

Buchanan saw me headed for the door. "Dave, hold up."

I stopped and waited for him. While I waited, I unsnapped my belt keepers, unhooked my Sam Browne gun belt, and hung it over my shoulder. It felt nice to get the weight off my hips.

Buchanan looked a little haggard, his brown hair not perfectly coifed like usual, and his brown eyes filled with fatigue. "Hey, ah, I called in the department shrink. She just got here. She said she'd like everyone present at the incident in one room for a group encounter. It's going to be in the station detective bureau."

"Is it really...I mean, is it mandatory?" I'd been through far worse in that slit trench lying alongside the beautiful and dead Jessica DeFrank wrapped in clear plastic, her eyes burning through to my soul. I wasn't sure anything in this world could be worse.

"Do it as a favor for me, please?"

I hesitated.

He said, "I'm worried about Siderites."

That was all he needed to say. I was so tired I had only been thinking of myself. Of course, I'd do it. I'd do anything for Siderites.

I nodded, half-turned to head to the detective bureau, now converted into a shrink tank, when he grabbed my arm and lowered his voice. "Dave, she's going to call on you first. I told her you were the anchor in this group, okay?"

I searched his eyes for the truth. Did he really think I was the anchor, or did he think I was the one who needed the shrink more than anyone else, and he was taking this opportunity to get it done?

Fatigue, like a warm, comforting blanket, snuffed out the ability to read a person. I couldn't tell which way Buchanan meant it. I nodded, "Sure, LT. I'm all over it."

I sat in the small circle across from Siderites, the rest of the chairs filled with Danny Dyer, the Apple Valley deputies who covered the back of the suspect's manufactured home, three dispatchers, and the department shrink, Peggy Hamlin. She looked fresh, as if it were nine a.m., just starting her day. She wore an expensive pantsuit, matching shoes, and a narrow gold bracelet on her wrist.

Hamlin opened with a long preamble about the purpose of the group and how it was so important to get out our feelings before we suppressed them. She droned on a little too long, and I tuned her out until she said, "Deputy Beckett, would you like to start us off?"

I snapped out of my fatigue-infused funk. My mind caught up with the question she'd put to me, "Ah...yeah, sure. The way I feel about what happened? Of course. I am extremely grateful that every one of us came out of it in one piece."

"Anything else?"

"Yes. This is a perfect example of how a simple call for service can quickly devolve into a violent confrontation where someone loses his life." I kept my eyes on Siderites. His mind was off somewhere else, and didn't acknowledge what I'd said. Then, a tear bulged and rolled down his cheek.

Ah, shit.

Hamlin kept the question moving around the circle until she came to Siderites, whose face was now streaked with tears, his eyes vacant. He wouldn't answer her question. He said nothing.

She got up, went over, and crouched down in front of his chair, her hand on his that rested on his knee. She spoke in lower tones, trying to get through to him. He finally returned from the far-away place he visited and looked at her. He nodded as she lowered her tone even more to where I could no longer hear.

She stood, turned to the group. "That's all for now. You guys were great. If anyone needs to talk, call my office, I'm always available. I'm going to stay here and talk with Ben awhile longer."

She'd very nicely dismissed all of us.

I stood. "Did you want me to wait? I could give him a ride home?"

She shook her head and pasted on a professional smile.

Now, the department *was* looking after Ben. I just hoped it wasn't too little too late.

I got up, walked out, drove to my station, changed, and drove home. I stopped at a liquor store in Hesperia where the clerk knew me from patrol. I picked up a thirty-two-ounce Miller Highlife. A sixteen-ounce just wouldn't do. The irony of the beer name, Highlife, wasn't lost on me.

The lack of food combined with the fatigue and the big beer, I drove a little blurry-eyed the last couple of miles to The Hobo. I pulled into the lot, and Dad's broken-down Ford Pinto was conspicuous by its absence. This instantly burned off my buzz. Dad was always at The Hobo.

Always.

I'd only been staying with him for eight months...no, now it had been eleven. Time was a weasel that slithered around, quick or slow, depending on her malicious mood.

I got out and found the cafe locked up tight. He never locked it because he was always there. Even at night, he didn't lock it. I warned him he was going to get robbed. He'd said with ferocious intent while swinging a thick-bladed butcher knife. "Seriously, sonny boy? You think some punk would dare come in here." He chuckled. "I'll serve 'em up as part of the breakfast special, eggs and asshole. It'll be a big hit."

Bold talk for a skinny old drunk.

I missed that skinny old drunk. I took out my key, opened the door, and turned on the lights. I checked around inside and found no sign of him. He'd cleaned up like normal, and at that time of morning, five-thirty, he should've already been open for business.

The front door chimed as customers came in. I looked out front to find two graveyard Rancho Cucamonga deputies hungry for coffee and breakfast.

I served them coffee, sat down with them, and reported a missing person.

My dad.

Chapter Twenty

A week, or maybe it was eight or nine days later, I woke not recognizing the strange bed chamber. I stared up at the bottom of a table littered with wadded-up gum and realized I'd yet again fallen asleep in The Hobo Café, in the booth where Dad always sat. I struggled up on an elbow to see the six-pack of empties; sixteen-ounce Old Milwaukee beer cans. I hated that beer, but I drank it in commemoration...more commiseration over Dad's absence. He had left once again. Fled my life as if I were some kind of leper. No word, no note. Nothing. Last night I realized he wouldn't be coming back, bought the beer, sat in his spot, and drank myself silly.

The night was moonless, and yet by the time I finished the sixth Old Milwaukee, an eerie glow illuminated the booth table. Nothing supernatural, just harsh imagination blended with regret and sorrow that played games with the mind. I sat there, hot tears burning my eyes and cheeks. I wished I'd had the nerve to talk to Dad, tell him how much he meant to me. Told him about Jessica DeFrank. Told him before he took it on the lam. Maybe he wouldn't have left. Was this my fault? Last time, he was gone for fifteen years. To look at him, that crusty old man didn't have another fifteen years left.

The night before, I'd fought sleep.

In my drunken stupor, as I sat in Dad's regular booth, I knew she would haunt my dreams as soon as I closed my eyes. Instead, I pretended Dad sat across from me, and I told him all of it, regurgitated every little fact, the sights, the smells...their eyes. All their eyes. Described the violence I'd encountered earlier in my career. The shotgun-suicide. The OIS, officer-involved shooting behind the Market Basket. The fatal car crash with Mom as a witness. The way the suspect from Lucerne Valley looked sitting there in the dark minus a nose, his eyes begging for relief. And, of course, the slit trench with Jessica DeFrank, the way she stared at me through clear plastic, her eyes inches from mine as the suspect, the shadow, tossed dirt in on top of us both. Told Dad about the guilt, the remorse that damn near strangled me every damn day.

The next morning, I sat up and looked out the window around the parking lot vacant of cars. The Hobo Café patrons, the regulars had all gotten the word their favorite eatery had closed down for good. They had to find someplace else to sate their appetites and regale them with crotchety wit and toothless threats about Tan Joe versus Black Joe and the virtues of chocolate chip pancakes versus strawberry Belgian waffles.

I struggled to my feet. I needed to find another place to reside. I could no longer stomach waking up and finding Dad gone. The year he'd let me stay in the café allowed me to catch up on bills and even save enough for first and last month's rent of a shabbily furnished apartment. As long as it was a dive with gold and crunching 70s high-low carpet. A place with yellowed walls that hadn't been painted in two decades and smelled of soured nicotine.

The payphone on the wall rang. I got up and shuffle-stepped with a drum-tight bladder filled with six Old Milwaukees. My head throbbed with pain in time with my heartbeat. I grabbed the receiver and listened, not in the mood for conversation. I needed to pee, and swallow four aspirin before my mood would have a chance to improve.

"Dave?"

"Lieutenant?" It was Buchanan from the station.

"Sorry to wake you. I know you worked swing last night."

"Not a problem, what's up?"

"Siderites missed court today. You seen him?"

I closed my eyes and put my forehead against the wall. "No, I haven't. I saw him at EOW last night when we gassed our cars."

"I was afraid you were going to say that. He didn't turn in his patrol car last night. It's still missing."

"I'm on my way in." I hung up before he could say no. It was my day off, and he couldn't ask, not without paying overtime. I hit the head. Then grabbed a thick slice of apple pie from the cooler, locked up The Hobo, got in my car, and drove.

Siderites had been put off work for two weeks per the shrink for mental health issues. She obviously saw something in him that needed attention or at least a break from the pressures and responsibilities of carrying a badge and a gun.

He couldn't take the solitude and came into work against orders. The watch sergeant either didn't know about his time off order or thought it better for him to get back on the horse that had kicked him in the head. In any case, after one shift he flaked off, left without saying a word, taking hostage a patrol car needed to protect the public. Disappeared into the oblivion we called life.

At the station, I stayed in plain clothes and drove another Hesperia patrol car all over that damn desert, looking for my broken friend.

Nothing.

Buchanan called up the airship to help in the search.

Danny Dyer said that the night before, Siderites mumbled something about going to Vegas for a little "wine, women, and song, and not necessarily in that order." Asked him if he wanted to go along. Dyer told him no, said it sounded like trouble.

I pulled his call history for the shift and didn't see any overt act that might trigger an emotional response. But who was to say what would in his delicate emotional condition.

Standing at the officer's counter, I looked up from the call history pages and realized I no longer carried that emotional trauma monkey on my back. The talk the night before in The Hobo, the talk I had wanted to have with Dad and had without him, somehow relieved a pressure valve. Now, when I thought about Jessica DeFrank I no longer got gut-punched with guilt and remorse. Instead, when the image emblazoned on my memory was called up, it triggered nothing more than a twinge.

I could live with that. Gravity had eased off the top of my head, and I stepped a little lighter.

The airship came up and searched, burning expensive av-gas.

Negative.

Buchanan decided to call off the impromptu search, buying into the theory that Siderites had probably headed to Vegas, the cop car being the quickest mode of transportation. Buchanan called Las Vegas Metro police and asked a favor, asked for them to look out for a wayward deputy we'd lost.

I kept the cop car burning county gas and continued my search for Ben. I stayed in the desert until dawn peeked over the horizon, changing the sky to pinks and yellows and blues. If I stayed out any longer, fatigue would pile up the patrol car.

I turned in the car and headed back down the valley to rent an apartment. I ended up in a low-rent district in the city of Rialto. The crooks all called it Rat-hole. The apartment complex, Castillo Del Mar, was a place with eight-foot wrought iron around the entire complex and an automatic gate for the parking area. Out front, gang graffiti littered the sidewalk, covering every square inch depicting every gang that ran the hood. This wasn't a place I wanted to spend time. Nearly dead on my feet, I signed the rental agreement, took the key and headed out to track down Dad.

Detective Sanchez, who'd caught the case in Rancho Cucamonga station, came up negative with his search of hospitals, jails, and morgues. I guessed that was a good thing. Sort of.

My mind hadn't been right with all that had been going on. Now the fog had cleared, and I realized, that first day Dad went missing, Darla had not shown up for work. She had to know something was up.

I found her address in the phone book and headed over.

Chapter Twenty-One

Darla lived with her mom in an older part of Upland about ten miles from The Hobo, the same house where Darla grew up. I couldn't imagine how old her mom had to be. I knocked on the door and, out of habit, stood off to the side. Two large trees shaded a front yard that needed to be mowed and edged, the grass and weeds beyond ankle-deep. On the other side of the door, the hardwood floor creaked, someone walking toward me.

I needed to know what Darla knew and, at the same time, didn't. Was I better off not knowing the where and the why Dad chose to disappear without a word? Chose to do it after only reconnecting with me for less than a year. What the hell happened? Had I driven him away? Was it something I said or did? He had been in the navy and moved around in his youth, his most formative years between seventeen and twenty-five. Maybe the simplest answer was the right one. He'd contracted a wanderer's itch in his youth and just needed to scratch it.

The door swung open. Darla stood, knob in hand, wearing soft cotton clothes that resembled pajamas, fluffy pink slippers, and a custom coffee cup labeled "Black Joe." She wore her hair down around her shoulders. I'd only seen her with it up in a tight bun covered in a hair net. This way made her look older, somehow more vulnerable, as if the ugly unrelenting beast called age might at any moment swoop down and take her. She still had that light in her eyes, but her expression said otherwise. She was in mourning, just like me, missing Dad.

Without a word, she stepped aside to allow me in. She knew the reason I knocked on her door. She closed it. I followed her into the attached dining area and she sat in a chair at the table. I did the same, still not a word said between us. The place was immaculate, no clutter, no dust and smelled of rose potpourri.

"You want some joe?"

I shook my head.

We looked at each other. I finally said. "You didn't show up for work, at least if you did I slept through it that first day after he…left. You had to have already known he took off."

She broke eye contact. "The day before, at the end of the shift, he told me not to come in anymore, that he was closing The Hobo."

"Why?"

She shrugged. "He wouldn't tell me, that cranky old coot." Tears brimmed her eyes and threatened to roll down her cheeks. Her sorrow over the loss of a friend, the loss of my dad made a lump rise in my throat. I didn't want to bawl in front of this woman. I was a deputy, for crying out loud.

I spent my days going from call to call dealing with other folks' problems, I knew how to put aside emotions and deal with theirs. Nothing but negative contacts. Always being called to their problems, cops seeing the worst of humanity. And the people dealing with cops during their lowest ebb. No wonder no one liked the police.

Her hand slowly moved across the table to a large, tatted doily. She reached underneath and pulled out a white envelope. One that had been waiting for me. She slid it over. "He said to only give this to you if you came looking."

I took it from her, the envelope still sealed with his initials over the flap, an illegible scrawl with circles and loops. On the other side, just the name: David. Not Davy. He knew I didn't like Davy and had made that distinction. This gave the envelope an ominous taint. I wanted to drop it, push it away. I was acting the fool.

Dad had not been a part of my life while growing up, and I had only known him for less than a year. During that time, he was crotchety, arrogant, and difficult to get along with, to say the least. Yet still, I came to love him in ways I had not anticipated.

How could he have just up and walked away like that?

Darla had not opened the envelope, which took great restraint and moral fiber.

"He said what?"

She shrugged again, not wanting to deal with the why of Dad's stupid game.

I turned the envelope in my hand over and over, unsure if I wanted to open it. I knew I would eventually. But in that moment, with him having so recently absconded, it hurt too much. The painful fact was that he'd just walked out yet again without so much as a goodbye. I couldn't deal with it, not until some time had passed to soften the blow. At least when I finally did open it, I'd eventually find out what he had to say for himself.

Obviously, he had not felt the same way about me that I did about him. That's what it came down to. Sure, it did. My fault. I'd opened myself up for this emotional crash.

"Thank you." I stood to leave.

"Wait?" She grabbed my hand that held the envelope, a simple paper envelope that had somehow turned warm in my hand.

"Aren't you going to open it?"

I couldn't shove the words out past an unwilling tongue and shook my head. I walked to the door and exited. She held the front door ajar, head half-peeking out. "You'll call me and tell me what it says when you do open it? Please, Davy."

Gosh no, I wouldn't.

That nickname again. Dad's nickname caused me to cringe.

I kept walking. I didn't want to make a promise I couldn't keep.

Inside the Tercel, I tossed the envelope on the dash to constantly keep an eye on it as I drove, watch it as if it were alive and would suddenly speak.

The sun reflected off the white as if Dad were saying, "Here I am, Son, open me and see my words."

My hand on the ignition, I sorted through my emotions, trying to understand why I couldn't open the stupid envelope. I was angry about him leaving. But most of all, what his words would say scared the hell outta me.

I was a fool. I carried a gun for a living, a master at sorting out everyone else's domestic issues, and couldn't handle my own.

I didn't want to go back to my dingy little apartment at Castillo Del Mar and sit in the gloom. I drove up the Cajon Pass headed to work. I'd nap in the car in the parking lot, then check out a patrol car and drive around looking for Siderites while hunting criminals.

My hands and eyes made the trip for me while I toyed with the idea about taking a day off and driving to Vegas to look for him and realized, in my mood, that would only result in trouble.

I pulled in and parked at Hesperia station, and before I napped in the car, I went in and checked to see if Ben had turned up. No luck on that front.

I checked my mailbox. Jimmie Poe had called the station. The pink "while you were out" slip said she wanted to see me before shift today, said it was important and to call as soon as I came in. Important was underlined three times with three exclamation points.

With all that had been happening, I'd forgotten about her. Those big traffic-signal eyes, those wonderful kisses. Warm lips. Moist tongue. How angry she looked when I left her standing out in front of that double-wide with the tweaker in the doorway looking on. She wanted to take those kisses to the next level and didn't understand my trepidation.

All of a sudden, I needed her. I needed to talk with her. Hold her. Bury my face in her neck, take in her scent. No words needed, just a good friend to hold on to.

I hurried to the officer's counter and dialed the number, one I recognized as an interior Victorville County station number.

She immediately picked up, "Detective Poe."

She'd said, Detective Poe.

She couldn't be a detective; she hadn't even taken the test. The test hadn't been offered for this year.

"It's Dave Beckett."

"Hey. Thanks for calling." She lowered her voice. "Where are you? Can I call you right back?"

"Ah, sure." I spouted off the Hesperia officers' counter phone number.

CHAPTER TWENTY-ONE

"Call you right back." She hung up.

I waited, tapping the counter. And waited some more. Doing a slow burn about the detective thing. I was a bigger person, and I was happy for her, but I had more time on, more experience. My mind automatically went to Cordova, making her an *acting* detective just to get my goat. Then I realized she'd made a helluva case with the arrest of the serial rapist, Nico Sumter.

The phone rang. I snapped it up, shoving down my rising jealousy and put a smile in my voice. "Poe? Acting detective, that's a good crack. Good job. I'm happy for you."

"Thank you. I couldn't have done it without you. Seriously, I owe you. Anytime you need something, all you need do is ask, and I'm there."

"What's with all the double-o-seven?"

"What?"

"Your voice changed when you said you wanted to call me back like you didn't want to be caught talking to me." I chuckled, "Am I that big of a pariah over there that you don't want anyone to hear you talking to me?"

She paused too long. It caught me up short. I *was* that asshole no one wanted to be seen with.

"Poe?"

"Ah, listen, I have a big favor to ask, and I know I have no right to, but I have no one else to go to. Will you help me?"

I knew how that felt. Maybe I could swap her for a hug, one of those hugs that snatched your breath away.

"Sure, kid, whatever you need."

Chapter Twenty-Two

Jimmie Poe nixed the first location I suggested: meet on the far side of the Roy Rogers Museum under Trigger. Instead, she suggested an intersection out in Baldy Mesa. The drive took twenty-five minutes from Hesperia station, the day warm enough to inflame the fatigue that tried hard to pull me into its arms and coo in my ear.

She sat in a plain-wrap detective car awaiting my arrival with a deep expression of consternation. I made a quick turn and pulled up window to window with her and shut off the Tercel.

All the while trying not to look at Dad's envelope but needing to know that it was there waiting for me. I put my head back and closed my eyes. I needed sleep. "How can I help you?"

When she didn't answer, I opened one eye and peeked at her.

"I'm sorry about Siderites."

I closed my eye. "He'll turn up. Won't do much for his career, though. That can't be what this meet's about." I wanted to pull the words back as soon as they left my mouth, sounding cavalier about an issue heated with emotion.

I didn't want to look, her blond hair in a bob, her brown eyes, those lips. The memory of those kisses.

I waited for her to ask for whatever it was she needed.

She finally worked up the nerve. "I know I have no right to ask this of you. I know it's…it's not right."

I opened both eyes, turned, and looked at her. "Poe, what's going on?"

"You know…well—"

"Just say it."

"Okay. I think Cordova's got it in for me."

I couldn't help it. I chuckled. "Join the club."

She scowled.

"I'm sorry," I said, "Tell me."

"He hit on me, and I rebuffed him."

I ground my teeth. The adrenaline woke me up. "And?"

There was more; there had to be.

"The captain made me acting detective after the Nico Sumter case. I'm working in the detective bureau, and everything was great until—"

"Until the thing happened with that pig that calls himself a lieutenant."

She nodded. Her chin quivered as she fought the tears.

In that moment, I'd do anything for her.

Anything.

"What's going on? How can I help?"

She turned her head, reached for something on the seat, and handed it to me across the two window sills. A manila folder with a tab that read, "First Fed Savings 211."

I took it. "A bank robbery?"

She nodded.

I opened it and found a face page and two measly supplemental pages with a crime scene description and interviews. "There's nothing here."

"Exactly. Cordova assigned it to me. Not the detective sergeant. Gave it to me directly."

"Wait. You're county. This happened in Hesperia."

"That's what *I* said. And he said, 'We're all deputies under the sheriff.'"

"What an asshole."

"I won't disagree with you."

"Just CR-3 it, clear it out as unworkable, no further leads. And it's true there's nothing here to work."

"He said that if I didn't make an arrest behind this case, I'd be back pushing a patrol car, taking calls. I told him that it wasn't fair and that there was nothing to work. He said, and I quote, 'You managed the Sumter rape okay, pulled that one out of your ass. Let's see you do it again."

"He said that?"

She nodded. "Said it just like that."

"He's taking you out and at the same time sending a message to me. Asshole."

She nodded again. "Will you help me?"

"With what? There's nothing here to follow up. No car seen, no fingerprints, no nothing."

Her jaw muscle started to work as she got angry. "We can't let him win. We can't."

"I guess you could—"

"What?"

"The only thing you can do with this dog of an investigation is re-interview the victim and witnesses." I looked at the face page. There weren't any witnesses, just the victim-teller listed. "This isn't even a four; it's a six and a half."

Cases were rated one through four in order of priority by the detective sergeant when he/she assigned them to the detectives. A one was a slam dunk with a suspect in custody, and the follow-up needed was only to firm up the case. Twos were cases with named suspects that needed to be tracked down and firmed up. Threes were long shots with maybe a partial license plate or a witness description of the suspect. Fours were labeled go-nowhere's. A total waste of time. Five or six didn't even exist.

"All I can do is re-interview the victim and hope that the deputy who took the first report missed something."

"Yep. And if you don't pull a miracle out of this victim, you're dead in the water."

She punched the steering wheel.

"Angry is good. You can feed off that."

"Will you go with me? I'm afraid I won't ask the right questions, that I'll miss something."

She believed that arrests, like what happened with Nico Sumter, weren't accidents. She was about to find out the hard way that you had to make your own luck. There was no such thing as a good fairy who dropped felony arrests in your lap.

I didn't answer, rolled up my window, and crawled over the seat to the other door as Poe brought the detective car around to my side. I locked all the doors and got out.

In her car, a cardboard pine tree hung from the rearview mirror that fought a losing battle with a reek of sour body odor and nicotine. The seat springs were broken in, and I sunk down. Riding too long, I'd get a lower back ache. They'd issued her the worst detective car in the fleet, which was standard for the acting detective slot.

She took off, driving to the address she must've memorized. She knew I'd go with her. I didn't know if I liked being so predictable.

I opened the file and read the statement of the victim-teller. She was handed a note that said to give her all the money and not to push the panic alarm. The note said no dye pack money and not to tell anyone for five minutes after he fled on foot. That explained why there weren't other witnesses, no one else in the bank even knew it had happened.

I read the report all the way through. Something niggled at my brain. Fatigue kept the reason from bubbling up. Fatigue. A dangerous partner when chasing a felon. "Wait a minute."

"What?" She took her foot off the accelerator. The car slowed. "What?"

"Keep going. I need to read this again."

She pulled to the dirt shoulder and waited. Other cars whisked by.

I read it slowly, word for word.

The bank surveillance photo of the suspect leaving; an unknown male wearing a dark jacket and a ball cap. He kept his head tilted down so the camera couldn't get his face. This crook knew what he was doing.

"There is ah...there's a time discrepancy."

"A what?"

"From the time stamp on the camera's freeze photo—the time the robber walked up to the counter, and the time he left, in comparison to the time the teller pushed the panic alarm. It was five minutes, fourteen seconds."

"The note said for her to wait five minutes before pushing the panic alarm.

That's what she did."

I looked over at her. "Think about that. Would you wait five minutes after you saw the guy flee the location?"

But that was all there was, nothing more for a good detective to hang her hat on.

Was there something else my subconscious had picked up and wasn't telling my brain's mainframe?

I looked at the three black-and-white grainy photos. The one was the suspect entering. Second: him at the counter. The third was one of his back as he fled. None of them of any use at all. Cordova had really stuck it to her.

I went back to the words on the report. There weren't enough words in the report for a wedding shower thank you note.

In the teller's statement, she mentioned she'd been a teller at a bank in Tampa Bay, Florida that had also been robbed. She moved west to start fresh. She said, "Bad luck just seems to follow me."

Being robbed should be in a teller's job description. That year, southern California had 2400 bank robberies. Bank robbery was a thriving industry. You worked at a bank, the odds were good you were going to get robbed, or at least know someone who had.

"Keep driving," I said. "I need to think about this before we interview her. The way to come at her is to spark her memory and give us something good. She had to have seen something we can use. Can you stop and get me a large cup of Black Joe?"

Chapter Twenty-Three

At the gas station market I got out into the air and sunlight, while Poe went into the store to get the coffee. She wore black Dickie work pants that fit her snugly over the top of a pair of Doc Martin boots. Her custom-fit white blouse hugged her body. When she moved a pleasant scent followed her. The boots did something for me, woke me up a little. I stood at the hood rereading the report for the fifth time.

She came out, handed me the coffee. I took the lid off and sipped the acrid, over-cooked brew, the caffeine a blessing. She stood by and waited.

Half the coffee gone, I got into the detective car. "You ready to do this?" She got in and started it.

She'd already checked the address in the Thomas Guide, memorized it, and drove to the location. The place sat on a dirt road, a rundown house cut up into three small apartments. The doors in the front didn't match the architecture and made the house cartoonish. No way the owner got a county permit for that messed-up dissection.

Poe knocked.

We waited.

The door opened to a heavyset woman with hair dyed blond, roots black in her part. She wore a rumpled dress that was more a muumuu, hiding eighty or so extra pounds in the folds of the floral material. Her muddy green eyes were bloodshot. She'd been crying. Poor girl. The emotional trauma of the robbery had really affected her. We were grade-A heels for putting her through the robbery all over again. And for what? This would get us nowhere. We were just going through the motions hoping for the best.

Poe would have to show she did something on the case even if it amounted to nothing.

I let Poe take the lead. She showed the woman her badge clipped to her belt. "Sheriff's department, ma'am. We're looking for Stacy McDowell."

"I'm Stacy. Is something the matter?"

"Can we come in," I asked, "We'd like to go over your statement from the bank robbery. It's strictly routine."

"I guess so, sure." She stepped aside. "The place is a mess. I took some time off at the bank. They said I could, after what happened. I haven't been able to sleep at all and I keep thinking about what could've happened if that guy had pulled his gun. I just don't know what I'm going to do if I don't get some sleep."

I knew the feeling.

She closed the door behind us. The apartment, more a small studio, had an unmade bedraggled bed in the living area. There wasn't a dining room and the kitchenette blended into the main room. The only other door, one to the bathroom, stood ajar. I wandered over, eased the door open, and checked to see if McDowell was alone. I didn't like surprises. Officer survival tactics never left me alone.

I sat on the couch next to McDowell, our knees not too far from the bed. Poe made herself comfortable in the easy chair next to the couch and opened the steno pad. She sat back, put an ankle up on her knee, and used her cocked leg as a desk. Later, I'd have to talk to her about awareness and being prepared even during benign investigations.

McDowell swept her arm toward the bed. "All I do is lay there. It's all I can do to get up and eat something. It's good for the weight loss, I guess." She let a weak smile slip out. "I don't feel much like eating anything at all."

I said. "You should see your doctor. This sounds like battle fatigue. You really need to get treated before things get any worse."

Me, of all people, giving her advice on emotional stability.

Fat tears brimmed and rolled down her freckled cheeks as she shook her head. I looked to see Poe's reaction. She stayed busy writing in the steno pad. What she wrote, I had no clue.

I wanted to get out of there as soon as possible. I took the digital recorder from my pocket, turned it on, and set it on the cushion between us. "It's okay, it's just for notes. We'll transcribe them later. Now, can you please tell us what happened? Try to think about each detail."

Fear returned to her expression, more in her eyes. She nodded and swallowed hard. "This man, he—"

"What did he look like?" Poe asked.

"He was about six-foot-tall, maybe even six-foot-three. Tall. And...and had like an Afro but cut short."

"So, he was African American?"

"Yes, I guess so. I think he—"

"Did you—" Poe caught herself and realized she was interrupting the flow to the interview.

"What? Are you new or something?" McDowell asked Poe.

Poe's face glowed red.

I turned my attention back to McDowell. "No, she's not. Please finish telling us what happened."

"There's not much left to tell. He waited in line and came to my window. Luck of the draw, I guess. It was all timing. He could've ended up at any of the windows. He had on these real big sunglasses and a baseball cap pulled down on his forehead. He handed me the note. I read it. I almost fainted dead away right then and there. I'm not kidding." She brought a shaky hand up to swipe at fat tears on her cheeks. "He had his hand in his coat pocket. I thought...I thought it was a gun. I thought I was dead. I really did. I gave him all the money from my drawer. He shoved it into his coat and walked out as if nothing happened. I mean, just like that, as if nothing happened. He didn't care what he done to me. He ruined my life. I'll never be able to work again. I just won't."

I said, "I only have a few questions left, then we'll be out of your way, Okay?"

"Sure. Anything I can do to help."

"What was on the baseball cap? Were there any markings or brands?"

"What? Oh." She looked off to the side, trying to picture it. "Ah...it was a

Buccaneers' ball cap. Yes, I'm sure it was a Buccaneers ball cap."

The bank photos had been too grainy to pick up the Buccaneers part.

I looked over at Poe to see if she realized the interview had not been fruitless after all, that we'd gleaned at least one unknown detail from the victim's memory. Poe didn't seem to catch on, or maybe it didn't really matter. How far would a ball cap get us? Everyone wore them, every color and brand.

"Okay," I said. "Why didn't you give him the dye pack?"

"Oh, because in the note, he said not to. I thought he was going to shoot me."

"I understand. Now, one last thing. Why did you wait so long to activate the panic alarm?"

"I did? I waited too long?"

"Yes, you waited over five minutes."

She shrugged. "I guess because I was so scared, and he told me to wait that long. I'm sorry. I didn't know what to do. Am I in trouble?"

I said. "We're sorry to have bothered you. We won't take up any more of your time." I turned off the recorder and put it in my pocket. I stood.

I said, "If you think of anything else, please call Detective Poe. And thank you."

I headed for the door. Poe had stood but hesitated; she had expected me to pull a white rabbit out of a hat. This wasn't a magic act, and there weren't any rabbits.

I kept moving.

I suddenly froze in the middle of the small living area halfway to the door, stunned. A jolt of adrenaline dilated my pupils and cleared away the fog of fatigue that had again rolled in, muddling all logic.

Poe had followed and bumped into me. "Hey, what the—?"

I stared at the inside door frame to the apartment. I turned and looked down at the rumpled bed, the two pillows. I stuck my hand in my pocket, turned the tape recorder back on. I smiled and turned back to McDowell, who had caught up to us in the small apartment.

"What's going on?" Poe whispered."

CHAPTER TWENTY-THREE

"A hunch."

I said, "Ah, just a minute. Ms. McDowell, you mind if I ask you one more question?"

"Sure." She stood close rubbing her hands.

"How long have you worked at First Federal?"

She came a little closer to us and stopped. "What? Why?"

Poe moved up as if she needed to be up close to hear. She wasn't catching on and didn't like it.

"I...I guess it's been what, four months now. Why? What does that have to do with anything?"

"Where did you work before?"

"Ah...Tampa, why?"

My back stiffened. I automatically went into a bladed stance, my body to hers in a classic interrogator's posture, preparing for an attack.

Poe caught the danger signs, and in my peripheral vision, she took two steps to the side in a flanking movement and rested her hand on the stock of her handgun sitting on her hip in a pancake holster. *"Beckett?"* She whispered.

I refused to look at him, kept my stare on McDowell, and didn't answer. I demanded, *"Where is he?"*

McDowell's eyes went wide in pure terror. She looked askance down at the bed. Just a micro-flash of a movement. Then yelped, "Don't hurt him. Don't you hurt him."

Poe said, "What the hell?"

She drew her gun and took a couple steps back. "Come out from under there. Do it now. Come out with your hands up."

I took a step back and drew my gun. I was glad to have Poe with me, the way she reacted to the threat. Pure professional.

I kicked the mattress. "Last chance, asshole. You come out right now, or I'm going to start pumping rounds into that bed."

A muffled voice. "Okay. Okay, don't shoot. Jesus, don't shoot. I'm coming out."

"Show me your hands first," I yelled.

Poe yelled, "No, you cover her, I'll take him down."

I turned and pointed my gun at McDowell.

McDowell screeched and stumbled backward, almost falling. "He told me to do it. He said no one would figure it out. It was his idea. *It was his idea.*"

Two hands appeared from under the bed. A skinny white guy with long, straggly hair scooted out. Black ink tattoos littered his body. He'd been in prison before, many times. He couldn't have been more than five foot six, a short crook, almost not big enough to keep.

Poe grabbed him with one hand, threw him on the bed. She put her knee in his back, put her gun away, and handcuffed him. The skinny tattooed man turned his head to the side and said, "You fat, stupid cow. You shouldn't 'ave even let them in. I told you not to let 'em in. This is your fault. All your fault."

"I'm sorry, Johnny, don't be mad. Please don't be mad at me."

Poe kept the suspect pinned to the bed, her voice a harsh whisper. "Son of a bitch. Son of a bitch. We got 'em. We got two in custody on a go-nowhere."

"Watch her," I said. "I'll call for a couple of units to transport."

"We did it, Dave. We really did it."

"You gotta believe me. It doesn't always happen this way. We just got lucky."

"I'll take lucky anytime." She beamed, her face flushed red with pride.

Chapter Twenty-Four

After the units arrived and we put them both in separate cars, she closed the unit door and turned to me. "Okay, now tell me what I missed in there."

I handed her the tape recorder with the suspect's spontaneous statement. "Tell you what?"

"Come on? What the hell just happened in there?" She pointed a finger toward the couch where we'd been sitting talking to McDowell. "What else do you think I'm talking about?"

I shrugged and smiled. "I guess we caught a couple of bank robbers."

"I know that part. Tell me how you knew he was under the damn bed?"

"I didn't have a clue about him being under there. When we were walking out, I saw the inside door frame."

"You saw the what?"

I pointed to the door. "The frame."

"Make some sense. Please, Dave? Quit messing with me. The door frame?"

I opened the bank robbery file folder and flipped to the photos captured by the bank's surveillance cameras, stapled to the back. "Look."

She peered at the photo. "I'm not seeing it. That guy's wearing dark clothes, every inch of his skin is covered. Hat low, sunglasses, keeping his head down from the cameras. How'd you make the connection between the guy under the bed, these photos, and a stupid door frame?"

"Look at the bank door in the photo. The door frame had bandit strips segmented in feet and inches.

"When a crook runs out, the witnesses can easily compare his height to the strip. They got 'em in fast food stores. We see them so often they're innocuous."

She still stared at me.

"Look," I said, "McDowell said the guy was six foot, probably six foot three. "Tall." Look, in this photo, when you compare him to the bank door frame, a blind man could see the robber wasn't any taller than five foot five."

"You caught a bank robber with a photo of a God damn door frame measuring strip?"

I shrugged. "I didn't know for sure until I asked her that last question about where she worked before."

She looked away from me as her mind worked out what I'd just said. She whispered, "Buccaneer's ball cap...and...she worked in Tampa. Son of a bitch." She kicked her leg out at nothing.

I nodded. "Yeah, I know. Real lucky."

"That was good. Really good. I would never have caught that on my own. I woulda walked away, leaving that punk hiding under the bed. Or worse, he could've shot me because I had my head up my ass. Like I said, I owe you. Anything you want. Nothing's off the table." She shot me a sly smile that gave me a little warm glow, woke a libido that had been asleep for too long, not really asleep, more focused only on Beth, my wife.

"Anything?" I tried to keep the innuendo from the tone.

She smiled again and winked.

Wow. But I thought about the implications, the mess it would make, her working as a detective and me working at an adjoining station, trying to make detective. Relationships with fellow officers didn't work.

"Okay," I said, "here's my ask, but you're not going to like it."

"Try me."

The units hadn't pulled away with the two crooks, and even though they couldn't hear us while they sat in the cop cars, I moved in closer to her. I gently took her hand and pulled her even closer. She didn't resist. I put my mouth near her ear so she could feel my breath and whispered my request.

She jerked her head back to look into my eyes, wanting to know if I was for real.

118

"Wait," I said, "I'm not done yet." I finished telling her, laying out my request.

When I finished and stepped away, she said, "You're kidding me, right? You sure?"

"Absolutely."

"I thought your request would be…well, not that."

"We can *still* do that thing you're thinking about."

She again shot me that endearing crooked smile that caused my knees to whither. We got in her detective ride, and she drove us back to my car. She'd have to return to the apartment and write a search warrant for the money hidden inside and the clothes the crook wore during the robbery. Especially the Buccaneers ball cap.

On the way, she kept talking about the arrest and how it would be great if we could partner up as detectives. That we'd tear the desert apart. "The crooks out here won't know what hit 'em."

It was a great idea. Never happen. But it was a great idea.

"I wanna see the look on Cordova's sour mug when you hand him the clearance with two pink booking slips."

"Yeah, you're right. That's going to be sweet."

The day had started out bad and ended on a high note.

Until we turned down the street where I'd parked the Tercel.

The Tercel was gone. The dirt turnout was empty.

Some lowlife criminal had snatched it.

At first, I thought we'd come to the wrong place. I shifted around in the seat to get my bearings.

"Ah, man, I'm sorry, Dave."

I punched the dashboard. I got out and wandered around looking in the dirt for clues and found shoe impressions for one person and tire tracks of a second car that had brought the little weasel to the turnout. A crime of opportunity, and they took it.

It was hopeless, a crime near impossible to solve. The car was gone for good.

Burglary was the number one crime in any police jurisdiction. GTA, grand theft auto, always came in a strong second. The Tercel wasn't worth parting out. They'd use it in other criminal acts and then discard it. In the desert, a lot of stolen vehicles were recovered in the aqueduct that transected the desert, water brought down from up north. Once a year, the water level is brought down for canal maintenance and reveals how active our criminals had been.

That's where my Tercel was destined, a deep-water nap.

I just realized I'd left Dad's letter on the dashboard.

I put my head back, closed my eyes, and let loose with a yell that hurt my throat.

Jimmie Poe put her hand on my shoulder to console me. I shrugged away and walked off further into the desert to be alone.

Jimmie waited patiently, following along the dirt road in the detective ride, not saying a thing, letting me work it out. What she must've thought, me throwing a childish tantrum over a stolen piece of crap car. She must've thought I didn't have two dimes to rub together. The truly sad part was that she was right about the dimes.

I finally got over myself, walked out of the desert, and got in her acting detective car. She didn't say a thing and headed back to the station where the two bank robbers waited to be booked.

We sat silent until we came to Mariposa. "Can you drop me at my station?"

The rule in hunting criminals was that if you catch 'em, you clean 'em. According to that unwritten rule, I should help her with the booking apps. I wasn't in the mood to deal with anyone, especially those two turds.

With every passing minute, I grew angrier about losing Dad's envelope and note. To hell with the stupid car. Cars can be replaced.

I had that envelope in my hand.

I had it in my damn hand!

Chapter Twenty-Five

The next day, I got up early and floundered around the apartment, at loose ends without a car. Pacing mostly. Missing The Hobo, the coffee, the social interaction with Dad, and the breakfast folks who all knew my name. I finally took a cab to Holt Boulevard in Ontario, where four used car lots sat in a row in direct competition. I needed all the help I could get.

I'd burned through all of my savings on the dive apartment, the first and last month's rent. I now stood vulnerable to the usury interest rates offered by the heartless dealers. What choice did I have?

I liked a little green Volkswagen bug, but the long, steep Cajon Pass ate cars without healthy horsepower and stout transmissions. I should've moved up to the high desert, maybe chosen a place close to Hesperia station where I could walk to work if I had to. But I couldn't work in the same place I lived, running into the same people, their domestic problems, their blatant resentment of me prying into their lives, stumbling on to the crooks I'd put in the slammer, out on bail awaiting a court date. That would be the last straw. Not to mention being absolutely pathetic.

I was quickly approaching rock bottom, my goal to make detective now moved in the opposite direction.

The slimy used car salesman filled out the sales contract with a smug grin. I used his desk phone to call the station to again check on Siderites' status and if my car had been found.

Before I signed on the bottom line, I hoped for an eleventh-hour reprieve; my car found abandoned, still in good running order, missing four tires. I'd even rejoice with only four tires missing.

The station clerk told me negative on both counts, no Ben, no Tercel.

No Dad's note.

She did say the lieutenant was looking for me. I pressed her as to why and could tell by her tone she knew and didn't want to give it up. I finally coaxed it out of her with the promise of a sushi dinner. Or at least I thought I had.

She said, "Thanks, but I don't want the dinner. It wouldn't be right, not under these circumstances." She hesitated. "Dave."

I waited for her words, for the other shoe to drop.

"The lieutenant wants you to come in an hour early for an internal affairs interview."

"Ah, shit."

"I'm sorry, Dave."

The silence sat fat and heavy over the phone line as rock bottom rose up and slapped me in the face. What had I done that warranted the shoo-flies to come sniffing around?

Department policy was that a person cannot be promoted while under investigation. And once the allegations are adjudicated and I drew some time on the bricks, the black mark would also knock me out of the running for detective for next year as well. A double-whammy.

I initialed and signed the contract for the used car salesman without even looking at the numbers, without even test-driving the vehicle I'd chosen. There wasn't any reason to. The dealer knew he had a sucker and tried not to smile too big.

I took the keys and walked out to the fifteen-year-old Ford Bronco, root beer brown. I got in and started it up. I shut it off, slammed the door. I walked back into the slimy dealer's office. I threw the keys at him as hard as I could. The metal keys struck him in the chest.

I scowled.

He rubbed his chest, his smile gone, replaced with fear. I could do that to people if the situation called for it. And this one did.

I said nothing and stared him down.

He held up both hands in front of him to ward off the impending attack, one he knew he more than deserved. "What?" He tried to play dumb.

I didn't say a thing and glared. I wanted to punch him. Force out all my aggression on the man with a crummy purple paisley tie that didn't match his brown tweed sports coat. The punch would for sure finish off any career I had left.

He finally gave in. "The gas, it's probably a little low."

I said nothing. He moved around his desk, giving me a wide birth, not losing eye contact, "I'll just go and give it a half tank."

I kicked the chair so hard it flew, dented the wall, and fell over.

"Okay. Okay, a full tank, I'll fill it up."

My foot throbbed from the kick.

Thirty minutes later, the Bronco galloped up Cajon Pass without slowing down. I loved the feel, the power, the engine hum. And I sat much higher than in the Tercel with a better field of vision.

But she could suck down the gas.

I should've cared more about what I was headed into. IAB housed the department headhunters, and they were better than good at their jobs, or they wouldn't be in their positions.

If I'd been a normal red-blooded American male, I would've been thinking about Jimmie Poe and nothing else.

Instead, I worried about Dad and Siderites. Fighting sleep. I'd been up too many hours straight. In that condition, I'd be a fool to come under the guns of a couple of departmental shoo flies looking to mount my head on their wall at the behest of Lieutenant Cordova. That's what the interview had to be about. That bastard Cordova, looking to get even.

I topped the summit and started down into the desert. On the horizon, dark clouds roiled on a freshening wind. Dad would have said, "Batten down the hatches. We're in for a real gully-washer."

Maybe even one like in 1969 that had flooded The Hobo Café, filled it to the top with mud.

I took the Main Street off ramp to the station. Instead of turning right, I turned left, drove over the overpass, and headed back down the hill. Back the way I came. Good sense won out. I'd sleep first, just a couple of hours or even three, enough to make it in time for my shift. When I woke, the world would've changed without me. Sure, something had to change. Dad will be back at The Hobo and apologize for his aberrant behavior. Siderites will have returned from Vegas, hung over and broke.

Everyone wins.

Then, with my life clear of problems, I could concentrate my endeavors where they should be with Jimmie Poe.

Before I crested the summit to head back down the Cajon Pass, fat raindrops spattered the windshield, and a strong wind buffeted the high-profile Bronco. All evidence pointed to a helluva storm. In many ways, hunting crooks mirrored fishing. Most of the fish hid under rocks and didn't come out, afraid of getting wet. Like the wicked witch of the West, they might melt.

But the real hardcore crooks, they carried a tattoo on their brain, a modified postal creed: "Neither snow nor rain nor heat nor gloom of night stays these couriers of evil from the swift completion of their appointed crimes." They possessed an insatiable hunger to wreak havoc on the unsuspecting.

My head nodded, chin dropping to my chest several times before I made it back to my new apartment. I'd jerk awake milliseconds before piling up the new used car, the fatigue now painful like a toothache.

I finally parked and had no memory of walking to my door. I dropped into bed.

Just before I slipped over the edge into the land of nod, I realized yet another department violation they would add to the laundry list. I didn't have the money to turn on a phone in the new apartment. Policy dictated that all sworn members have a phone and always be available.

Yeah, so fire me.

That was the fatigue talking.

I loved my job almost more than anything else. It was the only thing that kept me going. I'd sleep for a couple of hours and then call Lieutenant Buchanan, apologize, and tell him I was on my way in to handle my shift. With a couple of hours sleep, I could still make briefing. The IAB investigators would've tired of waiting for me and left.

Sure, a good plan.

Chapter Twenty-Six

I woke to darkness and checked my watch. Nine o'clock. I'd slept past the three o'clock briefing. Now I *was* in some deep shit. Dereliction of duty, and if the shoo flies wanted to, they could call it job abandonment, take my badge and gun, leaving me little recourse to contest it.

I shuffled over to the black-out curtains and pulled them open. Bright sunlight blinded me. I brought my arm up as a shield.

Ah, shit. I'd slept right through to the next day. It was nine o'clock in the morning. I needed a shave and a shower, but what I needed more was to find out if Siderites had returned along with the borrowed cop car. I walked barefoot outside and over to the neighbor's door. I knocked. If they worked like all the normal stiffs, no one would answer.

The door opened to a gal wearing a pink crocheted bikini that allowed peeks through to the more delicate parts of her young body. Her hair was brown but lightened, almost blond by the sun. Her green eyes were bloodshot, her pupils dilated. The stink of skunk weed wafted out the door. Thick marijuana smoke hung in a fog. On the coffee table was a water bong with two dudes sitting on the couch in front of it wasted beyond caring about the world that continued on without them.

I had intended on showing my badge to ask to use their phone but under the circumstances, that wouldn't work.

"Hi, I'm your new neighbor and—"

"Hi, new neighbor, I'm Trish." She offered her hand. I took it and smiled. "Come on in and meet my brother and my boyfriend."

"Thanks." I stepped in as she moved aside. She left the door open a crack, the only light in the dim room.

"You wanna toke?" she asked. She elbowed me, "First one's on the house." She had a beautiful smile and freckles that made her look younger than her nineteen or twenty-one years.

A pound of pot in a large Ziploc bag, all bud, sat on the dining room table. Felony weight. I lived next door, not just to some potheads, but to dealers as well. Internal affairs were going to love me even more.

"I, ah, just moved in and they haven't turned on my phone. Can I use yours to make one quick call?"

"Of course."

She pointed to the beige Princess phone mounted against the gold wallpaper. I dialed with my back to the empty kitchen and watched the dudes on the couch. The shirtless one with dark brown hair and a beard came around when he realized an intruder had entered their lair and now stood next to his pound of high-grade grass. "Trish, what the hell? Who's this? Why's the door standing open to God and everyone? Are you outta your pea-brained mind?"

Trish stomped over to the door and slammed it. "This is our new neighbor, be nice. He needs to use the phone. Be neighborly, all right?"

The room turned dimmer with the door closed, the marijuana reek, more intense.

Just as the clerk at Hesperia station answered. I said, "This is Beckett—"

"Hold on, please." She transferred me. "Lieutenant Buchanan?"

The clerk had shifted me right over to Buchanan.

Not good.

The shirtless dope smoker sat forward, his eyes going wild. "The neighbor! The new neighbor? Tom says he's a cop." His hand went in between the couch cushions and came out with a chrome .357 magnum, distinctive even in the low light.

I held my hands out with the phone in one. "Hold on. Take it easy. You don't wanna shoot anyone. I'm not here for what you think. I promise. I just want to use your phone, and I'll be on my way."

Buchanan's little tinny voice came out of the phone in the room, gone silent. "Dave? You code four? Dave? Where are you? Talk to me."

Lucky for me, the crooks on the couch couldn't hear him.

"Bullshit. Cops don't just walk away, not from this much dope." He pointed to the pound bag of bud. "Hang up the God damn phone. Now."

I hung up the phone and stood still.

"Do I look like a cop to you?" I held up a bare foot. Would I be standing here talking on the phone in a tee shirt and barefoot if I was a cop? Do you know any cops that would act this way?" I picked up my tee shirt to show him I wasn't armed.

Trish muttered, "Yum." She was loaded and had yet to grasp the severity of the situation.

I'd gotten under No-shirt's paranoia. The gun wavered and no longer pointed right at me, at least not at my chest.

"Tom, the manager, said you put on your application that you're a sheriff or some shit."

"Tom's a real nosy bastard. If you live here, you know that. I didn't want him sticking his beak all up into my business. So sure, I lied."

He nodded. "Yeah, old Tom can be an asshole that way." The gun lowered a little more.

"And if I was a cop, wouldn't other cops be busting through your door about now?"

The dope softened his survival instincts. He looked over to the door, kept his eyes there a full second before he turned back to me. "If you're not a cop where do you work?"

"I'm a short order cook over at The Hobo Café up on Foothill."

The other dope head came alive on the couch. "That place's awesome. Talk about some rad pancakes. Everyone talks about 'em. They're as big as...as big as my head. Come on, let's go. I got the munchies."

"Yeah," I said, "Everyone loves 'em. The secret ingredient in the pancakes is vanilla extract."

What made a good lie was the details. And at the same time, too many details will trip the liar up every time.

The inane fact about the extract convinced him, and he lowered the gun.

128

"Thanks," I said, "I didn't mean to cause you any problems. You mind if I use your phone? And maybe afterward you'll let me get some of this skunk weed on credit. You know, just until payday."

"Sure, man, go ahead with the phone, but no credit on the weed. It's cash and carry only, bro."

"I understand. But I'll be back on Friday to pick up some. You can bet on it. That stuff smells outta this world."

"Outta this world," trying to talk like a dope fiend would ruin my impromptu cover for sure. I had to shut up.

I dialed the station phone number, said my name, and was again immediately transferred to Buchanan.

"It's me again."

"You okay?"

"Yeah, I got it under control."

"You sure? It didn't sound like it."

"Yeah, what's the word on Siderites?"

"Nothing. The sheriff's getting worried, started a full-blown command post with four detectives assigned to it."

"Can I get in on that?"

"Where have you been, Dave?" His tone shifted to professional, all business.

"Ah...my dad disappeared. I have a missing out on him. I had to move into a new place. I haven't had a chance to do a change of address yet or have a phone put in. I'm at the neighbor's right now. I'll get it done tomorrow, I promise. I know it's no excuse. I'm sorry for missing my shift. I slept right through the night."

The other side of the line was silent.

I waited.

"Internal affairs needs to talk with you."

"When?"

"I'd go straight over there after you hang up."

"That bad?"

"With all that's going on, yeah, we couldn't reach you."

"I understand. I'll grab a shower and get over there."

"I'm sorry about your dad."

"He'll turn up, he always does." But that wasn't the case. Last time he left, fifteen years crawled by while I waited. I was just a kid. Thanks LT. I'm on my way."

"You be sure you are. I'll call ahead and tell them you're coming in. I'll try and tamp down their ruffled feathers."

"See you when I come in for my shift today at three." I probed him to see just how badly I'd screwed up. See if he'd agree to see me.

He didn't answer, instead he said. "Bye, Dave."

I hung up. I'd forgotten I was standing in my dope-dealing neighbor's apartment.

The hairy, shirtless man stood by the couch, the gun at his side. "You said LT. What's up with that? That's military for lieutenant and for the cops."

"Yeah, his name's Lincoln Thompson. Can you believe it? His parents must've hated him. Crazy chickenshit name, so he goes by LT."

Trish came over close, put her arm around mine, and said, "Give him a break would ya? He's our new neighbor."

"Thanks again for letting me use your phone. I gotta get to work."

I left less concerned about the gun that had been pulled on me and more concerned about losing my job. I didn't want my daughter going without if I got rubbed off the face of the earth. Beth, the ex, would raise holy hell if I missed even one child support payment.

What a mess.

Chapter Twenty-Seven

I had to find some way to move out. I couldn't be caught living next to gun-toting dope dealers. I couldn't arrange to have them arrested either. The revelation would enlist too many questions. I held strong to a good personal policy, I didn't get involved in law enforcement incidents off-duty and especially where I lived.

I shaved, showered, put on some clean clothes, and drove the Bronco to headquarters. I parked in the parking lot out front. I didn't have a card key to get into the back-secured parking. If I ever made it to homicide, that's where I'd park. That dream had danced off to the horizon and fallen off the edge of the earth. And the way it stood, never to return.

I should've put on a suit and tie. IAB adjoined The Office of the Sheriff. All the big brass walked by and clocked me, sitting in a chair in my jeans and button-down shirt, waiting to go in to take my medicine. Some very bitter medicine.

One lieutenant and five sergeants worked in the division; no detectives. A sergeant in a suit and tie, who I didn't know by name, came out and said, "We're ready for you now." Said it like he'd just finished adjusting the knotted rope on the gallows. He held the door open, then led me deeper into their lair to a sequestered interview room with a table and four plastic-backed chairs. The room didn't smell like a station interview room, sour body odor, and nicotine. This one smelled of fear, an emotion that exuded from the walls. Left behind by all those who had gone before me. And unlike station interview rooms, no one had marred the walls with lewd etchings or graphic graffiti.

38

A LONESOME BLOOD-RED SUNegment>

I sat down. Another sergeant joined my escort. He came in, introduced himself, and started a tape recorder. I didn't catch their names. At least they didn't stick. My thoughts ran too hot, trying to figure out what I'd done to land me in the spider's web about to be eaten.

They read my Miranda rights, then ordered me to talk, violating those rights, which was standard procedure since this was a personnel investigation. And as such, I wasn't allowed to lie. Any lie, and I'd automatically be tossed out on my ass.

"Did you want a member of the Sheriff's Association to represent you?"

"I'm sorry," I said. "I didn't catch your name."

"Look, we heard you're a smart ass. That's not going to play here. You understand? Keep it professional."

Just like that, they pissed me off.

I sat back and crossed my arms.

The guy in the blue suit, the one who escorted me in, laid two file folders on the table. He opened it and slid it over to me.

The DMV form I'd sent in on Cordova, requesting that he be reevaluated for his driving, shifting his driving privilege to "Pending." I couldn't help it. I smiled. Then chuckled.

Blue suit said, "What's so funny, Deputy?"

"Geez, for a minute there, I thought I was really in trouble. I thought I'd done something, violated some serious crime or policy without knowing about it. You scared the piss outta me. I'm laughing cause I'm relieved. I have no idea what this is. Seriously, you got the wrong dude."

Brown suit pointed at the form. "You're saying right now for the recording that you had nothing to do with this?"

I picked up the form. "What is this? I don't even know what it is."

I'd made them mad. Maybe they thought I'd just roll over and show them my soft underbelly, and they'd get me on tape copping to felony misuse of a government document. Forgery. Mail fraud.

I rubbed it in a little more. I laughed. "Oh, hey, this is a DMV reevaluation form and it's for Lieutenant Cordova. This is a good one, really. I wish I *had* thought of it."

132

They both glared at me. They didn't think it was funny. They wouldn't have another deputy head to mount on their wall after all. Not today, fellas, better luck next time.

Brown suit closed that file and pulled it away. He slid the other one forward without opening it. "I supposed you had nothing to do with this either?"

"I don't think so, but I don't know what it is." I opened the file and really started laughing. The file contained colored Xerox photos. One depicted a desk with a standard monument that declared, "Lieutenant Cordova." But someone had used White Out and made the "V" into a "B." Behind the sign was a framed family photo of Cordova and his wife, a Caucasian woman who I'd seen before, maybe at a department picnic. But someone had also cut out his wife and inserted a mug photo of a hardcore female crook with tattoos on her face, which included three black tattooed tears.

"Seriously, you think I did this? I don't even work at that station. And why would you think I'd do something like this to poor old Lieutenant Cordoba? I mean Cordova. I don't work for him." I leaned forward, lowered my tone, "But I have heard his troops don't think much of him." I shook my head. "You might want to ask around his station. There are a lot of suspects for this one."

Jimmie Poe had changed the desk monument and the photo at my request after she said she owed me and would do anything.

Blue suit reached over and pulled away the top photo to show the one underneath. I couldn't help it. I howled and slapped the table. Someone else had taken a magazine ad for Chrysler Cordoba cars, cut out Ricardo Montalban's face, and replaced it with Lieutenant Cordova's head. The caption read, "Drive a Cordoba with its smooth Corinthian leather."

This wasn't Jimmie, not for this one. Cordova's troops were now gunning for him as well. Who could blame them?

A knock came at the door. Brown suit reached over and opened it without standing. Another suit stuck his head in the door.

"Hey, they just found that missing Hesperia patrol unit."

I jumped to my feet. "Where?"

The suit looked at me like I had two heads. "Out in the middle of the Mojave Desert."

"Ah, shit."

II

Book 2

Four years later
1988

Chapter Twenty-Eight

I came in the backdoor to headquarters from the back parking lot and entered the department's homicide division. I worked alone and was no longer on one of the five, four-man homicide teams. Although four-man was a misnomer. Two women worked on the teams.

I wove my way through the cubical farm, headed for the captain's office.

One of the dicks, Frankenosa, spotted me, stood and yelled. "Here he is, the man of the hour. Hey there, birthday boy."

I'd hung the Frankenosa nickname on him, and he never missed a chance to return the favor. Years back, he fell off an ATV and cracked his neck pretty good. He had to wear a halo holding his head in place for a couple of months on light duty. The halo made him walk like Frankenstein. He was a great cop and liked to joke around with me.

Others stood. Some threw wadded-up paper balls, the air alive with missiles as they chided about how, in two minutes, I'd be bent over in the captain's office.

I'd been called into the captain's office yet again to have my ass chewed.

Not all that long ago, I was pulled from my regular homicide team and put on double-secret probation, a made-up term by the division captain. The deputy chief had wanted my head, but the captain stood up for me. Even so, he still had to dump me down a notch, down to the guy who investigated all the bone cases found in the desert. The very bottom of the barrel as far as homicide was concerned. At least I was still in homicide.

Bone discoveries happened once every two or three weeks. San Bernardino County, the largest county in the US, had twenty thousand square miles of desert. Lots of places to bury murder victims. It was said that if all the dead bodies buried in the desert stood up, the desert would turn into a forest, especially along the freeway corridor that led out to Vegas.

I was now officially known as The Bone Dick.

I truly did not mind it so much. I worked better alone. The bones almost always offered up intriguing investigations leading to many different cities in Southern California. And to suspects you'd never imagine would have the intestinal fortitude to off someone.

Today, I was called in from the field via pager—that horrible little electronic lease—to see the captain: *10-19 Charlie 911 911 911.* The captain's secretary had a bad case for the dramatic.

I made it to his open door and knocked on the door frame. He'd been writing something and leaned back in his chair. He smiled. A good sign.

Well, maybe.

"Close the door and have a seat."

"Ah, man. Really? A closed-door session?"

Not again. Not so close to the last one. I was doing so well lately. Or at least I thought I was.

Captain Hamond had just transferred in six months earlier. I'd worked with him when he was a brand-new sergeant in the jail. As a newbie sergeant in the jail, the job had a lot of career-ending pitfalls to negotiate. I'd gone against the unwritten line deputy rule and given him little hints on how to keep his tit out of the ringer. We became friends.

Or at least I thought we were friends.

He came to the job late in life and moved up the ranks quickly due to a maturity that helped him associate with the higher-ups. In his eyes, he thought me an errant child who couldn't stay out of trouble. A poor juvenile delinquent lost and in need of guidance. Some of that was true, but mostly, my methods took me to the edge of the black-and-white set down in the law. I sometimes dabbled in that narrow band called the gray area.

Okay, maybe more than sometimes.

I wasn't one to be restricted by rules. My way wasn't always necessarily illegal, it just caused grief for those who supervised me.

Captain Hamond had a sense of humor about it. Least ways he used to. I should've been reporting to a sergeant or, barring that rank, the division lieutenant. But Hamond wanted me all to himself to supervise and give "gentle, reassuring guidance." Yeah, right.

And it wasn't so much the friend thing. I'd gotten lucky with some of the bone cases and had improved the captain's clearance rate, which made him look good.

His hair had turned sparse and a little gray, his face a little red from too many cocktails after hours with the brass, a prerequisite to his meteoric promotions.

One time not long ago, I was out back in the parking lot when the captain and a deputy chief were loading up the trunk of a county car that belonged to the chief, preparing for a weekend getaway up in Big Bear. They loaded four one-gallon green glass jugs of white wine. The chief had seen me watching and had said, "Keep on walking, Beckett, and keep your smartass comments to yourself." I put my hand to my mouth and feigned a drunk's hiccup. I don't think I was close enough for him to hear.

I sat in the chair in front of Hamond and waited. He looked at me still with the smile, showing bleached-white teeth. He favored himself a lady's man. He knew his way around words and women. His greatest attribute was communication.

His office walls were adorned with framed photos of past exploits; in most, they depicted a much younger version with darker hair. In one, he squatted behind a narcotic seizure, a couple of pounds of weed, spread out on a green cloth with a couple of guns and some stacks of cash. I'd have taken that one down long ago. Nowadays, if a patrol cop didn't make busts that large every couple of weeks, they weren't doing their jobs. But to his credit, back then, that was a huge bust.

He finally spoke. "Do you have any idea why you're sitting in the hot seat, *this time*?"

I couldn't help it, I squirmed. I did respect and like him.

The detectives out in the bullpen had given me the clue to which boner he was talking about. So, I didn't need to ferret out that answer once they called me birthday boy. "Ah…" My voice cracked. I cleared my throat and let the lie fly from my lips. "No, Sir."

Hamond's smile grew wider. "Seriously. You're going to play that game. Come on, just this once, own up to it."

I forced a smile didn't move, and shook my head. "I…ah, really don't know what you're talking about."

He said, "I guess you have so many of these little problems, staying within the lines while coloring and getting along with others, that you don't want to say for fear of revealing the wrong one. One that I don't know about. *Yet.* Am I right?"

His tone still came out semi-jovial as if he liked this last caper of mine. The "birthday boy," caper. Or maybe it was his interrogation method, putting his prey at ease before striking at the throat.

He leaned forward. "Dave?"

I nodded. "Okay. Here it is." I hesitated, trying to form the story to present in the best possible light.

"I caught this gang killing. You know the one, the go-nowhere bag of bones out in Summit Valley. The guy'd been taped hand and foot and mouth. Shot in the back of the head three times. And like most of the ones I catch, he was buried in a shallow grave. Some guy's dog found it after the family parked with their RV and rode ATVs all over hell and gone. Dogs are most of my R/P's (reporting parties). The start of all my cases."

"Dave?"

"Yeah, right. Well, you see…" I adjusted position in my chair as I tried to tell the story that now sounded, even to me, a little…ah, rude and improper. Legally correct, but definitely rude. Captain Hamond in a previous talk, had told me he was making me his special project, and said he was going to "fix me."

Who said I was broken?

Who said I wanted to be fixed?

I said, "I know who did the killing. Just like everyone else knows who did it. Lil' Jo Jo. Joseph Jamison. Aka Sloppy Joe. Aka, Big Sloppy. Aka—"

"Dave, quit stalling."

I held up my hand, "And Jo Jo knows that I know he did it."

"How'd that happen? How did he find out, you know?"

"I…ah, knocked on his door down in San Bernardino and told him he was a killer and that I wasn't going to let him get away with it. That I wasn't going to stop until he was a permanent resident of Pelican Bay."

"Tell me, what section of the homicide manual does this…ah, method come under? The method where you tell the guy that you're chasing him?"

I tried to smile. It had to look forced. "Well…ah—"

"Never mind, continue. I've seen the written complaint from the doctor. I can't believe it. From a damn ER doctor." He'd raised his voice on that last part.

He took a breath and calmed down a little before he continued. "I just had to hear this one for myself. Hear how you'd try and explain it away."

In our last "Come ta Jesus session," Hamond had asked me to do him a favor. That in the future, when I had one of my urges before I pulled one of my Beckett specials, he wanted me to think about it first. Ask myself three questions: One, was this going to be something that could be called rude by anyone involved? Two, would it be morally objectionable? Three: he asked that I say it over and over again, trying to envision how what I was about to do was going to play in the press. And three—I kept quiet when his three things turned into four. Calling him on the counting error would…well…be rude, falling under edict number One.

Three: he asked that I go over in my head what it would sound like when standing tall in front of his benevolent captain. And would it give said captain angina.

"Okay," I said. "So, I couldn't nail Lil' Jo Jo—or to some, Big Sloppy. I didn't have any evidence. I mean zero. Nothing that even pointed to him. I needed someone to flip, give him up. I needed to find a wit to birddog some evidence. But his people are too afraid of him. And for good reason. Ask that cold cadaver in Summit Valley."

Captain Hamond waved his hand, indicating he wanted me to hurry up with the fairy tale portion of this meeting, so we could move on to the ass-chewing part. The penalty phase in my due process. Continue with the fairy tale I was trying to concoct on the fly that didn't sound nearly as good out loud as it had sounded in my head at the time. Maybe the captain's number three (four) things really did work.

If I employed them properly.

When I had put the plan into play, it had sounded so…so good, like why hadn't anyone else thought of it before. Right there, that should've been my first clue.

"I decided to go after one of Joseph Jamison's—Sloppy Joe's—cohorts, catch him holding some dope, and get him to flip. Work my case from the outside in."

"We've had this talk." He shuffled through his date book to the right page. "Yes, here it is, last month. In fact, I admonished you that: 'A homicide investigator is supposed to *investigate,* not *create*.' This isn't some sort of creative writing assignment, Dave."

I nodded and didn't want to answer because I had bent the search and seizure law just a tad, and to do so, I had to be…a little *creative.*

Just a smidgeon.

I started the fairy tale from the beginning.

Chapter Twenty-Nine

I enlisted Sergeant Jim Anderson to help me out, a patrol sergeant comfortable in his own skin. Black hair, large head, easy to smile. He owned a fast-food restaurant and made far more money at that endeavor than his cop paycheck. He remained on the job simply because he loved the work.

I was going after a tall dope fiend named Roscoe Simpkins, a member of the notorious Simpkins family. Roscoe sold dope to support his habit. Sold dope for Sloppy Joe. If I could catch him with enough dope, he might flip and give up information on his boss. He'd give up his own mother rather than go to jail and suffer withdrawals from his heavy addiction to heroin. And that wasn't just hyperbole about giving up his mother.

Roscoe chose his location well and set up shop on a concrete path known in the neighborhood as the Boardwalk. It ran perpendicular to three quiet residential streets in the City of San Bernardino. And to my knowledge, the only boardwalk of its kind for fifty miles in either direction. Roscoe kept two lower-echelon street urchins on his payroll who kept watch for him and whistled when Five-O—and, for that matter, anyone else the least bit suspicious made an appearance in the hood. With the lookouts and the location, Roscoe rarely, if ever, made it into the back of a cop car and on his way to jail.

I procured a grocery basket or "buggy," as my ex-wife Beth called them, and used a battered gray trench coat I kept in the trunk for disguises. I mussed up my hair, rubbed some dirt on my face, and pretended to be a meandering homeless person in search of a life lost. When I got into position, I surreptitiously called Sergeant Anderson on the radio and told him to go. He drove southbound two streets over, and really put his foot on the accelerator. The roar of his engine made it all the way over to me.

Roscoe naturally spotted the speeding cop and thought they were after him. He laughed, turned, and jogged instead of running because the boardwalk wasn't wide enough to accommodate a car. I waited for him on the next street over.

He jogged right toward me, looking over his shoulder, waiting for Sergeant Anderson's car to zip by, heading south at a high rate of speed. I drew my service revolver and stood in a shooter stance, waiting for him.

I said nothing and just waited for him to turn around to check where he was putting his feet next. When he finally did, I said, "Peekaboo, asshole." He skidded and almost tumbled to a stop as he tried hard to reverse engines. Even so, he was still able to listen to his little simian friend on his shoulder whispering a warning in his ear of the impending danger. Before I could get to him, he pulled his hand from his pocket and stuffed all the tiny balled-up toy balloons filled with heroin into his mouth.

The evidence I needed for the arrest. The evidence I needed to flip him and give up Sloppy Joe.

I grabbed him by the throat, but it was too late. He'd gulped them down. I handcuffed him.

"Damn you, Roscoe."

He smiled, opened his mouth to show his rotten teeth and lonely pink, white-coated tongue. He wasn't in danger of overdosing; street heroin was only nine percent pure. And knowing Roscoe, he probably even cut his batch yet again. Dope arrests were not predicated on purity, just on weight. Didn't matter. He'd outfoxed me. I'd been too smug waiting to rub it in when I should've simply tackled him when he wasn't looking. Now he'd gotten over on me and I didn't like it. Not one damn bit.

Anderson drove up as I walked Roscoe down the block. I tried to put Roscoe in the back of Anderson's sergeant's car. "Oh, no, you don't, boyo, you're not putting that skeevy relic in my car to smell it up to the end of time."

"Hey, Sarge." Roscoe whined, "This rookie here didn't get me with any dope. Tell him he's got to let me go."

My face flushed hot. The crook even knew I'd screwed up the caper.

I jerked on his elbow, pulling him along. Anderson put his car in reverse, backed up, following us. "That right? The all great and know-it-all Bone Dick got snookered?" He hit his steering wheel, laughing. "Won't this be a story to tell at briefing."

Right then, I should've been going over the three things (four) Captain Hamond had told me to do first before acting. Because that was when the evil little thought began to germinate, the idea in how to extract the heroin from Roscoe's stomach.

Roscoe continued to bump his gums at me the entire walk back to my detective car. Anderson had let loose with one more long, smug-laden cackle, then tired of the game and drove off.

I got Roscoe back to the detective car and strapped him into the front seat. I drove him to St. Bernadine's Hospital right off Waterman and not too far away from the jail. I took him right into the emergency room, still cuffed. "Wait. Wait," he said, "What the hell we doin' here, detective? No. No. Hell no. This ain't right. I want my attorney. You can't do this."

The admitting nurse approached. "What do we have here, Deputy, a pre-booking?"

"Yes. I'd like you to pump his stomach. He swallowed some evidence I need to get back."

She pulled her head back and shot me a funny look. "Detective, this is a hospital. We only do minor, non-invasive medical procedures for evidence gathering. We have never gone into someone's stomach for evidence of a crime. We won't do it now."

I opened my mouth to say the first thing that came to mind, that I was going to arrest everyone in the emergency room for not complying with a lawful order, PC 148. Then I did run that idea through the new three-part test. And I had to admit, this idea of mine did click on two, no three of them: it would sound rude; it would most likely make the papers; and it would most definitely give my captain angina.

I quickly shifted to another great idea that just popped up like they tended to do.

"Nurse," Roscoe said, "tell this peckerhead he has to let me go. He can't keep me if there's no evidence, right? Tell me I ain't tellin' it true?"

"Sorry, that's not anywhere near my wheelhouse." She started to walk off.

"Wait," I said, "Can you please get me a pre-booking medical release form and a doc to sign and clear my friend here to be booked in at the jail?"

She again looked confused. "Sure, put him right over there in that bay."

Twenty minutes later, the doctor appeared, looking over-wrought and harried, his hair mussed and his white doctor's coat wrinkled. The embroidered name said, "Doctor T. Willis." "What seems to be the problem here, detective?"

I took the clipboard from him and filled in Roscoe's full name. "I need you to pump this gentleman's stomach. He swallowed some evidence."

"Ah, no. You know as well as I do that is out of policy for this hospital and for any other hospital for that matter. According to the courts, a procedure of that sort will shock the public conscience."

It sounded like old doc Willis had spent some time in court. I said, "All right, then clear him for booking into our jail, and I'll be on my way." I held out the clipboard.

He smelled a rat. "What's going on?"

"Well, I'm a court-qualified expert in heroin intoxication, and this suspect is displaying all the objective symptoms of heroin intoxication."

Doc Willis nodded, took the clipboard, and signed it. "I can agree on your assessment of those symptoms."

"I'm also informing you that I personally witnessed this suspect swallow a handful of balloons filled with Mexican brown heroin. If even one of those balloons burst, he'll overdose and die." Not true, but very logical.

"Son of a bitch." He stood still, his mouth agape as his mind tried to rectify what I'd just told him. He tore up the pre-booking form. "Nurse, get this man a bed and pump his stomach."

I could only smile. If I said anything further, I sensed the good Doctor Willis might go off on me.

Ten minutes later, I had Roscoe's hands cuffed to the rails of the bed with a nurse pushing a tube up his nose, another nurse filling out the sheaf of paperwork needed for the hospital. When she got to the part where she asked him his birthday, he said, "It's today. Today's my God damn birthday."

Right then, I didn't hear the little voice *whispering* the three things that were really four. That voice was screaming it. When I applied the rules, the first one screamed, "morally repugnant."

All legal. But definitely morally repugnant.

Chapter Thirty

When I finished the story, Captain Hamond sat back in his chair, his mouth sagging open, a little stunned, just like Doctor Willis. Apparently, what I just told him was a little worse than what he read in the complaint.

Yikes.

I had hoped for a smile and a comment somewhere in the neighborhood of "Great job," or "That's the way to work the system." But he closed his mouth, and his jaw muscle started to work. He sat forward. The new weather report now: Impending storm on the horizon, take cover.

This time I might've crossed over that ever-elusive Rubicon and had ventured deep into no-man's land. I held up my hand to hold back the tirade in the offing. With my other hand, I yanked out of my back pocket a folded-up search warrant for Jo Jo's house. "Roscoe gave it up just like I thought he would. He told me JoJo thinks cops are all fools, 'asshats,' was his exact word. Roscoe said JoJo, after a killing, never throws away his favorite nine. That he keeps it hidden in his house. JoJo thinks it brings him good luck. Roscoe said JoJo told him he had eight bodies on that one gun. Maybe even nine or ten. JoJo couldn't remember for sure."

Hamond reached way over his desktop, snatched the warrant out of my hand, and read it.

I continued to plead my case. "Look, we get that gun and match it ballistically to the Summit Valley body dump. We got JoJo cold. And no telling how many other murders are going to fall once DRUGFIRE runs the shell casings. Hell, we might clear nine or ten off your big board." I pointed through his office window, out across the bullpen to the entire wall that listed the open/pending murders. The whiteboard was in a place the captain could see it every minute of every day, while he sat at his desk.

He looked up from the warrant. "He lives and sells his dope in San Bernardino city. That's not our area."

"But...but, if he dumped one body out in the county, maybe he dumped all his others there as well."

That one got to him.

His eyes diffused as he tried to calculate the odds, backing his dark horse—me—or throwing me to the wolves.

He finally smiled.

The odds came back in my favor.

"All right," he said, "I'll put off your public hanging, but you better damn well find that gun."

I stood, "No problem, captain. It'll be there. I can feel it in my gut."

"If it's not, you and your gut are going to be across the parking lot shuttling patrol cars to the auto shops for repairs. No bullshit this time, Dave. Get this warrant served. That doc called the sheriff himself, and the entire executive staff is breathing down my neck over this boner."

"I know. I'm sorry. I'm on it." I talked while I walked toward the door.

"And Dave?"

I froze, cringed. I turned back.

"Some lady from out in Phelan or Baldy Mesa asked for you, said you had come out there once before and recovered a leg bone?"

As soon as he said it, I remembered that particular leg bone was still rattling around in the trunk of my car.

Ah, the life of a Bone Dick.

Wasn't my fault, really. Right after I recovered the leg bone, I'd been given two weeks off paid leave. This after the shooting in a motel parking lot. I hadn't done any of the shooting, but the guy who'd been shot and killed, a cop from another agency, had been holding me hostage. He was also Jessica DeFrank's killer, who hit me in the face with a shovel, knocked me into the trench with Jessica. I had finally caught up with him, and he got exactly what he deserved.

In all the hoopla that came with that kind of mess, I forgot all about the leg in the trunk.

"This woman," Hamond said, "says she's got another bone for you."

"I'm on it. I'll take care of it as soon as I get Sloppy Joe in the can." I hurried out his door and closed it before he could bring up anything else.

I headed upstairs to get approval for the SWAT guys to help with the search warrant. Nobody in homicide would do it. When asked, they said, like they had in the past, "No thanks, we like our jobs." Comedians all.

I set the warrant service for one hour, the soonest the four-man SWAT team could get their gear together. Or so they said. They really wanted to eat lunch first. The team leader had muttered, "We shall kick no door before it's time." Trying hard to riff on an Orson Wells wine commercial and failing miserably.

Two hours later, we deployed on Sloppy Joe's house. It sat in a lower economic part of San Bernardino city. The house was a hundred years old or more and constructed of river rock and wide wood beams. SWAT hit the house hard using a ram on the thick front door. They secured the house and called for me to enter.

The house was empty. It was official. I was definitely in a slump. Old lady luck had left me out in the cold again.

Dad had once said, "Don't kid yourself. You make your own luck. So, quit sittin' there on your hands and go rob a bank."

At the time, I had thought he was joking.

The back door stood open when SWAT entered. The sole occupant of the house must've seen us coming up the street and fled before they got the perimeter set. It happens. I just hoped it wasn't JoJo who fled.

Murray Talbot, deputy chief Talbot's son, the corporal leading the SWAT guys, gave me a salute and headed for the front door with his guys behind him. "Good luck finding that gun, Dave."

"Hey. Hey, wait. Aren't you going to help me search?"

"Nope, not our job. We're simply the entry guys."

I followed them out the door into the yard. "Hold it." My mind spun, looking for traction, looking to make my own luck. "Okay then, thanks for helping with the entry. I really do appreciate it. I'll just stay here all by myself and search. I hope that killer, JoJo Jamison, doesn't come back when I'm here all alone."

Mike turned, laughing. "Really? You're throwing that card?"

I said nothing and shrugged.

"All right, guys, let's help this whiner find his gun."

"Wait. Can you move your cars? What if he does come back while we're searching? We'll want to grapple him up. And he'll split if he sees the cars."

You had to know when to throw the SWAT guys some red meat. "This guy has killed nine people, and he's going to be armed." Now, all the SWAT guys smiled. They hurried to move their two cars around the block.

We closed the house up and got down to the search with two SWAT guys watching our backs, peeking out the slit in the window curtains.

The interior matched the low-rent neighborhood. The hardwood floor was either bleached or dark in places from ground-in grime and lack of care. Some of the walls were kicked in; graffiti painted on everything, even the furniture. Except the living room and the kitchen, both pristine and recently remodeled. JoJo had put out the word not to mess with his stuff. Something wasn't right, though.

With three of us searching, I assigned rooms. Searches didn't happen in real life like in the movies. An investigator just doesn't casually walk about sticking his nose here and there until he or she finds something. A search has to be methodical, especially if you want to find what you're after.

I took the largest bedroom that smelled of feces, the reason the door had been kept closed. First, I searched the dirty mattress, under and around, then started at one side of the room, searching and throwing everything on the mattress. That was also when I found the source of the smell: little piles on the floor. My beautiful daughter would've called it poo." Human poo smelled much worse than the dog variety.

We searched until—

Someone knocked on the backdoor.

I ran out of the room, bumping into Murray and the other SWAT guy

151

called Mike. We hurried in a throng to the living room, where the other two SWAT guys had their guns out, looking to me for direction. One said, "It's not JoJo, what do ya wanna do?"

"Let's grab him and ask if he knows where to find JoJo."

Before I had a chance to think over the plan, Murray opened the door and yanked the visitor into the house. He yelped at the abrupt shift in his life, the brusque treatment that came from out of nowhere.

His name was Dan Hauser, a heroin addict there to buy dope.

Now, it made perfect sense. This was a dope house and not a place where JoJo might lay his head. He just visited, used it as a safehouse. Roscoe must've known that JoJo hid the gun in one of his dope houses, this one being the one Roscoe chose to give up.

Hopefully, the winner.

We sat Hauser on the living room floor after he failed to give us any actionable information and continued our search.

Until another knock at the back door.

We again met at the confluence of the bedrooms. Murray said, "This is getting ridiculous."

"Nine murders. Just keep thinking nine murders."

We made it into the living room just as Mike pulled another heroin hype into the house and closed the door. He used zip ties on this one and set him next to Hauser on the living room floor. While he dealt with both their complaints, we returned to searching.

Knock after knock came with the other two searchers not bothering to leave their assigned areas to check on the new visitors.

After a while, I needed a break from the smell and came out to check on the status of the two SWAT guys.

Twelve people sat on the living room floor, getting restless. I rummaged around, located a VHS cassette tape, and plugged it in. The tape played on JoJo's new rear-projection big screen. The dopers cheered when the title *Scarface* with Al Pacino came on.

That little voice whispered in my ear that I was yet again starting to edge toward the captain's angina thing.

An hour later, Murray Talbot in the room next to me sounded off. "Bingo."

I was on my hands and knees, feeling the wood floor for abnormalities—loose boards. I stood and hurried to him. He knelt next to an old hole kicked in the drywall. He pointed down into the hole. I took his flashlight and peered in, holding my breath, expecting to see a nine-millimeter. Hoping like hell to see a nine.

Instead, inside the wall sat a clear plastic lunch bag loaded with multicolored toy balloons, ones filled with heroin. Next to it, four red-rubber-banded bundles of US currency, thousands of dollars.

I kicked the wall. "Damnit."

Mike looked stunned, "What's the matter with you? This is a great bust."

"Yeah, if I was a narc, it's a great bust. You don't understand. My neck's out a country mile on this thing."

Murray chuckled, "Is that something new? You oughta be used to it by now."

"I'm sorry, yeah, you're right. Thanks for helping, for going along with this circus."

"Phew, you're starting to smell like the room you're searching."

I didn't answer, turned, and headed back to the smelly room. I kept his flashlight and rechecked the holes kicked in the walls. In the third hole, I yelled, "Bingo!"

Chapter Thirty-One

We got the gun.

Now, I only needed the arrest gods to stay with me long enough to find JoJo's prints on it. And of course, the ballistics to line up with the Summit Valley body dump and the other eight or nine purported to be on the gun. I was elated.

I came out into the living room holding the Berretta model 92f with my pen in the trigger guard so as not to smudge any prints. All the dopers sitting on the floor watching *Scarface* cheered as if we'd let them go now. The word had gone around about their term of detention, how it pivoted on finding the gun.

I held up my hand to quell the happy crowd. "We're not done yet. We're going to wait now until JoJo makes an appearance and we put the cuffs on him."

The crowd turned restless. Murmured threats of revolt.

"Hey, hey," I said, "These SWAT guys have guns. Big guns."

The first guy, Hauser, said, "Naw, they have to have a reason to shoot us. Come on." His hands still cuffed behind his back, he started to rise, struggle up from the floor in front of the big screen just as a shootout occurred with Al Pacino. They all turned back and cheered the bad guys.

I said to Murray Talbot, "Can one of your guys sneak out and buy all these turds some cheeseburgers and chocolate malts?"

Hauser had been the only one of the crooks listening and said, "And fries. We want fries, or we'll riot."

Talbot countered, "You guys are all legs and no arms. Your hands are zip-tied behind your backs. This is going to be a fun riot, more like whack a mole than riot."

"Man, that's just not right."

The others tuned back in, rejoining our conversation, and started giving meal orders for different things. I held up my hand again. "No, everyone gets the same thing, or it'll be a nightmare. But I'll throw in the fries."

I looked back at Murray. He shrugged and held out his hand. "I'm not footing the bill for twenty cheeseburgers, fries, and chocolate malts."

"Twenty?"

"My guys gotta eat."

"You just ate not three hours ago."

"That was three hours ago."

"All right, damnit. But I'm gonna remember this the next time you step into some shit and need a handout."

"Yeah, like that's gonna happen. You're the Bone Dick. When am I gonna need one of those?"

I didn't have near enough cash in my wallet, and my credit card was maxed out. I went over to the table and carefully set JoJo's nine down. I picked up one of the cash rolls found in the wall and peeled off enough money from JoJo's dope stash. The entire time, the little man sitting on my shoulder kicked me in the head, yelling, "Angina. Angina. Angina."

"Yeah. Yeah. But this is for God and Country."

"What?" Murray said.

"Nothing. Here you go."

An hour later, I stood back and marveled at the scene I'd created, twelve mopes sitting in front of a big screen cheering the bad guys, eating cheeseburgers, and drinking chocolate malts purchased with Sloppy Jo's money.

When the good guys on the screen got the upper hand, the deputies cheered, and the mopes booed.

Sweet Jesus, how this thing had spun outta control.

The phone rang.

"Quiet!" I yelled. The crowd quelled. I answered it and listened.

155

Nothing.

Then. "What you doin' up in my crib?"

"That you, Sloppy Joe."

"Beckett, you asshole, I tolt you not to call me that."

"I know you did. We're all sittin' in your pad eating food you bought with your dope money and watching your big screen. When you comin' home? I got a cheeseburger with your name on it."

Silence.

I whispered into the phone, "I'm comin' for ya, Jamison."

The line went dead.

Chapter Thirty-Two

I dropped Sloppy Joe's gun off at the crime lab along with the dope and the money. I wanted to pace up and down their hallway while I waited. I refused to leave until they did the gun examination. The guy at the counter very calmly said, "Then go ahead and have a seat. It'll be done in five days. Can I get you a sleeping bag? A toothbrush?"

I opened my mouth to reply with snark and remembered the new mantra: angina, angina, angina. I couldn't go back to HQ. The SWAT guys would have already circulated the story about *Scarface*, cheeseburgers, twelve skeevy hypes, chocolate malts, and a partridge in a pear tree. And I knew them. They'd over-embellish the hell outta the story, making me out a bigger fool than I needed to be. Any minute my pager would buzz and order me back to homicide PDQ ASAP, and a triple display of 911 911 911. Seeing those numbers would give *me* angina.

What I really needed was to have something in hand to bring to the captain when he did make his request to see me. A dog bringing something to his master and getting a pat on the head. Like I did with the search warrant in my back pocket. That thought reminded me that I had a leg bone in my trunk.

The nervous anxiety wouldn't leave me alone. I headed back up the Cajon Pass to the high desert. To the woman's house who'd turned over the leg bone and who told the captain, she had another bone. At least, once summoned to stand tall in front of Hamond, I could say I'd been active in the service of the king (the sheriff) and present the bones recovered in a new case.

It was something. Better than nothing at all.

There was always the chance the bone discovery would be a quick clearance kind of murder.

I made it up the Cajon Pass in thirty-five minutes and remembered the way to the woman's house. I transitioned to Hwy 138, then turned off onto the feeder, Sheep Creek Road, and eventually into the right neighborhood, a vast expanse of land sprinkled here and there with houses. I was in the foothills just below Wrightwood with a spectacular view of El Mirage, flat and white going on forever with little dust devils churning on through like young children chasing each other.

The closer I came to the woman's house, the more I remembered the last time I visited her. The winks, the salacious 'tude, her words filled with sexual innuendo. Real nice gal, just a little old for me. A retired school teacher who must've been a real pistol.

The homes lined up in twenty-acre lots with wide spaces in between. Sometimes, even fifty and a hundred acres of desert for separation.

I wasn't in a hurry to get to her house and decided to check the other houses in her tract first, work my way toward hers. I had to check them anyway.

I pulled up and stopped in front of a house where I knew someone was home. A man in shorts and tank top busied himself, wiping down a gorgeous '69 maroon Goat. A Pontiac GTO. A car I'd love to own. Yeah, and if pigs could fly. Easy forty grand sitting there.

This model was the one with four on the floor sitting atop a 396 with a four-barrel, all stock, all original.

Men and their toys, huh? He who dies with the most toys wins. This beaut mesmerized me the same as a bikini-filled beach.

Loud rock music playing in the open garage blared the Rolling Stones.

I got out and froze, waited for the man to stop using a chamois on the glassy maroon paint job, waited for him to notice me. A large German shepherd sat in the driveway, not far away, watching my every move. The man was so intent on getting the water spots off his show car that he never noticed someone parked in the dirt road in front of his place. The music had covered my approach. The lack of his spatial awareness and living in the middle of nowhere might eventually go against him if a criminal looking for a crime of opportunity entered his universe.

Rover growled.

The man's head jerked up. I held up my hands to show him they were empty. I stuck out my hip with the sheriff's star clipped to my belt. "Sheriff's Department. Can I talk with you for a minute?"

Something I said, the way I moved. Rover took it as an act of aggression and shot down the driveway right at me.

"Rebel! Out!"

Rebel skidded to a stop and sat not ten feet from me. Well trained. Good thing or I'd have had a chunk viciously extracted from my crotch. And I wasn't done using that equipment. Not yet, anyway.

"It's okay, he won't move now. Come on up."

I came up the sloping drive, keeping my eyes on Rebel's eyes.

"It's okay, the dog won't—Rebel, kennel." Rebel turned and ran off, disappearing around the house.

"Okay, well, that answers my first question. Do you have a dog?"

He smiled and wiped his hands on the chamois, taking a few steps closer.

"I work homicide, and your neighbor down the way, she called and said—"

"She called me too, and we talked. I know about the leg bone her Rots found. But that's been weeks now. You just getting back out here? Doesn't seem very judicious waiting so long."

"Yeah, I was a little tied up."

I didn't like the guy poking a stick at me, telling me how to do my job. I reached out my hand, "Dave Beckett."

"John Harold." He had a firm grip with callous skin.

He said, "After she called, I checked all around several times, even walked up to the wash behind the house back there." He pointed. "Didn't see a thing. Sorry."

"That's okay, sorry to bother you. That is one nice ride. I've never seen one so straight. And the paint job, unbelievable." I walked over to peek inside. Black leather seats and chrome.

He came along with me, smiling big enough to break his mouth. The same

159

as a proud grandfather. And he should've been. What a sleek ride.

He went back to work with the chamois on the chrome side mirror even though it didn't look like it needed it.

My beeper buzzed. I had to pull it off my belt to check, to shade the display from the sun. The captain summoned me forthwith. I was in it deep this time. He would suspend me, sure as God made little green apples. You just don't use doper's money to buy cheeseburgers. My only defense—JoJo would never file a formal complaint. Not that it mattered. A policy violation was a policy violation. And if Hamond wanted to push it, a crime of theft. I could lose my job and catch a conviction.

The cop job was my entire life.

"I better get going, John." I shook his hand one more time, turned, and headed for the car.

Maybe the captain just wanted to congratulate me on recovering the gun. Yeah, instead of chewing my ass. That could happen.

Naw, I was a goner for sure. Before I bought the burgers, I should've said that one out loud to check for rudeness. Damn, after the fact, that one sounded bad.

"Hey?" John said, from up by his car

I turned back to look as John came down the driveway to the dirt road where I stood in the open detective car door.

"Yes?"

He held out the chamois and said, "I forgot, Rebel never brought me a bone that didn't already belong to him. But he did bring me this chamois. I figured he just stole it from the neighbors. It's one great chamois. When you talk to everyone else, would you ask them if they're missing one? I'd really like to know where they bought it."

"Yeah, sure."

I started to get in the car when that primal instinct, that little voice, whispered in my ear. The words sent a chill down my back into my legs. I got out. "Hey."

John had started back up his driveway and came back.

"Can I see that?"

160

He handed me the chamois. The chamois was the softest sheepskin I had ever touched, a little dank and heavy from water absorption. It was larger than most and—"

The sun suddenly flash-blinded me. I turned instantly hot. Dropped the chamois as if it weighed a thousand pounds. I staggered back and grabbed the car for support. I reached into the cop car, fell into it really.

"Hey, deputy, are you okay?"

I pulled the radio mike from the clip and called for help. I needed anyone and everybody available to respond. I told dispatch to call out search and rescue. Told them to notify homicide, told them to tell homicide to have the division lieutenant respond code three, that this was a code twenty, a sensational event. That he needed to be on-scene when the circus arrived. I should've thought it through, but that's what panic could do to a person.

The dispatcher didn't ask any questions; she just replied ten-four Henry-eight. Search and rescue is responding."

"Cadaver dogs. I need cadaver dogs. Call Kern County and have them bring theirs as well."

The county sergeant got on the radio. He could hear the stress in my voice, so he talked plain, and not in codes. "Dave, whattaya got going? Talk to me."

I keyed the mic, "Not over the radio, Seven-Sam. Get up here now."

"Roger that. Seven Sam Two, show me code three to Henry-eight location."

"Ten-four, Seven Sam Three. Henry-eight, your notifications have been made. We're working on the cadaver dogs. Are you code four?"

My voice broke. "For now, until the circus comes to town."

Chapter Thirty-Three

I slid out of the detective car onto all fours and threw up in the dirt next to the chamois.

John said, "I'll get you some water. I'll be right back."

I had to know for sure.

I didn't want to touch the chamois again.

But I had to.

I crawled on hands and knees closer to it, the sun beating down, washing out all color in the world. My nose automatically cut off all scent. I didn't want to smell, not this.

Far off, the faint sound of sirens wafted on the warm thermal clines. Help was coming, but still miles and miles away.

With a shaking hand, I picked up the chamois, my fingers manipulating it, moving it around to the tattoo I'd seen.

Or maybe I had not seen it. Maybe my over-heated imagination had played an awful trick.

The sirens drew closer.

I found the spot, the faded colors, the two tattoos, one over the top of the other.

A wizard with a white beard and a tall wizard's hat. Below the hat were tattooed red lips, a kiss.

This could only belong to one person.

The chamois wasn't a chamois at all but the desiccated skin from Jimmie Poe's back.

A girl I had known.

A girl I kissed and had a thing for. A girl who had gone missing two years earlier, angry at the world.

A girl whose leg bone I had rattling around in the back of my trunk for the last month. I leaned away from the chamois and dry-heaved. I didn't have anything left in my stomach and gagged.

The siren drew closer.

I sat back on my heels and took in long breaths. I'd never reacted like that before. But this was an unusual discovery.

And in how I discovered it.

I wasn't at all ready for that kind of shock.

John returned with a pitcher of water and a plastic cup. I drank the cup all the way down. He refilled it and kept saying, "Are you all right? What happened? What's going on?"

I couldn't answer, not at that moment.

Behind my closed eyes, all I could see was Jimmie Poe's beautiful smile. Her wonderful touch, the way she smelled. Her soft voice. I gagged again but held it back.

A marked cop car slid to a stop behind my cop car. I crawled backward until my back touched the detective car. I sat back against it, hung my head, focused on the dizziness.

Sergeant Oscar Fuentes, Seven Sam Two, got out of his cop car and ran over. He saw the chamois, the throw-up, but most of all the shape I was in. He put his hand on my shoulder and spoke in a cool, even voice, "Dave, you okay? What the hell's going on?"

John Harold said, "He was fine one minute. Next thing I know, he had a seizure or something. He was ranting and shaking all over. He threw up. I got him some water."

Fuentes had been a sergeant in the county station forever. I knew him from when I worked patrol. We drank beers after shift together under Trigger. He knew me well. He pulled his handheld radio, as he said, "It's okay, Dave. Everything's going to be okay."

"No, I'm all right. Really, give me a hand up."

Fuentes put his hand on my shoulder to keep me sitting and spoke into the radio. "Seven Sam Two, I'm on scene, roll med aide for the Henry unit. And cancel all other responding units, put a hold on everything."

He thought I had sunstroke. Out of my head with mirages and wild images.

I broke away from him and crawled over to the chamois on hands and knees, ruining my slacks. Picked it up again.

I didn't want to. No way did I want to.

Fuentes followed along. "Dave, just stay down. I've got med aid en route."

I slapped his hand away and struggled to my feet. "Here. Look. Look at this."

"What is it? What are you talking about? It's just a chamois."

"Right here. Look. It's a tattoo. This is back skin to Deputy Jimmie Poe."

His mouth dropped open. His eyes going large. In all the years I'd worked with him, he had never reacted to anything because he had seen everything. His mind instantly caught up and understood the situation. He realized I'd made a positive ID based on the tattoo. He threw his head back and yelled, "Son of a bitch! Son of a bitch!"

He walked over to the detective car and kicked it hard three times, denting the passenger door.

More sirens approached.

His emotional spasm ended. He returned to earth, back to being good ol' Seven Sam Two, who had twenty-eight years on the street, most of them in the desert. He pulled the radio from his belt and spoke. "Seven Sam Two, cancel my last transmission. Have everyone respond, and I mean everyone. Get those cadaver dogs out here, NOW. She's not going to be in the ground one minute longer than—" He cut off, realizing he'd said too much. "Just get everyone here. Now. Stand by for a ten-twenty-one. I'm going to call you."

He turned back to me. "I'm sorry, Dave. I know you two were close." He turned to John Harold, "Sir, I need to use your phone."

He stood stunned. He'd overheard the revelation. He'd been drying the Goat with a desiccated piece of a beautiful woman's skin. His voice came out in a half-whisper. "In the garage, there on the wall. Is someone going to tell me what's going on?" He knew, understood, just didn't want it to be true. Wanted it to be put into clear and concise words in order to confirm it.

Fuentes ignored him and hurried up the driveway.

I carried the remains of Jimmie Poe over to the detective car and gently laid her on the backseat. I closed the door. I came around to the trunk to get some air and found two patrol deps from the county station standing there staring at me. I couldn't say anything to them and turned to John Harold.

"Mr. Harold, how trained is Rebel? Can he hunt by scent?"

"Hell, yes, he can."

"Call him."

John whistled, putting his fingers to his mouth. Off in the backyard, Rebel barked. He was coming fast. He pulled his hand down from his mouth and looked at his fingers he'd put in his mouth. He'd been touching the chamois.

I opened the detective's car trunk. I turned to the two deputies who knew enough to keep quiet. I pointed to the youngest one, the one in the best physical shape. "Strip down to your pants and your tee shirt."

"What?"

"Do it right now." His nameplate read R. Deakins, the other D. Rathbone.

Deakins pulled his gun belt, laid in the trunk of my car, and started unbuttoning his shirt.

"Second thought," I said. "Rathbone, you're going with him."

"Where we going? Sarge?" He said, raising his voice to the returning Fuentes.

Fuentes waved his hand, "You do whatever Dave tells you. This is his scene, his operation. I got everyone rolling, Dave. They won't be long."

Rathbone started catching up to Deakins stripping down. Deakins peeled off his body armor and put it in the trunk, his tee shirt soaked with sweat.

Rebel came running down the driveway and stopped at John Harold, who pulled a small pink ball from his pocket, showed it to Rebel for just a second. "Find it, boy." He teased Rebel, getting him in the game, playful. Playful dogs made the best scent dogs.

The two eager deputies stood ready in sweat-soaked tee shirts, green uniform pants, and black boots, polished to a high sheen. Not for long.

Now Fuentes got worried. "What's going on, Dave? Whattaya got in mind?"

"You two, pull your handheld radios." They did.

"Your job." I said, "is to follow Rebel and not lose him under any circumstances, you understand? You lose him, and I'm gonna kick both your asses." They nodded, still not understanding. I reached into the trunk and, with great reverence, took out Jimmie Poe's leg bone. I was never more the Bone Detective than in that moment.

I handed the bone to John Harold. "Have Rebel sniff it. Put him on alert. Have him track this scent. He's been to the body before. He knows where it is. He brought you...he brought you the chamois so he knows where to go."

Harold shook his head. "He should be on leash for this...I...I don't know. We'll lose sight of him. Then he'll just wander back, and we won't know where he's gone. No, I'm not going to—"

Fuentes nudged me out of the way, stepped up into John's face, "This is an official operation, consider you and your dog commandeered until further notice. Now let him sniff the damn bone."

Harold held onto Rebel's collar and put the bone under his nose. "Find it, boy. Go on, find it." He barked and yelped, trying to get loose.

I said to Rathbone and Deakins, "You understand what's happening now? This isn't a game. You stay with this dog. Under no circumstances are you to lose sight of him. I'm going to be right behind you. Run your asses off. You understand?"

They both nodded.

I turned to John Harold. "Let him go."

He let Rebel go. He took off in a flash of black and brown fur. In that moment, I wondered if I was thinking straight. Maybe we should've waited for help to get there. Maybe we should've kept him on a leash for the hunt.

But I couldn't do any of that. I'd let Jimmie Poe down. I had her leg rolling around in my trunk for a month and a half. I didn't do my job. Because of me, she remained hidden, four or five weeks longer than she needed to be. In that lost time, the environment had further eroded any evidence needed to catch her killer. I was playing catch-up and would not waste one minute more. No, it had to be this way. I had to find her right now. Use whatever means necessary.

Rathbone and Deakins took off in foot pursuit, sprinting after Rebel with me already falling behind. I yelled, "You boys, just keep him in sight. That's all I'm asking. Don't lose him."

From behind, Fuentes yelled, "I'll set up the command post. Go get 'em, Dave. Bring her home."

John Harold stayed with us for a hundred yards or so, then started to lag. The two running deputies stayed together. They first cut alongside John Harold's house, then straight into the desert in a bee line going up-slope. The sandy ground slowed all of us except Rebel. This was his home turf.

The deps white tee shirts grew smaller and abruptly disappeared.

What the hell?

I was a runner but older than those two youngsters. The sun blasted down on me. My breath came hard, and sweat burned my eyes. I ran on.

I came to the place where the deps had disappeared, a six or seven-foot-deep arroyo, a wash that in the monsoon season would be flooded to the brim with brown churning water. My homicide mind worked the problem all on its own. When was monsoon season? How long ago had Jimmie up and left, abandoning her job, angry at something personal? Left a note that said she was tired of the bullshit and was moving on. Tired of having IAB pushing their big noses in her business. Something I'd heard after the fact but still nothing but a rumor. Was it two and a half years? Three? How many monsoons had come through since then?

With the dogs bringing in her bones and...and her skin, what kind of crime scene could be left out there? Coyotes, ants, dogs. A lump rose up in my throat, making it more difficult to breathe.

I'd let her down.

Wait.

What if she was a suicide? What if she left the note some dark night, drove out here, walked out into the desert, and killed herself? But her car would've been found. Or it could've been stolen, just like my Tercel. I never got my car back; Dad's note, lost forever. Dad, lost forever.

Up ahead, the two deps' white tee shirts disappeared around a bend in the arroyo. I poured on the speed. I didn't want them to get too far ahead. I had to be there when we found Jimmie Poe.

Chapter Thirty-Four

Two days later, I walked through the cubical farm filled with homicide detectives, all of them pretending to be busy and not noticing me. This time, no one made jokes, spouted jibes, or threw paper balls. None of them apologized for what had happened to Jimmie Poe.

I'd stayed at the scene in the desert where we found Jimmie Poe—her remains—stayed for twenty-one hours straight. Until I was ordered to go home and get some rest. Captain Hamond had been the one to give the order. Out there in the desert, he didn't have his usual smile, in fact, he looked grim, like everyone else.

Exhaustion had made me loopy.

He also wouldn't let me drive home. Probably a good thing.

Later, I dreamt that Captain Hamond had driven me home. But that couldn't be right. He was a captain. In this dream, he rambled on and on the entire trip and scowled when he caught a glimpse of my digs, The Castillo Del Mar in Rathole.

Had to be a dream.

My body had thrown up its hands in surrender and wouldn't allow me out of my trance until I slept for twelve hours solid, not moving from the same position.

I got up to a ringing phone. The captain's secretary, Debra Ann, said the boss wanted to see me before I did anything else. "And that means *anything*," she said. Lowering her voice. "He's worried you'll go back out to the desert. He told me to be sure you knew the scene had been dismantled. No one's out there."

I showered, shaved, walked out my door, and realized someone had driven me home. I didn't have my detective car. Huh?

In a half-trance, I walked to the parking lot anyway and found my car. I checked on top of the left front tire, a homicide procedure used out at a scene. You always left your keys available in case your car needed to be moved and you were unavailable, stuck inside a house or up a mountain, or in some other structure where a body had been dumped. I found the car keys, got in, and drove to HQ.

The previous days flooded back on me in flashes, gruesome images that at any other crime scene would've been sedate, mundane even. But these bones belonged to my friend. That one fact shifted the world under my feet.

Two days earlier, I'd come running around the corner in the arroyo, the sun beating me into the sand, sweat burning my eyes, to find the two patrol deps three hundred yards ahead, bent over at the waist, hands on their knees trying to catch their breaths. Beside them, resting in the shade of the arroyo slope, sat Rebel. His long pink tongue lolling out as he wheezed. I loved him and hated him. He'd brought us to our target without delay, so Jimmie wouldn't be alone any longer than she had to be. He also was the one to bring his dutiful owner a remarkable chamois with a tattoo. One that changed my life and at the same time further defiled and humiliated my friend.

The bottom half of Jimmie Poe was gone, scattered across hundreds of square yards of desert, maybe even a square mile. Her top half was stuck in the top strata of the arroyo. She'd been buried in a shallow grave, a classic Bone Detective kind of case. A summer monsoon rain had come through and eroded the arroyo bank, exposing her legs right up to her pelvis. That's what protruded from the side of the arroyo, a few inches of her pelvis. Bleached white from the sun. Easy to see once you knew what to look for.

She was rolled into a hole, landing face down, and the dogs, Rebel in particular, wiggled in from the top edge, got to her back, pulled off the desiccated skin. When I first saw her remains, I wanted to go over and kick a lung out of Rebel for doing that to a woman I cared about. But it wasn't his fault. He was a dog doing what a dog was supposed to do.

I was a bone detective, and I needed to get my head back in the game, catch the bastard who did this. Do what a bone detective was supposed to do. Only I was tired then, standing in the bright desert sun. I stayed another twenty hours after that, while forensics did their thing.

Word had gone out someone found a buried deputy. News helicopters buzzed about. Annoying little gnats, looking to suck some sensationalism, suck some blood up from the desert floor, package it, and put it out over the airwaves. Off-road vehicles tried their best to sneak inside the perimeter, which wasn't set nearly wide enough. They were ruining any chance of recovering other bones. Assholes, all of them. Morbid, bloodsucking lookie-loos.

The techs finally, after too many hours, using small spoons for shovels, brushes, and whisks, working from the top down, made it to Jimmie Poe's head. They found two bullet holes in the back of her skull. Her soft blond hair, still in place, clotted with dirt. That meant it was probably raining when she went into the hole. Alone. With no one even looking for her.

We were the real assholes.

No exits. The bullets were still inside. The first real break. The first real evidence that confirmed it was a murder.

That was when Captain Hamond appeared out of nowhere, took me by the arm, and began whispering shit like, "Dave, you're dead on your feet. You need to get some sleep. We'll talk about this tomorrow. Come on now, don't give me any shit about this."

I was too tired to even reply and let him guide me along. He sat me in the car. As soon as my body stopped moving, I fell fast asleep and had no idea how I got home or into my bed.

Didn't hear or see a thing until the phone woke me.

I knocked on Captain Hamond's door frame. He looked up, no smile, not even a hint of one. I didn't care. I was fed up with the bureaucracy. The rules, regulations, and policies that tied my hands. The same rules that were about to keep me from doing real police work. Bench me because of a "conflict of interest." My relationship with Jimmie Poe.

I knew what he was going to say, chapter and verse. I closed his door and sat down in the chair facing him.

He tossed his pencil down and leaned back in his chair.

We stared.

My body ached from standing out in the desert sun. Then all the way through the night and back in the sun all the next day. The moon, rolling across the dark sky, then the sun doing the same as if time only counted in the high cathedral-like dome. As if time no longer applied on the ground. Ached from falling into bed and not moving an inch for ten hours.

On the way to HQ, I should've stopped for something to eat. I recognized that on top of everything else, I was *hungry*.

Hamond stared at me. "I know it won't do any good to tell you to stand down from this investigation."

"Damn straight."

He grimaced at my insubordination and leaned forward. "Deputy Chief Talbot wants me to put you on a desk right outside my office, like a chained dog." He raised his voice. "Because even he knows what an asshole you can be when it comes to taking orders and following the rules."

"This is Jimmie Poe we're talking about."

"Shut up and sit down. God damn you, Dave."

I took a breath and replayed what he just said. It sounded kinda like he might've been on my side. "I'm sorry, Captain. I'm…I guess I'm not quite awake yet. I shouldn't talk to you like that. You've been nothing but good to me."

The red left his face. Slowly fading away. He sat back in his chair. He waited, letting us both cool down, and finally lowered his voice almost to a whisper. "You know. And I know, no matter what I say, you're going to do exactly whatever you're gonna do. And to hell with your career."

I opened my mouth to reply.

He held up his hand. "Wait. Would you just give me a chance to talk, then I'll let you use your words to crucify yourself?"

I nodded.

He continued. "I also know that you, more than all these other swingin' dicks I got out there, will stop at nothing to run down the bastard who did this. You are unequivocally the best man for this job." He spoke through clenched teeth. "And I'm going to let you do it. You know why?"

He didn't let me answer. But I knew.

"Because I want this bastard like no other son of a bitch that has come before him. So, I'm going to wind you up like a little toy soldier and let you go do your thing. You understand what I'm saying here?"

"Yes. And thank you."

"I don't think you do, or you wouldn't be thanking me. Spell it out for me. I need to hear you say it."

I stared at him and said nothing.

He pushed a button on his phone without breaking eye contact. "Debra Ann, could you please come in here?"

Debra Ann opened his door and stood in the doorway, green dress, red hair. He still had not broken eye contact and said, "Detective Beckett, I'm ordering you to stay out of the Poe investigation. He handed me a file folder. "Your ballistics have come back on Joseph Jamison. Here's a warrant. Jamison is now wanted for seven homicides. Your assignment, as of right now, is to find and arrest him. And nothing else. You understand?"

I nodded.

"No," he said. "Say it out loud. Say you understand that you are not to involve yourself in the Poe homicide."

"I understand. I will not involve myself in the Poe homicide."

He looked up at Debra Ann. "Thank you. Now, please leave us alone."

She closed the door.

I smiled, the first one in a long time.

Chapter Thirty-Five

When the door closed, Captain Hamond said. "I've advised Sergeant Grimes—his team caught the Poe murder—I told him on the down-low that you'll be sniffing around the edges of this investigation and for him to turn a blind eye. Up to a point. You understanding me here, Dave? Go at this like a professional. Don't start right off kicking in doors. I want you to find this guy, before the brass gets wind of what's going on and shuts it down."

I stared at him and said nothing. Not being rude, but my mind was already running at high speed deciding on what to do first.

Hamond opened his desk drawer and handed me another file. "Grimes is copying me on everything his team is doing on Poe. I'll pass it on to you as it comes in. But I have to tell you, there's nothing here. There's nothing to sink your teeth into. It's a whodunit, plain and simple.

"In that file on JoJo, he has a couple of houses up in the high desert. Known associates. If anyone asks what you're doing up there, use that file as cover. Low profile, Dave."

"I understand. I can do low profile if I have to."

"Yeah, right."

I stood to leave, to get to it.

Hamond said, "Too bad Captain Cordova is up at the county station, I don't have any sway with him. In fact, he can be a real prick, so steer clear of him."

"I understand and appreciate the opportunity. I know what you're putting at risk."

But he really wasn't putting anything at risk. He had not risen to captain without learning how to play the political game. How to get a sensitive job accomplished without getting any blowback spattering him. He covered himself with a witness, Debra Ann.

"Now," Hamond said. "IAB wants to talk with you. They're waiting."

"Internal Affairs? Whatta *they* want?"

Hamond shrugged. "Hell if I know. You know those guys upstairs, all personnel matters are hush, hush. Double top secret. Executive staff only. I'm command staff."

I turned and stepped toward the door.

"Dave?"

I turned back.

"If you're worried about cheeseburgers and chocolate malts, it's not that. I put the kibosh on it. Told them I gave you permission to use the money and that I'd chit it out with buy money later on. Don't do that shit again."

"Yes, Boss. Thank you, Boss."

"Quit with that Boss shit and get outta my office."

"Yes, Boss."

He smiled and threw a pencil. I dodged it and slipped out the door.

I retreated back through the cubicle farm, not wanting to talk with anyone. This wasn't the proper way to deal with grief, but it was my way. I headed upstairs to Internal Affairs.

Twenty minutes later, I was escorted to an interview room. One pristine without graffiti, one with a new table and comfortable chairs. Too small and claustrophobic with what I had going on in my head. The images. The leg bone that had been rolling around in my trunk.

After sitting for forty-five minutes waiting, the room started to close in even more. Coupled with the anxiety over the need to get started hunting Poe's killer, I opened the door and fled. Out in the hall, James Sampson, a new sergeant in IAB, raised his voice. "Hey, where the hell you goin'?"

"I'm tired of the bullshit games. I know what you're trying to do, putting me on the back burner to simmer. But unlike you, I have real police work to do."

This was an IAB sergeant.

I should've listened to the words before they spewed from my mouth.

Sampson hurried, got up in my face. "I'm sorry over what happened. I really am. But if you don't go right back to that interview room, you will be suspended pending investigation."

"For what? What have I done this time?"

He said nothing.

Had I not wanted to get to the Poe investigation as soon as possible, I'd have walked away. To hell with him. I hesitated to let the fat silence work on him a little. He was rotund; his jowls and cheeks were flushed red. His new suit looked as if he'd just pulled off the sale tags. I worked with him briefly on the street. He was a paper deputy, just did what he had to do to get by. Answered his calls, did an average job. But never pulled anyone over, too afraid of running into something dangerous.

I turned my back to him and walked to the interview room. I sat down as he closed the door. Anger started to fester.

IAB was a promotional position for those on their way up the ladder. Anyone assigned to the division was on the fast track. Three kinds of deputies moved up the ladder: the disciplined, conscientious deputy, known as the worker bee. Next came nepotism, the Brass Babies, sons and daughters of the executive staff, given a hand up. And then there was favoritism, known as The Brown Nosers. Sampson fit in the last category. His mentor or rabbi, or Juice Card, was none other than Captain Cordova. No wonder Hamond didn't know why I was summoned. The strings were being pulled by Cordova from all the way out in the desert. I remembered how he had taunted Jimmie Poe by giving her the bank robbery investigation, telling her she solved it or got flopped back to patrol.

I yelled at the door. "I'm staying five minutes more. Then—"

The door reopened. "Then what?" In came Sampson and Pedro Ramirez. Ramirez was one of the worker bees in the division, and I trusted him. At least, I used to. Something happens to a person when he crosses over into the rat squad.

They sat down in chairs with their backs to the door. I had my back up against the far wall, the table between us.

Ramirez wore his black hair cut close on the side walls; his dark brown eyes, almost black, could burn a hole right through a person. They got the paperwork out of the way, having me sign the waivers and giving out the verbal admonishments for the tape recorder. Which scared me a little. Maybe I did need a rep. But I wanted to get out of there as soon as possible.

Ramirez sat back, taking a moment to get his interview strategy lined up as he assessed me.

He patted a thick file he'd brought in, one of two. "You know this took me a while to get through. You've had quite the colorful career."

"Hey, look, can we just dispense with the small talk and get right to it? I got a murderous thug to track down."

Sampson shot me a crooked smile. "Sure. Why not?" He opened the second file and pretended to read from it. I wasn't at all sure he knew how to read, at least not at an adult level. One two, buckle my shoe might work better for him.

Sampson said, "Did you arrest Nico Sumter, two and a half years ago on February 2nd?"

"This is about something that happened two-and-a-half years ago? Are you kidding me?" I got up to leave.

Ramirez stared, unmoving, his voice calm, "Beckett, sit down. We're trying hard to not file a homicide charge against you."

I sat. "Homicide? You have got to be kidding. I haven't killed anyone. What are you—?"

"Nico Sumter, remember him?" Sampson said.

The name tickled the tip of my brain. I did know him but couldn't bring it to the surface. "Not right off. You have a photo?"

"You arrested him for rape, you and Jimmie Poe?"

I eased back down in the seat. "Ah, shit."

Chapter Thirty-Six

That reminder about me and Jimmie arresting Nico did it. The arrest flashed in my memory. Jimmie Poe's face, her elation for taking a class-one predator off the street, and at the same time giving her a needed boost to an acting detective slot.

"Yeah, sure, I remember Nico Sumter. He committed a rape, was convicted, did his time and got out. Stalked the same victim again. Laid in wait and again raped her. So, yeah, I was there when we arrested him. What's that got to do with a murder charge, and why now…I mean, with all that's going on with Jimmie Poe?"

I was missing something, an important piece of the puzzle and couldn't figure out what.

"Two-and-a-half years ago—" Sampson started to say, but Ramirez put his hand on Sampson's arm.

Ramirez said, "Nico Sumter was killed in prison."

I said nothing and waited for the other shoe to drop. They were holding all the cards.

They, too, waited. Cops using the same interrogation techniques on another cop didn't work too well.

"Okay, I'd say I'm sorry, but I'm not. What does all this have to do with me?"

"Just before Poe disappeared, we called her in on this same matter, interviewed her."

I sat forward in my chair. "What are you saying? Did you have her caught up in some kind of bullshit beef about a guy she arrested who got killed in the joint?

"Wait. You stopped investigating because you thought, at the time, she was despondent and left the job, disappeared to avoid all this crap?" I poked my finger on the file. "Then, when we found her with two slugs in the back of her head, you realized you'd screwed up and took another look at this bullshit case. Am I getting close? Now you need to hang it on someone or have egg on your face, and I'm the perfect patsy. I had nothing to do with killing Nico Sumter in prison. I haven't even thought about that turd until you just brought him up."

Ramirez said, "We're here to ask two questions. Just two. *If* we get the right response."

"I just told you, I didn't kill him. How could I? He was killed in prison. He was inside, and I was on the outside. Next question."

"Not for long," Sampson muttered.

Before I could react, Ramirez jumped to his feet, grabbed the door, and opened it. "Get out."

Sampson looked like someone had pissed in his Wheaties. He stood and hesitated, waiting for a reprieve, not smart enough even to apologize.

"Out."

He left. Ramirez closed the door and sat down. He leaned over and turned off the recorder. This was out of policy. This was the old street cop in Ramirez stepping in to take over.

I asked. "Pedro, what the hell's going on?"

"We reopened the IAB investigation. Looking into the formal complaint from a family member that said a deputy had something to do with Nico Sumter's death. We sent Nico's booking app to Quantico along with your handwriting template we had in your file. It matched. Before you say a thing, Dave, think long and hard about your answers."

That was the only friendly warning I was going to get.

He turned on the tape. "Detective Beckett, did you fill out the booking application when Nico Sumter was booked by Jimmie Poe for rape? This application, right here?"

"Wha—" I shut my mouth as my mind spun out of control trying to figure out what he was driving at, where this could lead. It didn't make any sense.

"For the tape," Ramirez said, "I'm showing Detective Beckett a copy of the booking application." He slid it across to me.

My eyes scanned the document and fell upon the third line from the top labeled, "Nicknames and Aliases." It all flooded back in a rush. The air in the room turned thick. Back then, I was a reckless, devil-may-care street cop doing stupid things. But for the right reasons. I'd matured since then. At least, I hoped I had. Now, I would never have done something so sophomoric.

In the slot, I had written as a nickname: Bey Bey Wraper. Like he was some kind of rap star. A kind of joke.

But it wasn't a joke. I purposely labeled him.

I knew it then.

I knew the consequences and didn't care. Nico had it coming.

Nico Sumter was killed in the joint because criminals have a code. You don't mess with women, and you certainly don't mess with children. Your fellow inmates killed you for it. Nico's victim was only seventeen the first time he raped her. That means he violated both unwritten rules in the criminal code of conduct: women *and* children.

Far worse was the fact that Jimmie Poe had been called on the carpet for something I had done. A stupid little thing. Three short words in one box on the booking app. Could that have caused all of this hate and death? Had Jimmie Poe died at the hand of Nico's relatives because of me?"

"Is this why I'm here? You're looking at possible suspects in the killing of Jimmie Poe, and you found me instead? To take some of the heat off."

I got up. "This interview is over."

Ramirez remained seated, looking up at me. "Detective Beckett, I'm advising you to sit back down."

"I answered your questions. Your partner harassed me, made an insipid little comment—he threatened me, implying that I'll be in jail soon for killing—"

Ramirez's hand shot over and clicked off the recording. "Sampson's not a bad guy. He just doesn't know when to keep his mouth shut."

"You tell him for me, I meet him out on the street, I owe him a rap in the mouth."

"*Did* you fill out the booking form?"

He was a fool thinking I'd incriminate myself, say something against my penal interest. I had my hand on the door, ready to flee. I needed air. I stopped. "You said you sent it to the FBI. Was that a bluff?"

He shook his head, "No, we did and got the analysis back."

I smiled. "If you had enough probable cause, you'd have already arrested me. Now I'm sorry, Pedro, but I gotta jet."

I walked out of the interview room and into the hall, my knees weak. I had to get further away. I leaned against the wall for support to breathe free air again. I had never come so close to going to the joint. It wouldn't have been for twenty-five to life, though. The DA would've cut a deal. I would've drawn seven years at the most. But even so.

Was that what Jimmie Poe had been thinking when they had called her in?

No. She knew she hadn't filled out the booking app, that I had. The tan and green wall of silence that said, never rat on a brother dep, would've been tearing her insides out. She hadn't said anything to me and dealt with it alone with no one to lean on. Had she only told me, I'd have come forward. I always owned up.

I'd put her in the jackpot. Me. Mr. veteran cop who thought he knew it all.

I was a little too arrogant, all-knowing. No one was smarter than me. Yeah, right.

When I filled out that app. I knew there was a slim possibility that I'd catch some blow back. When I came to that one box, I changed hands and wrote it with my left. The FBI report would confirm that I filled out the app. But that one box on the app would be listed as inconclusive. That's why I was walking around free. The story of my life. I was always an inconclusive kinda dude.

I'd built in my own get-out-of-jail-free card. Now, I just had to deal with the guilt. Enough guilt to pile-drive me right into the ground up to my chin.

I had to know what happened with Jimmie.

Did she die because of me?

Chapter Thirty-Seven

Out the door and down the hall from Internal Affairs, I headed for Human Resources. I couldn't allow Jimmie Poe to get into my head. I had to keep my feelings for her separate or risk losing all control of the investigation. Losing sight of the suspect who did this to her. Once I found him, I'd unleash the pent-up rage in all its ferocity.

At that point, my career wouldn't matter.

I opened the door to HR, stepped in, and over to the short counter. A woman dressed business professional in a pantsuit with a matching blouse smiled, got up from her desk, and approached. "My name is Mari. How can I help you?"

I showed her my badge, flashed it, not wanting her to get a gander at the number, an old habit. "I'm working the murder of Jimmie Poe, and I need to see her personnel file."

"Oh." She lost her smile, her eyes staying on mine as she tried to decide on an appropriate way to decline the request.

"I know what you're thinking. I know what you're going to say. Personnel files are confidential and can't be released. I understand all that, but I'm putting you on official notice that she has been murdered. Now, most of those silly rules no longer apply, right?" I shot her my best Dave Beckett, the Bone Detective smile. It wasn't true, but I wanted to give her something to hang her hat on.

She, too, pasted on her own version of a faux smile, held up one finger, and backed up to her desk. She dialed a four-digit number and whispered a few short words before hanging up. She stood by her desk as we both waited for her boss to appear, the outcome a forgone conclusion.

A woman larger by half came from around the cubical wall. She approached the counter unsmiling. A rhino on the charge, snout down, ready to take on this unfriendly interloper. "I'm sorry, but Mari was correct in telling you that under no circumstances can we release a personnel file."

I swallowed my rising ire and tried hard to keep my tone even. "Did I mention that Jimmie Poe was a deputy sheriff for this department?"

"No matter. The law is the law."

I closed my eyes and corralled the words that came to mind, sifting through all the other options that weren't appropriate. Hamond's method didn't work in this situation. How could he expect it to, not under the circumstances? I opened my mouth ready to spew the chain of expletives interspersed with a few choice obscenities, when I clamped my teeth together and yanked the phone set on the counter over to me. I dialed the four-digit inter-officer number. Debra Ann answered.

"Tell Hamond that I'm upstairs in HR about to burn it to the ground." Hamond came on. "Here," I said, "talk to this woman." I handed the phone to the HR supervisor.

The rhino took the phone. In a few seconds Hamond would wipe away her smugness, and I'd do my best not to gloat but would anyway.

She listened intently. She said, "No," and hung up the phone. She turned heel and walked away, more a trot, elbows away from her body. I tried hard not to imagine her gait as a goose-step. The phone rang. I scooped it up before Mari could and held it away from my ear. Those same expletives and obscenities I'd successfully tamped down came blaring through the phone, Captain Hamond on a tirade directed at the rhino. I was slightly elated that this time I wasn't the only one to invoke his wrath. I waited for a pause.

I wasn't in the mood for levity, but this one was too sweet. "Why, Captain Hamond, did you stop and think through those awful words before spewing them out in public?"

He slammed down the phone. I cocked my head to the side and smiled at Mari. I knew Hamond. He didn't suffer fools. I fit in that category at the top of his list. But this time, the rhino took the first-place trophy.

I checked my watch and marked the minute and second hand. From his office, Hamond would step across the hall into Executive Staff Country and speak with the in-house county attorney, who'd, in turn, call the rhino back, and tell her just how the cow ate the cabbage. That would fix it.

Two minutes forty-five seconds later, the light on the phone blinked. An incoming call. The light stopped blinking. I held my breath, waiting.

On the other side of the cubicle wall, the rhino let loose with a resounding "No." Then, "I don't care who you are. I don't work for the sheriff's department. I work for the county." The light went off, corresponding with the phone being slammed down.

I leaned over and whispered to Mari. "For a...ah, tall woman, she has quite the Napoleon complex."

Her hand flew up to her mouth to hide her smile lest the rhino charge around the cubical wall and catch her. Mari didn't leave. We both waited, knowing there'd be more to the developing saga. Mari had a nice smile, and under different circumstances, I might've flirted with her.

Time crawled by with anticipation over which powers would rise above in the tug of war.

Four minutes, twenty seconds later, the line on the counter phone again lit up. The rhino answered. "Human resour—"

Silence.

Then, from the rhino: "Yes...No...I'm sorry. It won't happen again. Yes, I understand." The light on the phone went off. We waited. I counted internally, one Mississippi and so on.

Finally, from the back: "Mari, come here, please."

Mari shrugged, smiled, and disappeared behind the cubical wall. The disembodied voice of the rhino floated over. "Here, he can look at it. But it stays in this office. No exceptions. And I don't care who he calls."

Mari reappeared with a thick file. I took it from her. We both smiled. Not wanting to risk further ire of the rhino, I headed for the door, opened it, and whispered, "I'll bring it back when I'm finished with it." I winked.

She said. "Oh, my God." And chuckled.

What a hypocritical world. No one liked it when I broke the rules or laws, but it was okay when the brass did it. HR rules were supposed to be sacred. Solid. Impenetrable.

Until they weren't.

Chapter Thirty-Eight

I headed over to the staff lunchroom, one used by the entire building, huge with vending machines, two refrigerators, two coffee makers, counters, and two sinks. I took the table at the far end to stay away from a trio enjoying their coffee break. Too early for lunch.

I took in a breath and opened Jimmie Poe's file, and realized I knew almost nothing about her.

The tab read: Judith Eileen Poe. (Aka, Jimmie)

The file was broken into sections based on chronology: Her application to be a deputy sheriff. The results on her six tests to become a deputy (written, oral, physical agility, psychological, polygraph, and background). Then came her performance evals from the academy. She did well in every category, but not outstanding. She was sanctioned twice for tardiness and warned a third would mean termination.

After graduation, she was assigned to the women's side of Central Jail for six months before going out to patrol at Victor Valley station. The file contained her six-month FTO training period and her patrol performance evals. She was awarded a meritorious conduct medal for the Nico Sumter arrest and another for the arrest of Stacy McDowell and her boyfriend for bank robbery. I paused and processed the McDowell arrest. No way could those two idjits be involved in her killing.

Next came a memo that said to check with IA for an open investigation into a policy violation/criminal case. After that came the paperwork necessary to officially fire her for "job abandonment." In the back of that section was a copy of the goodbye note Jimmie had left.

Nothing in the file jumped out at me.

Not in the cursory perusal.

I flipped back to the background to learn a little more about her. Where she came from, where she grew up. What her friends and neighbors thought of her. Things as her friend I should've already known.

Nothing there unexpected. Everyone thought of her what I did, a great gal, who'd give you the shirt off her back.

A deeper dive revealed that she was raised by her sister. Her father left when she was too young to know him, and her mother died from a protracted battle with melanoma.

Jimmie graduated high school, took a couple years off where she...I turned the pages, looking to fill the time gap. Jimmie disappeared for those two years, from age eighteen to twenty, without an explanation. The background investigator didn't even try to find out what happened during those two missing years.

She resurfaced again to live with her sister while she attended junior college majoring in Admin Justice. From there, she applied and was accepted as a deputy sheriff trainee.

Other than the missing two years, nothing rose up, and bit my nose as a lead. Not the smallest inkling.

Had she been a criminal, the term would've been: "She's as clean as a Safeway chicken."

Based on the file, Jimmie Poe was a true victim. Victimized by the system. Victimized by Cordova, who pulled the strings to have her taunted by IAB over something I had done. His direct involvement wasn't written in black and white, but gut instinct said he was the man behind the curtain. Jimmie had shunned him, and he'd gone after her, tried to steal her acting detective slot. If I got the chance, I'd knock the wheels off his little red wagon.

I put aside the HR file and opened the homicide investigation. I read the first page, starting with Crime Summary.

Nothing there either. Short without any substance at all. Which irked me. This was all that remained of her life, a crime summary.

Crime Summary:

Victim Poe was found in a shallow grave, (see 'location box,' on the 49 for GPS coordinates). For explanation in how Poe was located please refer to detective Beckett's supplementary report under this case number. Detective Beckett was following up on a report of 'a found human bone,' that was ultimately determined to be victim Poe's right femur.

Only half of victim Poe's remains were located. Animals and seasonal flood water carried off the missing half (see attached diagram for additional information where other bones were located by local residents in the surrounding area). Coroner estimates the victim had been in the ground for two-plus years. More information to follow pending completed autopsy.

At the time of her disappearance two years five months before the discovery of her remains, there was speculation that Detective Poe fled her job to evade a criminal filing for second degree homicide (for further see attached investigation). Currently there isn't any reason to believe the Nico Sumter homicide is related to hers.

Evidence:

What appeared to be two expended 9mm rounds were located inside victim Poe's skull. Those bullets were sent to DRUGFIRE for ballistic examination and classification.

Witness Statements:

None at the time of writing this initial report. Victim Poe appeared to be a loner. Detectives responded to her apartment, but it had been rented out twice since Poe resided there. None of her neighbors remembered her. She led an unremarkable private life, making a timeline difficult to establish.

Detectives are still looking for victim Poe's sister who sold her home in Upland, California two years ago, shortly after Poe left her job with the sheriff's department and disappeared.

I thumbed through each supplemental page that followed and found nothing. Only leg work, shoe leather, and documentation of same, as if the detectives on Grimes' team were just going through the motions, checking the boxes and nothing more.

No one was looking for her the way they should've been. Any other cop murdered, a command post would've been established; detectives pulled from all over the county; the gang team, the violent crimes team would've been all wrapped up into one huge coordinated effort. The department would've untied the purse strings with unlimited overtime. Cops would be turning over rocks and throwing everyone in jail until someone gave up a clue. If a keeper of the peace goes down in the line, how could the public feel safe?

Had Hamond seen some kind of invisible writing on the wall? Understood no one was really going out of their way to find her? Was that why he'd said, *"I'm going to wind you up a like a little tin soldier and send you out after this bastard."* Told me in so many words to go forth and pillage?

But why wasn't the department pulling out all the stops? Jimmie Poe was a great gal, an excellent cop, and—

Of course.

The department didn't want the black eye. They believed she was culpable in the Nico Sumter killing in the state pen. Why unearth something better left buried?

Oh my God, they actually believe she and I had conspired to kill Nico. That was why Hamond had called me in and had gone against the party line. He wanted to give me one last chance to clean up *my* mess.

I got up from the table, walked over to the window, and looked out at the mountains: Mount Baldy, Day Canyon, the Cajon Pass, and the outline of an arrowhead large as a city block on the side of the mountain. Delineated by white oak trees. The symbol used for San Bernardino County, the Indian arrowhead.

I stood and stared.

I *was* culpable. I *had* filled in the aka box, knowing full well what that could mean for Nico Sumter. But was that what really got him killed? Or was it the jury of his peers who found him guilty in a due process trial that threw his perverted sociopathic ass into the can to keep him away from

190

other victims?

I didn't have time to mull it over. I had to wedge my fingers under a few rocks and flip 'em over, find out who pumped two little lead pills into the back of a beautiful woman's head.

"Beckett?"

I turned to find Corporal Murray Talbot Jr. from the SWAT team standing in the doorway to the lunchroom.

A dark thought flitted through my mind: was he there to arrest me for the second-degree murder of Nico Sumter?

Chapter Thirty-Nine

I drove my sheriff's detective car, following the SWAT guys up the Cajon Pass to the high desert. Captain Hamond had sent Murray Talbot Jr. to find me. An anonymous phone tip that came into homicide ratted out JoJo Jamison. The tipster said Sloppy Joe was laying his head up at a house in Victorville County area and gave the address. Said Sloppy Joe was angry and "wanted to shoot that punk-ass detective Dave Beckett."

That was all right by me. Let him try.

The drive would take forty minutes with a little bit of traffic. Too much time to think about how Jimmie's leg bone, for two months, had banged around in the car's trunk. The noise begging me to pull my head outta my ass and listen to what Jimmie had been trying to tell me.

Thoughts of Jimmie and her goodbye note automatically led to the memory of Ben Siderites. He drove his cop car out to Needles, a desolate corner of San Bernardino County, and parked under a narrow railroad trestle. Did it so 40K, the sheriff's airship, would have a difficult time spotting it. He stripped down to his tee shirt, uniform pants, and boots. He laid all his gear on the front seat of his patrol unit...and just walked off into the desert. Took six weeks before someone had noticed the car.

If you have never hiked out into the desert, the vast expanse of sand dunes, sage, and salt cedar, and not experienced how it can immediately swallow you up, then you can't begin to imagine the task, the manpower needed to search. And the longer the delay in starting, the fewer the odds of success.

Cordova had been the one to push Siderites over the edge of sanity. The way he hunted him hounded him. All because Siderites arrested Cordova's cousin or nephew.

Cordova.

Again.

During a large military maneuver out in the desert by 29 Palms Marine base, one soldier was not picked up from his post when the war game ended. It wasn't until everyone got back to base that the soldier was missed. The military, with its enormous amount of resources, leaped into action, throwing at the problem an untold amount of manpower, helicopters, and off-road vehicles. They also filed a missing person report that activated the sheriff department's search and rescue. The coordinated search went on for days, long past the time a human could survive without water in the blistering heat. The Marine Corps' tenacity in refusing to give up might've been due to the blackeye given to their mantra: "No one gets left behind."

Except when they are.

Even with a solid starting point to search, the soldier was not found. In fact, the search was eventually scrubbed.

An obstinate sheriff sergeant, one who spent his entire career out in the desert, recalculated where the soldier could have possibly walked and extrapolated a line of progression and found him. The remains. The reason the military had not found him was that the soldier had actually done the impossible. He acted like a true marine and, with great fortitude and will to survive, had hiked miles outside the projected search zone. He was found by the sheriff's sergeant a hundred yards from a main highway. The sad irony; he had almost made it out on his own.

The Siderites search didn't have the vast resources of the military. The searchers had no idea which way Siderites would've gone. All points of the compass needed to be searched. Vast expanses of empty desert covered. The most important part of the search equation the searchers only whispered about was that *Siderites didn't want to be found.*

The search flared bright in the news for a couple of news cycles, then shifted to something else. The American people needed fresh misery and sorrow to commiserate over. That's all the news offered: rendered down hate and discontent that allowed viewers to internally say, "Man, I'm glad that wasn't me."

Like the marine soldier, the search was eventually shut down. And like the Joshua Tree sergeant, on my days off, I had returned again and again looking for my friend. Never to be found.

* * *

Our little caravan of three cars, mine and the two cars carrying the SWAT team, pulled over and stopped at The Summit Café. Murray said he preferred the cover of darkness when approaching a house that might contain a murderer with seven kills. We ate lunch and waited the two hours. Wasted time that I could've been searching for Jimmie's killer.

I stood at the payphone in the café, burning up quarters, following leads, tracking down Jimmie's sister, who had disappeared. I called the realtor who sold Jennifer Poe's home in Upland. I bamboozled personal information from the escrow company, and then the notary public who certified the sale. I discovered that Jennifer Poe had been married and divorced. I called county records to confirm it. Even though after the divorce, Jennifer took back her maiden name, I ran her married name, Fitzpatrick, through records and found something odd. Jennifer had at one time been committed for WIC 5150, welfare and institutions code for gravely disabled and/or unable to care for one's self.

I paused, standing by the pay phone over the newest discovery. A 5150? Could Jennifer have killed her own sister over an as-yet undisclosed family squabble? Then realized that was just wishful thinking, a way to assuage my over-heated guilt. Deep down, I knew it could only be those three words I wrote in the aka box on the booking app. I'd killed her. It came round-about, but I killed her just the same.

I went back to working the phone while the SWAT guys lounged in the booth, drinking coffee and telling each other embellished war stories. I called the bank Jennifer used in escrow for the sale of her house. They wouldn't talk to me, wouldn't divulge personal information. I talked with Sherry Johnson, the bank's assistant manager. I started at the beginning.

I told her all about Jimmie, the two cases we worked together, told her what we meant to each other. Then I told her about the murder, about the bone-rattling around in my trunk. Sherry Johnson was quiet on the other end of the line as she wept over the tragedy I described. And finally, I told her about the chamois, the words like broken glass in my mouth.

She ran a check on Jennifer Poe and found her account *inactive*.

Crap.

She also said that Homicide had served the bank with a subpoena earlier in the day and that she had not yet called them with the same information.

Maybe Grimes' team was working the murder harder than I gave them credit.

Just when she was about to hang up, I said, "Wait. Wait, Sherry, please, one more question. Please, just one more."

Sherry said nothing. Sniffles came over the line.

"Sherry, can you please run her through your bank records as Jennifer Fitzpatrick?"

She didn't reply. Clacking of computer keys came over the phone line. Then. "Huh?"

"What?" I held my breath. But couldn't wait and asked again. "What?"

"There's recent activity on an account under that name with the same date of birth and social."

I closed my eyes and put my head against the wall next to the payphone. Chasing down Jimmie's sister didn't give us a killer. It didn't give us anything really except maybe entries into the timeline leading up to Jimmie's murder. If you have nothing at all to work with, this mere wisp of a lead looked like a solid finger hold. One needed to flip over the rock where the real clues lie.

"Do you have an address?" Please, please have an address.

"What does this name have to do with your murder?" Back to the obstinate protector of record.

"It's Jennifer's married name. She left it behind when she divorced, went back to Poe. It was just a guess on my part. Please, do you have an address?"

Sherry hesitated and lowered her voice. She was venturing deep into a bank policy violation, one that could easily get her fired. "One-oh-five-thirty-eight Hickory Street, Hesperia, California."

"You're kidding me? She's actually up in the desert?"

"Please, Detective Beckett, keep this to yourself."

"I won't tell a soul, and I owe you a very expensive dinner."

"That's all well and good, but it doesn't help with the guilt of telling you something I'm not supposed to. I feel terrible."

"I'm sorry about that, but look at it this way: you may have helped me take one step closer to figuring out what happened to Deputy Jimmie Poe."

"I hope so. Good luck, detective."

Chapter Forty

I dumped my detective car in a strip center off Bear Valley Road and got in with Murray. The other four SWAT guys followed us in two cars. Darkness had fallen, taking far too long to squeeze out the last vestiges of dusk. I wanted to cold-knock Jennifer Fitzpatrick's door at 10538 Hickory and had to tamp down that anxiety. I also wanted to be the one to put the cuffs on Sloppy Joe. Once he was firmly ensconced in Pelican Bay, he would never get out.

We drove west on Bonanza, then south on Petaluma. Murray pulled to the road's shoulder, shut off his headlights, and reached under the dash for the toggle switch to kill the brake lights. The other units followed suit the same as cloned robots.

Earlier, one SWAT guy did a drive-by to scout the location on Petaluma. He came back to the strip center and drew a diagram of the house and surroundings from memory. Murray cut up the plan and assigned me to cover the back. He wanted all his guys going in the front. JoJo was too dangerous to take for granted. Normally I wouldn't mind the back. The rats jumping ship almost always came that way and gave me the best chance to say, "Peek-a-boo, asshole."

Not this time. I wanted in on taking JoJo down. Insisted on it. He assigned Phillips to the back, who scowled.

I said to him, "We gotta knock and notice. You're going to be in the cat-bird seat. They'll all be funneling your way."

He lost his scowl and nodded.

Murray and his merry band of knuckle-draggers had trained and trained

197

for just this type of dynamic entry and would hit the house too hard and fast for the rats to even know what hit them, let alone have time to flee. I'm not a backdoor guy, not where Sloppy Joe was involved.

Petaluma sat in the middle of an area called Mountain View Acres, an island of county area surrounded entirely by Victorville city. The city didn't want to annex it due to "costs" (in air-quotes.) The area didn't have any curbs and gutters, or streetlights, no improvements whatsoever, and if annexed the city would have to shell out big time to fix them. An excuse to cover the real reason. The folks who lived in Mountain View Acres...just weren't the type Victorville wanted in their city. "Scalawags, carpetbaggers, and pirates, all," according to the Victorville mayor caught on a hot mic during a city council meeting. So, it remained county, and the county sheriff's station serviced it instead of the deputies who worked the Victorville City contract.

If I had to pick a place for JoJo to be hiding, this would not be a big-money gamble.

Murray took his foot off the brake and accelerated. One of the other deps in the car behind us asked dispatch to limit radio traffic, that we were hitting the location.

I'd hit houses many times in the past, and it never got old—the thrill of the hunt. The threat of the unknown where at any moment, violence could jump up and slap you in the face.

Murray pulled over two houses north of the location. Everyone exited, easing the doors closed until they clicked. None of their gear rattled or reflected any ambient light. The SWAT guys lined up in their stick, long guns hanging off team slings. I got in back of the line. If working homicide had not been as cerebrally engaging, I, too, would be one of those SWAT guys on permanent assignment seeking out the worst of the worst.

Chain-link with a double gate surrounded the property, an acre lot. No one in the stick slowed to check if the gate was locked, they vaulted the fence. I followed a second slower. The end SWAT guy, Phillips, took the back of the house.

In the yard in front of the front door sat a junker, a 60's model Chevy, up on four blocks with weeds all around, positioned on purpose to stop bullets from drive-by attacks, a latter-day Fort Apache.

We deployed on the door.

Murray leaned over and whispered. "You sure you want to give 'knock, notice?' It'll hang our asses out."

I nodded. "By the book."

To do a breach entry without knock and notice required probable cause delineating the possibility of violence and a signature from a judge. When cops give knock and notice, it's the same as telling the crooks grab your guns, here we come. It wasn't fair, but the rules and laws heavily favored the bad guys, contrary to what the press want the public to believe.

Murray pounded on the front door and yelled. Not so much for the occupants, but for the neighbors to testify later in court that they heard it.

"Sheriff's department, search warrant, demand entry."

I automatically started counting, one Mississippi, two Mississippi—" Case law accepted twenty seconds after the announcement as notice given. Plenty of time for the crooks to arm-up, barricade, point their guns at the front door to wait for the cops coming through.

Too many times I'd waited in that same position for that slow twenty seconds to tick by, thinking it was absolutely insane that we had such a restriction. In my mind, the occupants would be flipping over couches and refrigerators, pulling sawed-off shotguns from the closets, lining up to engage in a free-for-all slaughter.

And each time, we still went in after waiting.

Murray said out loud, "Nineteen, twenty. Hit it."

The guy with the ram stepped in front of the door and slammed it hard, letting go of the ram, allowing it to penetrate, and becoming the first to enter. A quasi-decoy.

Each man entered and buttoned-hooked either right or left, opposite of the man in front of him. I ended up going right, running the wall.

Even with the twenty-second lag-time, two suspects—late on the upswing—fled the living room, one going for the kitchen. Another going to the back room. A third sat on the couch, stoned out of his gourd. I chased the guy to the kitchen. Yelling, "Stop. Stop. Show me your hands. Sheriff's department. Show me your hands."

He ran into the kitchen and turned to face me. He held a gun in his hand but down by his leg. Sweat beaded on his forehead, his eyes wild, trying to make the decision to be a hero in prison and drop a cop or be known for punking out. Would he will his hand to rise up and his finger to pull the trigger?

I yelled louder. I screamed at him to drop the gun. I should've pulled the trigger. I had the legal right and the moral right. I just didn't have the emotional ability to pull the trigger. So I screamed some more.

The SWAT guy, who'd secured the rock head on the couch—zip-tied his hands—stuck his shotgun from behind me along my side, the barrel long and black and absolutely lethal. He didn't yell. Didn't say a thing. He quietly waited for the fool who refused to drop his four-inch Colt Python .357. To move so much as an inch. Take an aggressive step. Do anything other than his fingers releasing the gun and letting it drop to the floor.

But this bad guy still hadn't made up his mind yet, hate for the cops glaring in his eyes.

The entire encounter took no more than three seconds, feeling more like a full minute.

I slide-stepped toward him twice, went up on the toes of my left foot, and booted him in the chest with my right. At the same time, I came down with my gun barrel across his head.

He went down the same as if I'd shot him.

Only he was still alive.

I dropped to my hands and knees, gasping for breath, and grabbed his gun.

The SWAT guy behind shoved me out of the way in the small kitchen, flipped the crook over, and zip-tied his hands together. Then, set him up so he wouldn't die from excited delirium.

I sat with my back to the greasy oven, breathing hard, shaking all over. I should've pulled the trigger on him.

And at the same time, shouldn't have.

A moment, a split-second decision sure to take up residency in the corner of my mind, never leaving and constantly rising up at the most inopportune moments to haunt me. The same as the incident in the slit trench with the dead little girl, Jessica DeFrank, behind the clear plastic, her eyes pleading with me. Events nightmares are built upon.

The SWAT guy got down on one knee in front of my face, his eyes even with mine. "Are you outta your frigging mind?"

That's when my eyes reengaged, and I recognized him. Murray. "What? Ah…Yeah. Go ahead and put me down as outta my friggin' mind."

Chapter Forty-One

In the kitchen, I struggled to my feet and shuffle-stepped back the way I came. Murray met me at the front door, put his hand on my shoulder, "You okay?"

"Yeah, sure. No problem."

"We get him?" I asked. "We get Sloppy Joe?"

"Naw. Not here. But it's another one of his rock houses, plenty of coke and guns. A chunk of change, too, stacks of Ben Franklins. It's a great pop. Worth the trouble, without a doubt. We'll get JoJo. We keep hitting his houses like this. He won't have anywhere to go. You want the pinks, or do you mind if my team takes 'em?"

The pinks were the back copy of the sensitized booking app. The mark of a hardworking street cop was oddly gauged on the number of pinks.

I was already in homicide, going nowhere fast. "Sure, you can take 'em. Let me get some air, and I'll help you with the search and seizure of the evidence. I can't stay too long, though. I still need to interview a wit over in Hesperia off Hickory."

"Sure, take all the time you need. Mike says that for a second in the kitchen, it got pretty hairy. I got meds en route to check on the crook. You did good. Real good. You had every right to cap his ass."

I could only nod and step out into the night air as the entire scenario rolled back on me, replaying every move. Every extended moment.

I kept going on out to the street just as the paramedics arrived. Murray cut the lock on the chain link and opened the gate, so they wouldn't have to vault it. Two county patrol units arrived to assist in the transport. I stood out on the shoulder next to a thick-trunked cottonwood tree sucking in the cool desert air, enjoying being alive. Enjoying not being a killer of man.

Far off, two or three blocks down Petaluma, came a car northbound headed our way, the engine roaring. The car used the entire road, starting at one shoulder, crossing over the middle of the road to the other shoulder. A dangerous drunk driver.

I turned and yelled at the two deps in the street and the one medic. "Heads up, this guy coming up the street is really duce."

I stepped back close to the tree for cover if need be. A car had a hundred times the killing power of a handgun. And this driver was acting the fool, driving toward two cop cars in the street with their overhead rotating red and blues, lighting up the pitch-black neighborhood.

The car slid up and stopped. One of the patrol deps headed for the car to make the arrest said, "Ah, shit." He turned heel, retreated, got into his marked patrol car, and took off, not wanting any part of it.

"What the—" I turned back to confront the violator, who stopped parallel to the cottonwood tree in his maroon Crown Victoria. The driver's window whirred down.

Cordova.

Son of a bitch, it was *Cordova.*

The Captain from Victor Valley Station. He'd heard the call on his radio, heard I was out on Petaluma for a search warrant. He just had to come over and harass me.

"Beckett, what in...the hell...are you doing in my jurisdiction? You need... to un-ass this area, immediately Mister. And by that...I mean, right now. Get your ass back down in the valley where you belong." His words came out slurred and elongated, disconnected.

In another one of Hamond's talks, he pointed out that I didn't possess enough tact decorum, or diplomacy to survive in today's law enforcement.

This time I didn't have to play the scenarios over in my mind like Hamond asked me to a moment before I made a major boner.

Not this time.

This decision came easy, one that I would not question the rest of my life for not making the right choice. Right was right.

"Sir, please step out of the car."

Murray appeared at my side, took hold of my arm, tried to pull me away. His voice a harsh whisper, his mouth close to my ear. "Beckett, damn you, back off. Don't do it. I know what you're thinking in that little pea brain of yours, and I'm telling you, begging you not to do this. It's a career-ender."

I should've thought about his words and, for at least a microsecond, consider them. But the thought that did pop into my pea brain was that I was also hanging out to dry Murray and his merry band of brothers. They would be forced to make a career-ending decision as well: Back the captain and survive to play another day, but at the same time be blackballed by every other street cop for ratting on a fellow street cop by not bearing witness. Or, do the right thing and be good witnesses to the arrest of a sheriff's captain for duce. Double jeopardy in the truest sense.

The dark desert night didn't afford the light needed to see the invisible scales of justice.

Cordova chuckled after hearing what Murray whispered. "Beckett, you don't have enough hair on your balls to arrest a sheriff's captain. Why I'd have you before a board of deputy chiefs before you could say—"

I yanked open his car door. "Sir, I am not going to ask you again. Please step out of your car. I'm going to administer a field sobriety test."

Murray, behind me. *Son of a bitch, Beckett.*

Cordova wore the suit he'd worn during the day while fulfilling his admin duties as station captain. Only now, the dress shirt lay half buttoned, exposing his sling-shot tee, his tie hung haphazardly around his neck, and his belt was unbuckled. His face was flushed red, and he had bloodshot, watery eyes. He was so drunk he even fulfilled the elements of PC647f: a gutter drunk. He had no business behind the wheel. None whatsoever.

He rolled out of the car and used the door for support, swaying from side to side. He tried to point at me. "I'm a sheriff's captain. You...You are nothing but a punk-ass detective. Who...whom after tomorrow will be working the motor pool. You can, God damn count on it."

I grabbed him, spun him around. "I'm arresting you for drunk driving.

It is my opinion that you are too drunk to complete an FST and to do so might harm yourself."

He tried to resist and pull away but was too inebriated. I cuffed him and walked him over to Murray's car, the car I arrived in. I'd left mine at the strip center.

Murray said, "I'm gonna make a phone call."

I yelled at his disappearing back. "You do what you think is right, Murray."

I jerked the captain's arm and took him back to his own car. I strapped him into the front passenger seat, following policy. I got in the driver's side, adjusted the seat, put it in gear, and drove, headed for the county station to book the captain. The good captain let his head droop against the window where he drooled and immediately fell asleep.

I picked up the radio and said, "Sixty-two Henry-eight, I am ten-fifteen with Seven-Charlie for 23152a."

The dispatcher came back with a stunned tone. "Ten-nine your traffic, Henry-eight?"

Oscar Fuentes, Seven Sam Three, the patrol sergeant who was out at the scene when I discovered the chamois, cut in before I could answer the dispatcher. He said, "That's negative, Henry Eight, you will transport to central jail for that booking."

At least someone was thinking straight.

I had apparently put my brain in neutral. It would've been wrong to book him at his own station.

One night, while drinking under Trigger, on the north side of the Roy Rogers museum, Oscar Fuentes had told me his theory on criminality. How he thought crime really worked the same as a virulent virus that spread from one person to another. The severity depended on your moral compass that worked as your immune resistance. And like a virus, the very first crime could be tracked back to patient zero. Where it had all started.

Cops were merely immunologists or surgeons who excised the malignant growth from society, quarantined the most infected (in prison) from the rest of us. The cops tried to keep the virus from spreading.

If that were truly the case, then Cordova had the virus and needed to be segregated from the rest of the uninfected.

Chapter Forty-Two

Seven Sam Three was right about booking the station captain in his own station; it fit squarely into Hamond's accusation that I lacked decorum.

I said, "Ten-four, Seven-Sam Three. I'm en route to central." I should've asked him if he'd call my captain for me, but I didn't think that mattered. The whole sheriff's department would know in the next twenty minutes or so. That's just the way the rumor mill worked.

I moved my head till my nose stuck out the cracked open window and caught the outside slip-stream, the reek of metabolized alcohol too much to deal with.

I couldn't have passed on the arrest even if I wanted to for fear of angering the arrest gods. If I passed this one up I would've been cheated out of felony arrests for years to come. That's the code of the street. You can't pass up the Marys (misdemeanors), or you'll miss out on all the Franks (felonies). Marys and Franks sounds like a picnic dish you ate with homemade ice cream on a hot summer day.

I made it down Cajon Pass in record time: thirty-seven minutes.

Two other Crown Vics, county cars, waited for me on the free side of the jail's sally port. I pulled in behind them as the drivers exited. Deputy Chief Murray Talbot Sr. from one car and Captain Hamond in the other; both apoplectic, ready to burst a vein.

But I had them over a barrel. They couldn't punish me for doing what was right—and at the same time doing something absolutely wrong going against the tan and green culture. I'd jumped into no man's land all by my lonesome, and they couldn't touch me. At least not right away.

But once some time had passed with lots of water under that ugly bridge, they'd handle their problem child. My first misstep and I would be that guy shuttling cars for automotive. Or even worse, the guy who had to send the letters out to the photo-red light citations and deal with all those angry phone calls. Ugh.

Neither the captain nor the chief said word one. Hamond came up and stood next to me and fumed, his anger radiating like the noonday sun. While Deputy Chief Talbot went to the passenger door to Cordova's Crown Vic. Talbot saw, and immediately understood the situation. He couldn't open the door without the jack-in-the-box popping out. "Wes?" He yelled and tapped on the window.

I opened my mouth to tell the chief how drunk Cordova was when Hamond shoved his fist in my stomach. Not a sock, just a good shove.

All right then, let them deal with it. I did my part, got a dangerous drunk off the street.

The chief eased the door open, moving his hand inside the door to keep Jack-in-the-box from acting the clown. I wished I had a camera. I'd need something to show my grandkids how I had sealed my fate and lost my job.

The chief had put his time in on the street and used a pain threshold maneuver, rubbing his knuckle on Cordova's sternum. Cordova rose up out of his stupor and looked around, lost. Then looked up at Chief Talbot, "Murray, what the hell are you doing up in the desert?"

Another car pulled in behind the three Crown Vics and parked; all of us just outside the sally port to the jail. A woman wearing denim cut-off shorts and a tee shirt, no bra, got out of the car and, without a word, headed for the car with her husband. Slack skin from a disrupted sleep filled her glum expression, making her difficult to recognize.

She hurried over to help Chief Talbot with her husband. I caught another glimpse of her face, a soured scowl with down-turned lips and flashes of anger in her eyes.

Something clicked in my memory. Clicked in the part of the brain used to identify criminals, that rarely, if ever failed me. I'd seen the woman somewhere else and couldn't place her. Before my wife Beth left me, we were active in the sheriff's department's social circle, attending all the events, the huge barbeques, the picnics, and, most important, the annual sheriff's rodeo. We met too many fellow cops and their wives to remember and put a first name with the face. That had to be where I'd seen her. Now, the guilt returned over the grief I'd caused her. The late-night phone call, getting dragged out of bed to come pick up an errant husband who didn't know how to say no to the next drink.

Chief Talbot and the woman got Cordova poured into the family car, a blue minivan. I fought the urge to stop her, tell her I was sorry. That my feud with her husband had bled over into her life. She drove away before I could work up the nerve and make the move to apologize.

Had Cordova been a borderline drunk there might've been hell to pay that night. But how could they possibly fault my actions, the shape he was in?

Chief Talbot walked over and stopped in front of me. His stare shrank me down to three feet tall. He finally said, "That was a helluva job tonight up in that kitchen on Petaluma." He pointed in the direction where Cordova's wife just drove away, "But that right there proves you to be the asshole we all think you are." He walked off. So few words, and yet he had still cut me to the bone.

I took a step to follow, to offer a half-hearted rebuttal, but Hamond again shoved me in the stomach, harder this time. "Did you at least get a line on JoJo Jamison? Or did you just concentrate on making fools out of the entire department?"

"Nope."

He moved up closer to my face. The reek of Johnny Walker Red on his breath. I only recognized it because I had, at one time, filled my dance card with Johnny Red. Scotch, an acquired taste, an acrid liquid rust over ice.

"Listen very carefully," he said. "You are to drive this car." He pointed to Cordova's Crown Vic, "Straight up to the desert, no deviations. Not so much as an inch. No victory laps around Hesperia station, Apple Valley station, or the County station. You are to leave his car parked in the captain's slot at his station. You are not to say a word of this to anyone. And I mean not one *God damn soul*. As far as you're concerned, if anyone asks, it never happened. Do you understand?"

"Yeah, I got it."

"Dave, tell me you understand."

"I said, I got it."

"That's it? That's all you have to say for yourself? That you got it?"

"Did you see how drunk he—"

He held up his hand to stop me from talking. "Don't. If you don't understand how you just shit the bed big time, then kid, you are truly lost." He turned and headed for his car.

I hated disappointing him. I liked and respected him too much. In my situation, had Hamond been up there, seen Cordova driving, he would've called the deputy chief who would've driven up and taken charge of their delinquent captain. But there again, either the laws are for everyone, or they aren't. If they're not, then we've taken one giant step toward anarchy, or at the very least, a bifurcated society.

I said to Hamond's back. "I got a line on Jimmie Poe."

He froze and slowly turned around. Came back. "You what?"

"I got a good solid line on Poe."

He tried to hide a half-smile, but it didn't work. "How the hell did you do that when I got my best team on it, had them shaking the bushes for three days now? And you've only been dickin' around with the JoJo Jamison warrant for what six-eight hours?"

I shrugged. "You know me. I mean the way I work. I had some downtime. I worked the hell outta the phone. I pleaded, cajoled, and you know, out and out lied to a whole shit-pot full of people to get what I needed."

He stifled a chuckle. "Then quit standin' there and get on it, you asshole."

Chapter Forty-Three

I drove Captain Cordova's Crown Vic back up the Cajon Pass, thinking about how the executive staff would handle Cordova's driving policy violation. They couldn't just sweep the whole stinky mess under the rug. What would happen when the next street deputy was arrested for drunk driving and brought before the board of deputy chiefs. Past practice would bite them all in the ass. I smiled at the conundrum I'd put them in. They sat behind their desks shuffling paperwork from one side of their desks to the other. Let them deal with a real problem for once. Although that problem did have my name written all over it.

I topped the summit and started down into the Victor Valley; the city lights a carpet of spangles twinkling in the dark.

When I remembered 10538 Hickory in Hesperia, I socked the steering wheel. Captain Hamond had ordered me not to deviate from a direct course in delivering Cordova's county ride to his slot at the county station.

Although that victory lap concept of his *was* a great idea. Why I hadn't thought of it. It would be a wonderful boost for morale. Like all those ticker-tape parades on VE day.

Yeah.

A foolish dream.

But how much trouble could I get into just going to a house in Hesperia to knock on a door and talk to Jennifer Fitzpatrick about her sister Jimmie Poe?

By the time I made up my mind, Main Street in Hesperia came up fast. I cut the wheel hard across three lanes to make the off ramp.

Ten minutes later, I turned down Hickory, where Hesperia still had not gotten around to putting in curbs and gutters, or streetlights. Hesperia had only recently incorporated and was more than fifty square miles; soon to be a hundred, when they finally annexed Summit Valley.

Driving south on Hickory, the little warning, the lizard part of my brain all of a sudden lit up. A red flag that said to pull my head out of my ass and to pay attention. Something was off kilter and in a bad way. I'd worked the streets long enough to listen to that latent instinct.

I pulled Captain Cordova's car over to the curb, shut off the headlights, and shut down the engine. I rolled the windows down and listened, sniffed the air. I tried to let my brain relax and allow the information buried deep bubble to the surface. I started the engine, took my foot off the brake, and let the car roll down the right dirt shoulder. The tires crackled and popped on the small pebbles.

I closed in on 10538 Hickory Avenue. Three houses down, I braked hard. It wasn't that address that had sent up the emergency flare. It was the house across the street.

The house and surrounding environs, the fenced two and a half acres that belonged to the house. And the acreage lots on both sides of 10541. All of it belonged to none other than Leo Archuleta, Dog Willy, a card-carrying member of The Baldy Mesa Disciples of Hate. Archuleta was half-brother to Big Babe or Tito Harris, the president of the club. The Disciples of Hate had been associates of the Hells Angels for years, hoping to get patched over. It would never happen, though. The Disciples of Hate had too many mixed-race members. The HAs strung them along, doing their dirty work. The DoH's main bread and butter was stealing and chopping cars. They made an art form out of the way they dodged the police. At least most of the time. Other members had their places out in Baldy Mesa and Phelan, twenty-acre lots filled with derelict cars and trucks that camouflaged the stolen ones. Cars that only stayed there hours at a time until they got parted out. Or sat there before transiting to Mexico.

Archuleta, across the street from Jennifer Fitzpatrick, Jimmie Poe's sister, was just a coincidence. In a fledgling city still rife with criminal activity, every Hesperia citizen had a one in six chance of being within a three-block area of a bad actor.

I'd tangled with Archuleta twice in the past. Once, I caught him in a fresh rolling stolen that hadn't yet been reported; just a lucky grab. The second time was for possession of meth, enough for a sales beef, and another stolen car. I knew where he lived from the grand theft auto arrest, knew that he had a rap sheet for violence; ADW, attempted murder, times three, arson and armed robbery. A real charmer.

One cold winter night, I drove by 10541 Hickory and spotted Archuleta out in his garage wrenching a primered truck up on blocks. It didn't have a front license plate. The truck was backed in, the garage door open. I couldn't see the plates and didn't have probable cause to contact him on his own property. I'd violate his rights by simply walking onto his property. I needed probable cause and didn't have any.

I parked the marked Hesperia patrol car in the street in front of his house, got out, and turned the spotlight on to illuminate the hood of the cop car. I set out my posse box filled with all my report forms on the hood and began writing delinquent reports due at EOW. I ignored Archuleta, and he ignored me. After a few minutes, I espied him out of the corner of my eye; he'd looked up and watched me. I picked up the radio mic I had looped around the spotlight, looked up and down the street as if trying to decipher a geographic problem. I didn't key the mic but pretended to use it, lips moving to a silent dance.

Archuleta's expression turned to one of consternation. I put the mic back and returned to handwriting a couple of mundane go-no-where house burglaries. The bane of a patrol deputy.

After a few more minutes, I again did the same radio maneuver.

Archuleta threw down a wrench, went into his house and into his kitchen. The curtains were open, the light on, back-lighting him. He picked up the wall phone and dialed. Had to be calling his half-brother, Big Babe, to tell him that some dumbassed cop was parked in the street in front of his pad. He waved his arms and hands, angry. He paused to peek out the kitchen window to see if I had left, his movements indicative of someone in the throes of acute methamphetamine intoxication. Someone who'd been up for a couple days straight without any sleep, agitated and paranoid.

He slammed the phone down and came into the garage, his hands on his hips staring at me. He finally yelled. "Beckett, you asshole, what are you doin' parked in front of my house? You can't do that. Get the hell outta here."

I didn't look up and kept writing, a little surprised he remembered me from the stolen truck I caught him in. I picked up a burg report face page and pretended to be reciting something to the dispatcher from it. He had no idea that I wasn't really saying anything, not even keying the mic.

I ignored him and went back to writing, doing my job, and not violating anyone's rights while parked on a public street. Archuleta couldn't handle it any longer. He stomped down his driveway, opened his gate, and came out to my cop car.

He'd stepped out into public and became fair game.

I turned to confront him head-on and shone my light in his eyes. I observed other objective symptoms of meth intoxication, his dry and caked mouth, bloodshot eyes, and dilated pupils. Huge pupils. They barely reacted to the flashlight and almost covered his entire iris. I said, "Leo, my man, you are under the influence of a controlled substance. You're under arrest."

He pulled back to swing on me. I was ready for him. I caught his arm, spun him around, and slammed him on the hood of the cop car, messing up the burg reports I was writing, smearing them with his oily face. I got him cuffed and secured into the back of the patrol car, him yelling bloody murder the entire time. Said that his brother Big Babe, Tito Harris was already on the way, said Babe was going to kick my ass. Said when he got loose, he was going to kill me.

I had been threatened with great bodily injury and death a number of times and mostly discounted them as part of the job. But Archuleta was a different kind of criminal. I would log the threat on the front page of my arrest report in case he made good on his promise. Then the cops coming up behind looking for a killer—detectives who'd pull all my past reports—would find Leo's name, and just as important a motive.

214

I shut the car door, muffling his obstreperous language, and walked down his driveway to his garage. The law allowed me to search any areas the suspect had immediate access to prior to the arrest. The truck in his garage was stolen with the VIN, vehicle identification number, removed. When I filled out the CHP180 to tow the stolen truck (policy dictated that I had to do an inventory search), I found a baggie of meth.

Curiosity caught the cat on this one. Big Babe never showed up to kick my ass.

* * *

I pulled Cordova's car in front of 10538 Hickory, the house dark at ten forty-six in the evening. Jimmie Poe had already waited too long for me. I didn't want to put off this witness's interview any longer. I opened the car door and got out.

Chapter Forty-Four

When I left my detective ride on Bear Valley Road, headed to Mountain View Acres in Murray's car, I also left all my gear in the trunk. I wore my green sheriff's windbreaker with large white letters on the back announcing to one and all that the wearer was a deputy sheriff. I had my pocket notebook, my *Streamlight*, my *Smith and Wesson* model 66 .357, and two-speed loaders. But for a homicide detective, I was all but naked. No 35mm camera, no tape measure, sketchbook, different size envelopes for evidence, evidence markers, disposable gloves, shovel, brushes; the list went on.

I moved through the moonless night on the dirt shoulder without the use of the flashlight; that would've made me more of a target than I wanted to be. My head on a swivel, I watched for any developing threat, especially from across the street at Leo Archuletta's. He could easily still be in prison on one of the previous cases I had hung on him. I hadn't seen him in two years or better. Or he could be in on a case another cop hung on him. I wasn't the only one out there on the prod in the hunt for criminals.

The door to the house north of Jennifer Poe's opened. No interior light behind the occupant. A bad sign. He or she also knew a little bit about tactics. I stopped and waited by a telephone pole to see what the homeowner had in mind.

The shadow inside stepped out, something long and dark in his hand. A rifle or shotgun.

I left my gun in the holster on my hip and said just loud enough for him to hear, "Sheriff's Department."

"Prove it."

I slowly raised my hands and went against instinct, turned my back to him, so he could see the bright yellow reflective letters on the green windbreaker. Enough ambient light for him to see it.

"That's a step in the right direction, but any Tom, Dick or Harry can buy a damn jacket with writin' on it."

"Put your gun down and I'll show you my ID and badge."

"Not gonna happen. Looks like we got ourselves a Mexican standoff."

I raised my hands higher and walked back toward him. "Just take it easy, Mister. I'm one of the good guys. I'm here to interview your neighbor about a homicide. I work Homicide. My name's Dave Beckett. That's Beckett with two t's."

I stopped at his gate. "I'm going to reach inside my pocket and take out my badge wallet."

"Make it real slow. I'm a little twitchy tonight."

I pulled out the badge wallet, opened it, and shone my flashlight on the gold sheriff's star.

"Good enough for me. Sorry about that, Beckett, but with those yahoos across the way, I can't be too careful. They harangue me any chance they get. They'll be the death of me, you wait and see if they ain't. But I won't go down alone, I promise you that much."

"I understand. Is Leo out of prison? I put him there a couple of times. It just doesn't take."

The man chuckled and walked toward me, "Yeah, he's out. The man's a cockroach, nothing'll kill him off." He offered his hand, "My name's Walter. You can call me Walt."

He remained in shadow. I couldn't make out his features or his age. I took his hand and shook. He was old, real old without much meat on his hand or finger bones.

"You say you want to interview Jen about being a witness to a murder? That's a fool's errand, Beckett."

"Why's that?" Cherry tobacco smoke emitted from his breath and person. A pipe smoker. Didn't see many of those anymore.

"She's blind as a bat."

"She's what?" I'd heard him, okay, it was just the shock of it.

"Yep. Only been livin' here six months or so. I do what I can for her, when she'll let me. She's real headstrong, that one. I tried to warn her about that nasty lot across the way. I know she wouldn't have rented the house if she could've seen that nest of snakes for herself. That big bastard, Big Bubba's been sniffin' around her and I hate it. That's why I keep a close eye out and my gun handy."

"You mean, Big Babe?"

"Could be, my hearing ain't what it used to be."

"You know if Jennifer is up this time of night, or does she go to bed early? Her lights aren't on but if she's blind they wouldn't be."

"You don't listen too good for a homicide dick, do you, Beckett? I jus' told ya, Bubba is sniffin' around her, makin' a play. I tried to warn her off, talked till I was blue in the face, but she won't listen. Blind doesn't make you dumb, and beauty can only protect you so far. She's about to take a serious fall, and there's nothing I can do about it. He hurts her though. It'll be his last conscious act."

I covered a smile. The old man couldn't stand up to the likes of the men in the Disciples of Hate.

Headlights lit up Hickory Street, a truck coming south, a jacked-up GMC by the headlight pattern. The truck passed us and stopped out in front of Jennifer Poe's house. I turned back to Walter, "You're shittin' me?"

"Son, you gotta be quicker on the draw, or one of those ol' boys like we got across the street is gonna take you off at the knees."

The truck door opened. Out stepped a big man, based on his shadow. He wore a biker's cut—a denim vest common among the outlaw bikers, and in the light of day, you'd see patches signifying his rank within the organization. Big Babe had been the sergeant of arms for years, and from what I heard from another homicide detective working a murder, Babe had been moved up to vice pres, or even pres. Which made him even more dangerous.

The shadow came around and opened the passenger door. The interior light came on, illuminating the passenger. A brunette with long hair, and even longer legs in a navy-blue dress and short heels. He took her arm and helped her from the truck, treating her like a porcelain China doll. Which revealed the most important bit of information: Big Babe was in love. When it came to women, outlaw bikers treated them as chattel. Unless strong enough emotions made them go against their stated creed. Jennifer Fitzpatrick, nee Poe was a fool, but maybe not as big a fool as Walter thought.

I took a step headed their way, when Walter grabbed my arm. "Beckett, ya damn fool, never get between a beast and his feed bowl. Let it play out. She hasn't let him in her house yet, and tonight won't be no different."

Walter had lived a long time by the rules laid down in the call of the wild. He was absolutely right. I couldn't afford to have another miss-step, especially not in the same night. A cop walks up on Big Babe, out with his girl, and he has no choice but to protect what is his, even if the threat is only perceived and not real. He'd rip my head off and hand it to me.

I waited with Walter while Big Babe walked Jennifer to the front door, hating that a vulnerable woman, any woman for that matter, was making the mistake of her life. Big Babe walked with his head turned our way, on alert to a possible threat. A predator smelling another predator.

Walter lowered his voice. "You mind I ask you what murder you're talkin' about? And how our Jen could possibly be involved?"

"She's not involved. It's her sister, Jimmie Poe. We found her remains."

He kicked the dirt at his feet. "Dat gum it! I didn't know she had a sister. I hate seein' anyone get that kinda bad news, especially that special girl right there. She's got enough worries on her plate."

Walt was right. Babe didn't stay long. Jennifer Poe was playing hard to get. Good for her. But that left Big Babe sexually pent up. A man like Babe wasn't restricted by civilized rules and could blow off steam, unrestricted and violently.

Big Babe walked out to the truck, never taking his eyes off us. He got in, started up, and made a U-turn, his headlights swinging around the dark street to head north. He drove by us, my hand automatically going to the gun under the green windbreaker in a holster on my hip.

The GMC truck drove a few feet past and took a hard right east into his brother's secondary driveway, a double-chain-link gate that led to the two acres behind the house, the open land cluttered with all kinds of motor vehicles. The truck's headlights lit up the back lot. Big Babe got out to unlock the gate.

I took a step forward, stunned. My mouth dropping open all on its own.

I walked fast at first, then broke into a jog headed for Captain Cordova's Crown Vic.

Behind me, Walt yelled, "Beckett, what the hell?"

Chapter Forty-Five

My hands fumbled with the door handle, got the door open. I sat on the bench seat and hesitated, thinking it through, the ramifications.

To hell with it.

I picked up the mic. "Sixty-two, Henry Eight, I'm out at 10541 Hickory, roll one unit to back."

Dispatch came over the air, "Any unit to clear and respond to assist Sixty-Two, Henry Eight, at 10541 Hickory, Code one?"

The radio lit up with three deputies from Hesperia station responding to help. I couldn't wait. I had to move. If Big Babe got into the house or even into the lot behind the house, the situation would double in complexity. Search and seizure, probable cause, and the like. I grabbed the handheld radio from the charger and popped the trunk. I ran to the back of the Crown Vic, pulled on the gun rack for the unit shotgun. Locked. I slammed the trunk and yanked my Smith and Wesson .357.

I yelled. "Tito Harris, Sheriff's department. freeze. Don't you move."

Big Babe came around the truck to see who just called him out. He stood bold. Defiant.

I walked in the middle of the street right toward him, gun pointed at his chest, still a hundred feet away, moving in.

Big Babe, a monster of a man, had a long black beard and was ugly by anyone's standard. That explained why he was so enamored with a beautiful blind woman, his one and only chance at moving up in class.

His biker cut was shiny with dirt and grease. He held out his thick-muscled arms. "Whatta think ya gonna do now, you punkass? Huh? I didn't do nothin' wrong. And I'm right here. Come and get it."

The front door to 10541 Hickory opened. Out stepped the homeowner, Leo Archuletta, Dog Willy, a length of rebar in his hand. Who kept rebar in their house? With him came another biker thug I didn't recognize. Three against one.

Leo yelled, "What's goin' on, Babe?"

"This shitass cop thinks I did something, pulled a gun on me. I got nothin' in my hands. He can't do a damn thing."

Leo walked across his yard, stepped onto the asphalt close to his step-brother. "That's the asshole who arrested me right outta my own garage. The cop I was telling you about. I got eight months over all that bullshit. Now he's back pullin' his same shit. Not this time. I ain't gonna let it happen again."

The incident was quickly spinning out of control. "All of you lay down on the ground. Do it now. Do it right now!"

I'd have to shoot one, if not all of them, to regain control. They knew the rules of engagement better than any rookie cop. I keyed the mic on the handheld, "Sixty-two Henry Eight, I've got three at gunpoint, expedite my back."

The dispatcher didn't have to repeat what I said, but she did. Far off in the distance, sirens came on headed to Hickory, to an officer-needs-help-call. Their engines winding out, their suspensions taking a beating on the rough desert roads, their brakes fading more with each quick stop, all racing to get there first.

Oscar Fuentes, the sergeant from the county station, said, "Dave, whattaya got?"

"Sam, I got three uncooperative Disciples of Hate, at gunpoint."

"Hold on, I'm only two minutes out."

Big Babe said to his brother, "Throw down that hunk of iron, he can't shoot if we got nothing in our hands. Come on, let's take him and then get the hell outta here."

No one in their right mind would advance on a cop with a gun in his hand.

Bikers were rarely, if ever, in their right minds.

Leo tossed down the rebar and, with his buddy, moved closer to Big Babe. As a group, they started to move toward me, closing the twenty-foot gap.

Behind me, a gunshot went off too close. I startled as did the bikers.

The back tire on Big Babe's truck blew out. The truck listed to the side.

Walt came up beside me, his shotgun smoking. "He can't shoot you all, but I sure as hell can. You turn around and lay on the ground jus' like he says, or the next one, I'll pump right into your gut."

"Crazy ol' coot," Babe yelled. "I've had it with your shit."

Walt racked the shotgun and pointed it right at Babe. "Take a step and try me, big man. I'll cut you in half."

Someone in the neighborhood must've been on the phone with dispatch. Dispatch came on the air. "All units responding to Hickory, we have shots fired! Shots fired on Hickory!"

Down the block, a cop car slid sideways, coming around the corner, siren blaring, red and blue lights bouncing off the houses.

The three outlaw bikers eased down to the ground and laid flat.

I got on the radio, "Sixty-two Henry Eight, code four, backup is on scene, shut down all code threes."

I didn't want anyone piling up their cars because of me.

A uniformed deputy skidded to a stop, jumped out with a shotgun, and racked it. He came over to the back of Babe's truck and used it as a barricade. He aimed at the three on the ground.

Walt had somehow disappeared, melted back in the shadows. I owed him a case of beer.

Two more minutes, five more sheriff's patrol cars choked the street, cops with their guns out.

Oscar Fuentes, the county sergeant out of his area in Hesperia, came up. "Whatta we got, Dave?"

"I'm thinkin' a chop shop."

He scowled at me. "You're thinking we got a chop shop? Aren't you supposed to be working homicide? How did you get here?"

He wanted to know if we had a legal right to be holding three bikers at gunpoint in the middle of the street without probable cause.

"There's a stolen car in the back lot."

"No, there ain't!" Leo yelled from face down on the asphalt. "That bastard shot my brother's truck tire. I want him arrested."

Fuentes took hold of my arm and guided me out of hearing range and, at the same time, ordered the patrol deps to cuff and secure all of them.

He turned to me. "I didn't hear you run a plate, or even hear a plate come back on the radio as stolen. I'll ask you again. How'd we get here? We gonna have to let these fine, upstanding Hesperians go? You shoot that truck tire, Dave?"

Oscar Fuentes knew me well, or at least he used to. Prior to me arresting his captain for drunk driving, he wouldn't have questioned anything I had going. But I had not shown good judgment that night, and he no longer took me at face value. I couldn't blame him. I'd have to work hard to regain that trust.

"I didn't shoot the tire. You have my word on that. The blue car back there," I shone my light on a small car amongst thirty-five or forty others, "That one right there, is stolen."

"Dave, it doesn't have any plates. How do you know it's stolen? Did you go back into the lot and pull the VIN?"

He was asking if I'd violated the homeowner's constitutional rights of search and seizure and trespassed to get the probable cause I needed to make an arrest.

"Oscar, that's *my* car."

A slow, wicked smile appeared. "And you have detained these three Disciples of Hate. Very nice." He turned, walked toward the three on the ground. "Get these turds in the cop cars, keep 'em separate. Then one of you, call your station, get the on-call detective out here for a search warrant. You three get in that house and secure it pending the search warrant. And watch yourselves. Make sure you announce."

He came back and looked me in the eye. He whispered, "Dave, how did the truck tire get shot?"

Chapter Forty-Six

I stood in the middle of Hickory, the narrow street clogged with marked patrol cars and more on the way to see what had happened. Cops were no different. They liked nothing better than to lookie-loo. Especially if they didn't have to take any paper on it. The deps without an assignment stood in a half-circle, not coming any closer as if some sort of force field surrounded me and Seven-Sam. They wanted to ask if the rumors were true, if I had really arrested Seven Charlie for drunk driving?

I would never answer that question. Hamond asked me not to. The arrest would enter the annals of often-told war stories. The kind of stories no one believed but often recycled after drinking plenty of beers underneath Trigger the rearing horse on the north side of the Roy Rogers Museum.

I answered Fuentes' question, who shot Big Babe's back truck tire. I said, "Don't know. I was standing here with my gun pointed at those guys who were already coming at me when a gun went off. I didn't see who shot it."

That was the truth. I hadn't seen Walter shoot. Just heard it.

I pulled my green sheriff's windbreaker aside to show him my handgun. "That tire was hit with double ought buckshot, and I don't have a shotgun. If I had to guess, the shot came from a good citizen over in the shadows. Someone in this neighborhood is tired of these assholes ruining their lives. I need to check out my car."

Fuentes didn't believe my story, and as he followed along, he tried to decide if he'd let it stand. "You sure it's your car? They made a ton of those shitbox Toyotas."

"It's *my* shitbox Toyota. Trust me on this."

When Big Babe had made the turn into the double gate, his headlights scanned across the cars in the backyard. The car all on its own didn't click. Instead I spotted the damage first before my mind registered the type of car and color. The unique damage that happened in the incident on Main Street, when from behind me came Siderites with three CHP cars in a slow-speed pursuit. He'd sideswiped the Toyota, leaving a unique artwork in the crumpled metal that I had seen over and over again each time I got in to drive it.

Siderites had been drunk at the time.

The irony. Cordova had given me shit about talking the CHPs into letting Siderites go. He wanted to rack me up over Siderites driving drunk, the fact I had not arrested him.

Fuentes heard me chuckle and asked. "What's funny?"

"Nothing. Just happy to get my car back."

"Dave, that car was a piece of shit when you bought it. Now it's been sitting out behind someone's house rotting for three years. It's not worth the money to tow it away. That's why it's still here. If there was a dollar to be had from that hulk, the Disciples of Hate would've already squeezed it out."

"Yeah, but it's still my car. I got a lot of memories in that baby. And beyond that, it's the principle of the thing."

"You haven't shown a lot of principles lately, Dave."

"I'm allowed a boner here and there, aren't I Sam?"

"Heh, if that's the case, you're all full up for the next seventy years."

I didn't have the nerve to tell him about how my father had gone missing. How he left me a note that I hadn't had the guts to open. Like a fool, I left the note on the dash. Dad had disappeared three years ago, never to be heard from again. The car stolen before I could read that damn note.

I couldn't let myself hope too much that the note was still somewhere in the car, not after three years. The field rats would've used the car for one big nest and the envelope with the note as nest stuffing.

No.

No way was that note still in there.

But I had to look.

Three years ago, when Dad up and disappeared from The Hobo Café, I filled out a missing person's report and entered him and his Ford Pinto into NCIC and SVS. Two weeks later, his Pinto turned up in San Bernardino City, two blocks from the Greyhound Bus depot. But no sign of Dad. Every week, I called Detective Sanchez at the sheriff's Rancho Cucamonga station to prod him, get him to recheck the morgues and hospitals, to do anything at all.

Now, out of nowhere, a chance to find out what happened fell in my lap. I almost didn't want to know if that note still existed. Didn't know if I could deal with the added disappointment. I'd held out hope for three years that I or someone else would come across my Toyota Tercel, that it hadn't been junked and crushed, or taken to Mexico.

And here it sat in the backyard of a house that belonged to a Disciple of Hate in the city of Hesperia, where I used to work. Some big-time cop I turned out to be. Why had I not looked for crooks with past records of stealing cars? Hell, I had even arrested Leo Archuletta twice before for GTA and still had not thought of knocking on his door. Finding the Tercel at Leo's house wasn't a stretch at all. The DOH clubhouse was in Baldy Mesa, just a few miles from where the Tercel was stolen. And DOH's bread and butter, their most common method to earn money, was grand theft auto.

Had my subconscious been shielding me, a primeval kind of protective sheath? I didn't believe in that kinda crap. Cop work was ninety percent instinct, ten percent curiosity. Both of which took a holiday on this one.

We came to the blue Tercel sitting in between a crumpled green Ford Mustang and a gray VW Rabbit, the three of them all but obscured by a thick layer of desert dirt and blow-sand, the desert trying its best to reclaim what it was owed for the ruined environment.

I took a deep breath, held it, and opened the door.

Chapter Forty-Seven

Back when I'd parked the Toyota in the dirt turnout and gotten in Jimmie Poe's acting detective car, I had left the note from Dad on the dashboard. The car thief who took the car may or may not have torn it open looking for cash to a grandchild, or a birthday check. Then simply discarded it on the floor. That's how I envisioned it.

Oscar Fuentes looked over my shoulder, curious. I didn't know why. There was nothing to see in a broken down, musty car. He had his own instinct on high-alert.

The ignition on the steering column had been punched. Most likely with an autobody slide-hammer—a dent puller, a common tool that continually circled in and out and around a car thief's world. The Toyota could now be started with a simple slot screwdriver. But my car would never again enjoy the aerodynamic wind over its hood and roof, or the passing asphalt beneath its tires. Once rescued from the clutches of Leo Archuletta, my little Toyota was destined for the junkyard. Crushed into a small cube. Recycled to create a newer vehicle with clean lines, a car hungry to drive the roads and highways.

I was stalling, waxing poetic. I didn't want to discover that note was long gone. I leaned in, shone my flashlight around inside. In the footwell on the front passenger side, fast food wrappers and other clutter rose up six or eight inches. The note could be anywhere in that mess. Fuentes laid an empty black leather glove on my shoulder. How did he know I wanted to search further than a cursory glance? "Thanks." I pulled it on and swished the trash, then piece by piece, I picked up and placed it on the seat.

Close to the bottom, I froze. An envelope. Crumpled. Dirty from being stepped on, smeared with grime. It sat just out of reach. I climbed in a little more and gently brought it out.

Nothing inside.

Just the envelope.

The right envelope though, with dad's writing on the front that said, "Dave."

I dug back into the pile on the floor with more vigor, tossing piece after piece onto the seat until I came to it. A balled-up paper.

That had to be it.

I squared myself in the driver's seat holding the note with great reverence. Three years didn't seem like such a long time, but to me, it had been three lifetimes.

In my peripheral vision, Fuentes took a step back to give me privacy. Life on the street gave you instincts. You grew them out of the need to survive. He knew I'd been after something other than the car and that I found it.

The outside world fell away as I opened the balled-up paper and smoothed it out.

> Dave,
>
> All my life I foundered, lost, looking for I don't know what. Never finding it. At every turn screwing things up beyond repair. My world a total mess. My fault. No excuses. My biggest mistake was running off and leaving you and your mom. That time gone forever. My biggest regret.
>
> The crime they held me accountable for, I never told you about. But as a cop, you could find out if you wanted to. A senseless crime, one committed out of heated tempers, neither one of us wanting to back down. Stupid male testosterone. That's neither here nor there. Just so you know that I had been lost for a very long time.
>
> Until I found you. Or you found me. I'm not sure which. Fate took a hand that day you walked into The Hobo for a plate of pancakes and eggs.

I worked in the back away from the public for a reason. You can probably figure out why. You have a natural cop's instinct. I was afraid my past would catch up to me. I was tired of running. I wouldn't have stayed near as long had you not shown up. Even so, I stayed too long.

I want you to know I would've stayed forever with you living in the back room. You and me talking and drinking those nights while the moon shone through those front windows. They were some of my happiest days on this planet.

But it wasn't to be. Konstantina's people came looking for her. The woman who owned The Hobo. She owed them money. Big money. Bad people who blamed me for her disappearance. Said I assumed her debt. I couldn't blame them, not the way it looked. Me present, her gone without a trace. Me the sole beneficiary of The Hobo.

I had a choice to make. Flee like I have all my life when the going got a little rough? Or tell you. Like I said these are bad people, Dave, and I already have enough regret. I couldn't live with myself if you were harmed in anyway over one of my messes.

So, here's to you.

My only son.

I love you.

P.S. Don't come looking. You'll never find me. I didn't have the heart to tell you my real name, only the one your mom knows me by.

The note caused a lump to rise in my throat and tears to burn my eyes.

He had never told me he loved me.

His written word was nothing like the way he spoke. The note sounded like someone else entirely. Or had I just made up my mind what kind of man he really was, putting a square peg in a round hole. Classifying him as an ex-con-short-order fry cook. Not seeing past his flawed criminality. Instead of seeing him like I should have, as a father.

Finding the little blue Toyota was the same as finally finding Dad. Not the disposition I hoped for. Sad. How his heart filled with regrets now transferred by osmosis over to me. He didn't want me to find him. Said he had another name. Of course, he did. How else could he have eluded me for so long? I could find him now if I really tried. I just needed to interview Mom. An extensive interview teasing out long lost memories, things Dad had said, things he let slip. Build a profile.

But did I want to go against his last request in the note?

Hell yeah, I did.

I struggled out of the car and walked through the dirt to the double chain-link gate. The dark street was now lit up with flashing amber lights and headlights of the parked cop cars.

Across the street, Walter stood in the yard of 10538 Hickory next to the blind Jennifer Fitzpatrick, speaking quietly.

First things first.

I'd deal with who killed Jimmie Poe.

Chapter Forty-Eight

I moved across the street, avoiding two separate throngs of deps who stood talking quietly and glancing sideways as I passed. I was a pariah. I'd gone against unwritten rules and arrested one of our own. Even though some—most really—didn't care for Cordova, I still crossed a line, one I could never cross back. How could they trust me during a critical incident where decisions had to be made in split seconds? What if someone chose wrong in that split second? Would they think I'd instantly slap the cuffs on them? Ridiculous on its face but still an undeniable truth. Perception and myth worked the street just as hard as the coppers.

I'd made a huge error that was just now manifesting itself. I had done the right thing for the right reasons, but in the tan and green world, that didn't matter. I would have to watch my back at crime scenes, lay low for at least a little while until some of the heat faded.

I hoped Walter had not told Jennifer about finding Jimmie's remains, and at the same time, I hoped he had. Even so, Jennifer would still have questions. Ones I wanted to avoid at all costs. The most shameful of which, the bone in the trunk of my car rattling around for weeks.

And the chamois.

Especially the chamois. Thinking about it still caused the gore to rise up in my throat.

A county contract tow truck arrived to tow away my little blue Toyota. My faithful steed that had gone missing and had been found only to be taken to the crusher.

I opened the gate to 10538 Hickory and followed the concrete walk up

232

to Walter and Jennifer. She wore a thick, pink pleated robe and slippers. Her long brown hair hung past her elbows. In the darkness of the night, impenetrable sunglasses obscured her eyes. In her hand, she held a long white cane with the red tip.

She was definitely blood kin to Jimmie Poe in stature and in smooth skin and delicate hands. I wanted to see her without the glasses, see her eyes, her cheekbones. I wanted her to look like Jimmie, the cop I had worked the streets with.

The wonderful girl I had kissed.

Walter said, "This is the guy I was telling you about. He didn't back down from those thugs. This is Dave Beckett, a detective with the sheriff's department."

She offered her hand. "Nice to meet you, detective. I understand you have some information on my sister's murder."

I took her hand and looked at Walter. He shook his head. He had not told her.

"Nice to meet you as well. Do you think we could go inside and talk?"

She let go of my hand. "No. I'd prefer to talk out here in the fresh air. I don't like being inside where everything is so still. Not if I have a choice."

Walter walked off. "I'll leave you to it. Call me, Jen, if you need anything."

"Thank you, Walt. You know I will." She waved an awkward hand, one not directed enough toward Walt.

She said, "Well, detective?"

"Please, call me Dave. I'm here because I…ah, found your sister out in the desert in a shallow grave." The words in my throat caught. I pushed them out too fast for fear of not being able to say them.

She nodded. "I thought that might've been Judith. The news never revealed the name. I guess you folks held back that information until next of kin were notified? That would be me. And no one could find me, right? How did you finally track me down, detective?"

She spoke casually about something so heated and emotional. At least for me, it was. Time was the only thing that healed the loss of a loved one. Three years must've been enough for Jennifer Fitzpatrick to put to bed the regret, the loss, the missing piece to her family. A sibling who she had roomed with while they were adults.

My dad was still alive. I had not put to bed my feelings about him. On the contrary I just reopened a fresh emotional wound.

"Did you uncover any leads as to the son of bitch who killed my sister?"

Ah, the emotions bled through her defenses. She wasn't such a cold fish after all.

"No. I'm here to put together a timeline of her last day. Can you help me with that?"

"*Now* you people want to work the case? I've tried and tried to tell you she wasn't just missing, that someone had done her dirty." She'd raised her voice. Some of the deps out in the street looked over. Dirty Dave, doing it again. Now he was harassing a defenseless blind woman. My rep was taking a major hit.

"You sure you don't want to go inside?"

"No."

"Okay. Just take a moment."

"Don't try and handle me, detective. I won't be handled by you or anyone else."

I let a pregnant pause settle between us before I started again. Let things cool down.

"Can you tell me, when was the last time you saw your sister…ah…I'm sorry, I mean, contacted your sister?"

"I know I'm blind, *detective*. Don't patronize me by doing the soft shoe around my challenged eyesight. You're telling me that you didn't recover any kind of evidence at her…her gravesite? How was she killed?" Her voice caught at the end of that last question.

I wasn't the case agent and was only assigned to nibble around the edges. I didn't want to screw up the investigation. Grimes and his team would most definitely be following up right behind me.

If I told them about her.

But Hamond was for sure telling Grimes once I briefed him. And I had to brief Hamond.

"I…ah…I'm really not at liberty to tell you anything about the ongoing investigation. Just that she was murdered and—?"

She turned using her cane. "You can kiss my ass, detective."

"Wait." I couldn't believe how the interview had devolved so quickly. She came off callous and hard and, at the same time, vulnerable and needy. I'd never dealt with anything like that before.

"She was shot in the head. Twice."

Jennifer Fitzpatrick froze, her back stiffening. She didn't turn back and still faced the house. "I guess I asked for that. I'm sorry I'm being such a bitch." Her head dipped a little, and her shoulders shook as she silently wept.

I didn't like to see women hurt. When a woman cried, I felt helpless and would do almost anything to fix the problem.

"It's late," I said, "This is a lot to take in. Why don't I come in the morning, pick you up? We can go to coffee and just talk about Jimmie."

She slowly turned around, her sunglasses in the dark made her pale skin glow. Glistening tear tracks ran down her cheeks. In that lighting, the whole package made her out as a kind of alien, someone who didn't belong in the same world where I stood.

"Dave? Being blind sharpens my other senses and my survival instincts. Your tone of voice just shifted. You knew my sister, didn't you?"

I said nothing. Angry for some reason for being found out. Angry at myself for the unacceptable job I had done investigating the first bone handed to me in this case. Angry that I had further hindered my ability to go after the killer by arresting a sheriff's captain. The doors that would now be closed to me.

I let that anger out for a little walk and spouted. "What the hell are you doing going out with Big Babe? Do you want to end up like your sis—"

And it hit me just like that. She was a square peg being jammed into a round hole, and I hadn't seen it. How had I not seen it?

"Sweet Jesus," I whispered. "You're out here…you're renting this house… you're dating Big Babe because you're hunting your sister's killer."

Jennifer pulled off her sunglasses, her gaze to the right of me unfocused. She had beautiful brown eyes. She allowed me to see her face.

Her words came out hushed. "Keep your voice down. Let's go inside and talk?"

Chapter Forty-Nine

I followed close behind Jennifer Fitzpatrick as she entered her dark house, using her white cane as a wand in front of her. A faint wisp of sweet perfume followed in her wake. Once inside, I stumbled along in the darkness.

The revelation that she was investigating the death of her beloved sister, Jimmie, was almost too shocking to believe. This vulnerable woman had ventured deep into a violent underworld to find her sister's killer. Blind, no less. To do so, she had, without concern for her own safety, sought out and dated the biggest, the ugliest Disciple of Hate in that outlaw motorcycle gang. The nerve. The fortitude.

"Oh, so sorry," she said. "I always forget the time of day. Let me turn on some lights." She moved the loop on the white cane down her arm and clapped her hands. Several lights came on, illuminating the living room. The house was a small rental, probably a two-bedroom, one bath. The furniture, cheap and old, had to have come with the house. The kitchen, dining room, and living room all blended into one small area. The homeowner's parent had probably passed away, and they had rented the house "as is."

Jennifer made her way to the couch and around the coffee table without the use of the cane. She'd memorized the house pattern. Confident on her home turf. She sat. "I'd offer you something to drink, but like I said I'm not happy with the sheriff's department as a whole. And you being a member... Well, those feelings have festered for close to three years now.

"My sister deserved better than what she got. Now, please tell me how you knew her."

Her head followed my movements by sound, her eyes lagging behind in their tracking. I sat in an upholstered chair, the fabric worn thin, the wood on the armrests in need of varnish.

"I don't think I will. I think it's time you quit running a game on me and answer my questions. What does Big Babe have to do with Jimmie's killer?"

She leaned back and said nothing.

I'd gone at her too hard.

I couldn't let the impasse keep me from getting the information. This woman thought she knew something, and it had to be more than anything I had, which was a big fat zero.

What kind of nerve did it take for a blind woman to uproot from a nice neighborhood in Upland, and then purposely move across the street from an outlaw motorcycle gang member. Then spark up a relationship, all to uncover a killer?

And now I'd faulted her for playing word games in an interview?

"Okay, I'm sorry. I came off a little brash. I knew your sister from working the street. She was a great cop."

"I figured as much. But I want more. Details, please."

I squirmed a little. Jimmie's leg bone kept rising up in my thoughts. I kept pushing it back. "I ah…assisted her on a couple of cases."

Jennifer homed in on my voice, and now her eyes came close to locking in on mine. She sat forward on the edge of the sofa. "Wait. You're not talking about Nico Sumter and Stacy McDowell, are you?" She smiled for the first time, and it lit up the room as bright as the noonday sun. What a beautiful woman. No wonder she could turn Big Babe's head. All she needed to do was fire that smile at him. A near-lethal dose of feminine wiles brought him to his knees. Made him as malleable as clay, made him a babbling idiot.

I knew the feeling, the babbling idiot part.

She said, "You're Cracker Jack."

"Beg your pardon?"

"She called you a Cracker Jack cop. Said she'd never seen anything like you. The way you went after the bad guys. A real cracker jack patrolman who should've been working homicide. Hell, she said you should've been a supervisor in Homicide."

She lost her smile. "If that's the case and you actually are Detective Cracker Jack, where the hell have you been? She's been gone for years now. What have you been doing all this time?"

I squirmed a little more, the room suddenly turning hot. It was a fair question that cut right down to the bone. "I'm on it now. And to answer your question...me and your sister...we...ah—"

"Kissed. Judith said you really know how to kiss a girl. She said your kiss tingled all the way down to her toes. Damn near knocked her socks off." A partial of that great smile crept out, only a little crooked this time. Women trusted each other more than men when it came to secret intimacies.

I couldn't answer her. I fell into the remembrance of that first kiss. The warmth from the memory flushed my face. I was glad Jennifer couldn't see my embarrassment.

"I've answered your question, now please tell me why you think Big Babe is involved with your sister's death?"

"Because it only makes sense."

I waited for her to elaborate. It made no sense at all. Maybe Jennifer was a little over the edge, paranoid, and seeing a conspiracy at every turn.

She said nothing more.

"Please, quit playing these word games. I'm with you now, doing my best to catch whomever did this."

"I don't know if I can trust you."

I again waited.

Nothing.

The woman might be nervy, bold, and fearless, but she was starting to give me a major pain in the ass.

"This isn't a game," I said. "Like you, I'm angry that Jimmie has been killed and that she had not merely been missing. I'm willing to do whatever it takes to find her killer."

"She was afraid of losing her job. Did you know that? And I never liked that nickname, Jimmie."

"No, I didn't know that. I didn't know about the internal affairs investigation until recently."

More grief and regret.

I was the one to fill in that damn booking form, putting in the three words, Bey Bey Wraper. An arrogant, sophomoric move that triggered the whole mess.

"She loved her job. In fact, she loved her job more than she loved you, Cracker Jack."

The bottom dropped out of my stomach, her words the same as a gut punch. "She...she told you that...that she loved me? We hardly knew—"

"She said you two just clicked. She also said you felt the same way. That the thing you had together might well have been the real McCoy. That it could've gone the distance. Is that true?"

Anger again rose up, the kind that manifested into stupid mistakes. Anger to mask the huge loss. The grief. My stumbling errors. How had I not followed up that kiss?

I did love her.

That love had laid latent without a voice because Jimmie scared the hell out of me. I'd been burned once by Beth, and at the time, that stove had still been too hot for a second attempt.

"I'm tired of playing your silly games. Either you're going to help me, or you're not. You again just shifted the narrative away from the information I'm trying to get from you. That I need from you to track a killer."

"That right, Cracker Jack?" The crooked smile.

"Quit calling me that. You want to play stupid games. Okay, I'll play. How's this? I can very easily leave here and drive to the jail. I can tell Big Babe you're working him like a chicken bone. That you only want something from him, and it has nothing to do with romance. And once you get what you want, you'll discard him like a pair of his two-week-old underwear."

She sat back, shocked. Her mouth sagged open. Tears filled her useless but beautiful brown eyes that would forever and always stare off into oblivion. An oblivion only she could know.

I got up, hurried over, and sat next to her. I took her hand. She didn't shy away. She reached out. I hugged her. She was warm and firm. I needed the hug as much as she did. I gently rubbed her back.

Until I realized she'd just done it again, shifted the narrative right under my feet, right under my nose. I'd fallen headfirst into her trap. Sweet Baby Jesus, she was good. She was right about how blindness sharpened some other skills. Her ability to manipulate men was off the charts.

She moved her face up close to my ear, her breath hot and moist. I shivered. She whispered. "Cracker Jack, you really want to know the reason I rented this house? The reason why I flirted with Tito? Big Babe, as you call him?"

I nodded, too bound up to speak, fighting off the desire she sparked with her warm, moist lips touching my ear. Her breath. Her words. Calling me Cracker Jack.

"My sister was scared. Scared to death after she met you." Jennifer lightly moved her hand up and down on my arm. It sent more shivers up my back.

My voice in a whisper cracked. "After she met me? She was afraid of me? Why?"

Jennifer huffed warm breath in my ear. This time, it had the opposite effect. She was trying too hard to manipulate, to mold me into conformity. I pulled her away and looked into her eyes for the truth that would not be forth coming, not from there.

I took her by the shoulders and gently shook her. "Tell me."

The Cheshire smile again. "She fell in love with you. Her love for you caused all of this. Caused her demise."

"What? How? You're holding something back. Tell me." What she said couldn't be true, at least not in the way she was thinking. Love didn't kill. Love bound together two people with hope for a better future.

"After you met, and she fell in love, she came to see me. She was upset. I'd never heard such fear in her voice. I didn't understand, not from her. She was a rock. Not afraid of the devil himself. I kept asking what was wrong. She wouldn't tell me. Finally, she said that to really love you, she had to have a tattoo removed. Removed before she could be intimate with you."

"She what? You mean the wizard and the kiss tattoo?" There were those two damn tattoos again. They ran throughout the whole case. They were what I spotted on the chamois. That day now seemed like a thousand years ago.

Jennifer shook her head, her eyes oblivious to mine. "No, I didn't know she had *those* tattoos."

I shook her again, even more gently this time. "What tattoo are you talking about?"

"DOH. She had a tattoo, 'Property of DOH,' removed from her ass."

I sat back, stunned. "DOH? *Son of bitch.*"

The Disciples of Hate.

Chapter Fifty

I couldn't stay in Jennifer's living room any longer. The walls moved in, squeezing out all the air. I got up and half-stumbled from the house, mind spinning, not engaging on any one item. Not wanting to. Out in the street, I stood leaning against the telephone pole in front of Walter's house.

Steve Laramie, a Hesperia station detective—we worked patrol together—came out of Leo Archuletta's house. Spotted me and came over. He wore a blue long-sleeved chambray shirt, denim pants, and his black patrol boots. The overtime detective's attire. He kept his Glock service weapon in a brown leather shoulder holster. In his hand, he carried the standard stamped-leather-covered San Bernardino County Sheriff's notebook.

"Hey Dave, nice work on this one."

A tow truck pulled out from the side of Archuletta's house, dragging along the blue Tercel that had been the Egyptian-like tomb for Dad's note.

I shook Steve's hand and mumbled a greeting, my mind still trying hard to process the fact that Jimmie Poe had been a DOH *groupie*. The knowledge of how groupies were treated—pass-around girls until someone in the group took them as their "old lady."

In her background history, that's where her missing two years had gone. She'd somehow hooked up with that bad element. It also meant that in those two years, she had not had any police contact, or she would've automatically failed her background.

Steve said, "Hey man, you okay? You look like you've seen a ghost."

"Huh? What? No. Yeah, I'm cool. Just got a lot on my mind."

"So far, we've identified eight stolen cars and trucks, and two motorcycles. Since you're working homicide and all, do you mind if I count the CHP180s? I could use another pin."

"Yeah, sure, no problem, take 'em."

California Highway Patrol, in conjunction with the California Insurance Board, had a program where they awarded any cops in the state a plaque and a pin for the number of stolen motor vehicles recovered. The department approved the pins to be worn on the uniform shirt. The pins changed color with the higher number of vehicles recovered, combined arrests, and chop shops. The three arrests, the cars, trucks, and motorcycles recovered at Archuletta's place equaled a pin all on its own. Quite a coup.

All at once, I realized something glaring that I'd been missing, that my mind had covered up. A concept too emotionally painful to accept. The tattoo, "Property of DOH," meant Jimmie Poe belonged to that gang forever. It meant she had never wanted to be a cop in the first place. She'd been wound up like a little tin soldier and sent out to infiltrate the enemy camp— The Sheriff's Department. She was a planted spy for the Disciples of Hate. If the DOH could land a spy embedded in the Sheriff's department, one with great information, the Hell's Angels would have to patch them over.

I muttered, "Ah, shit."

Steve said, "Yeah, I know what you mean."

"What?" He couldn't possibly know what I was thinking.

"Did you really hook and book Seven Charlie on a duce?"

I stared at him, not needing any more drama piled on top of everything else. "Whatta ya talking about? Of course not."

I'd technically only detained him. I was stopped before I could book him.

Steve leaned in, smiled, shook his head, and pointed. "Hey, cowboy, that's his car you're driving?" He walked away, his hand raised in the air. "See ya on the street, Dave. Thanks again for the 180s."

Captain Hamond had ordered me to drive Seven Charlie's car straight to the Victor Valley station. No detours. No victory laps. Instead, I'd driven Cordova's county car straight into a steaming pile of shit. By morning, the entire county would have heard that ugly rumor that wasn't really a rumor.

I needed to go back in and finish the interview with Jennifer, but I had a feeling I had already gleaned all the information she had on the matter. I started walking toward Seven Charlie's car. I still had to drop it off as ordered. With each step, I continued to put all the pieces together.

The focus on Jimmie Poe's murder had shifted and now pointed directly at the Disciples of Hate. If a motorcycle club member, in particular one from the Disciples of Hate, tries to leave the motorcycle club without proper approval, that member is severely disciplined or killed. Usually killed as an example to the other members who might court the same rebellious ideals.

If Jimmie Poe had the tattoo "Property of DOH" removed from her bottom, that would be all the evidence needed by DOH to prove that Jimmie had turned traitor. Turned double agent.

I kicked in the side of Seven Charlie's car, dented the right rear passenger door. They killed her because she no longer wanted to be an infiltrator. A spy. They killed her because of her love for me.

My fault. All of it.

The next piece fell into place all on its own.

I knew who killed Jimmie Poe.

Now, I just had to prove it.

I got in Seven Charlie's Crown Victoria, started it up. Just as Seven Sam Three, Oscar Fuentes, dressed in his tan and green uniform, opened the passenger door and got in. He stared at me. He smelled of Old Spice and nicotine. I'd never seen him smoke before. He was a closet smoker.

"I'm sorry, Dave, I've been ordered to escort you to Victor Valley station. To make sure you turn this car in and that you don't continue in this crazy victory lap. That last part is a quote from your captain."

I glared at him for a long moment, put the car in gear, and drove. I was going to be suspended pending termination. Hell, if I were the captain that's what I'd do.

I took Hickory north, weaving in and around side streets to get to Bear Valley Road. Then I'd turn left on Bear Valley and take it to the 15 freeway north.

Seven Sam Three, Oscar sat silently watching the passing terrain and homes. I wanted to talk to him about all that had happened, all that I had just found out. But it would put him in a precarious position as a witness at my Board of Deputy Chief's hearing. And then, once I was terminated, he'd again have to testify at the Civil Service Commission hearing. If I chose to take it that far. I wouldn't do that to him.

I finally made it to Bear Valley and turned west. The streetlights created a kaleidoscope inside the car, flashing glimpses of Oscar.

He continued to stare out the side window and said, "You know what I've learned over the years about this job? Learned about crime?"

"I'd like to hear it."

He turned to look at me. "The thing about murder is that it's often contagious. It tends to spread like mono at a high school in the springtime."

He didn't know I figured out who killed Jimmie Poe, but he knew I would. This was his warning, an admonishment not to do what I had in mind.

I said nothing.

"Are you hearing me here, Dave? Don't get yourself in a crack you can't climb out of."

I took my eyes off the road and looked at him. "I think it's already too late for that, Sarge."

He stuck out his hand. "Then *vaya con dios,* my friend."

I took his hand and shook it.

He wouldn't release my eyes. I drove blind and took my foot off the accelerator. The car slowing all on its own.

He said. "I'm an old war horse, and it's time to take to the pasture. If and when you do this thing, keep me in mind."

I nodded.

He looked forward. "Watch yourself, Dave. Don't hit that mailbox."

Chapter Fifty-One

I woke to the phone ringing, a headache, and a dry mouth. The same as if I sported a category-four hangover. By the time I had rolled in from the high desert the night before, I'd been too tired to imbibe and fell face-first into bed. The symptoms came from dehydration and a critical fatigue factor. Emotional distress. The person who coined the phrase, "You can never die from hard work," was a fool. The cop job kills a person a little more each day.

I rolled over and answered the phone. Debra Ann, Captain Hamond's bearer of bad news. "Dave—"

I interrupted her, "Don't tell me. His eminence requests my presence. I'll be there in thirty minutes." I hung, not wanting, at the moment, any further contact with humans, even the kind and generous ones.

Forty minutes later, I entered the homicide cubicle farm and wove my way through over to the captain's office. Few detectives sat at their desks. They'd divvied up the leg work needed on the Jimmie Poe investigation, and it was now all hands on deck helping out Grimes' team do follow-ups.

Over to the right on the big white grease board that listed the current homicide cases, the name Jimmie Poe under "victim" and the word "open" next to it glared at me the same as a high-intensity spotlight.

I approached Debra Ann's desk. She held my eyes and shook her head, giving me fair warning.

"Morning, Deb." She didn't like being called Deb.

She smiled anyway and held up her hand as a guide, that meant go on in and hope you have a nice beheading. I could read the signs.

I entered, closed the door and sat down in the hot seat in front of his desk.

Fatigue hung off Captain Hamond like a wet wool blanket, his skin sallow, his eyes bloodshot with dark half-circles under them. "Don't look so chipper," he said. "You've finally done it. You've hit rock bottom. You've taken my generosity and stomped it into the ground. In fact, you've gone so far beyond…never mind. You're on the desk until further notice. This morning the members of the Sheriff's executive staff were arguing over which scut job they'd transfer you to. I think the resident deputy in Trona won. So, pack your bags, buddy boy; you just earned yourself some freeway therapy pending your board of deputy chief's hearing."

"Seriously, for doing my job." I really didn't have a defense. It had been bad luck to run into Big Babe the night before while driving Captain Cordova's Crown Vic. It even sounded bad just thinking back over the way things hadn't fallen my way.

Hamond rose, putting both hands flat on the desk. He opened his mouth, ready to spew invectives of a caustic nature. A needed pressure valve or risk implosion.

I interrupted him, stood, holding up my hands. "I give. You got me, copper. I'm tired of fighting the crooks and the bureaucracy both. You win. Trona sounds lovely this time of year. Quiet. Out of the way." I turned to leave.

"Wait?" Hamond said.

I turned back to face him. "What?"

"That it? That's all you got? That wasn't at all gratifying, you just rolling over like that. I had an entire rant ready. I've been working on it all the morning."

"You really have a tough job. You outta get out more."

He lost his half-smile and scowled. "What in the hell were you doing out on Hickory last night arresting bikers while driving a car I told you to drive straight to Victor Valley Station? Which by anyone's definition would be considered a victory lap."

I came back and sat down. "It wasn't meant to be. I was just minding my own business and kinda fell into that mess."

Hamond, still standing, picked up a memo and read from it. "Minding your own business, you say? Holding three Disciples of Hate at gunpoint, shooting out a truck tire, and recovering twelve stolens? That's minding your own business?"

"I can explain. First, I didn't shoot that truck tire."

"Oh, well, that's a relief. You created a major incident while driving the car that belonged to a captain you shouldn't have arrested in the first place!"

"Yeah, I know. It does kinda sound bad when you put it that way." I stood and turned for the door yet again. "I'll just go pack my bags. I'm Trona bound. I won't cause a big stink about it." A play on words because Trona was a tiny burg out on the far edge of the Kern County / San Bernardino County border. A town placed there for no other reason than to support a chemical plant that filled the air with a God-awful reek similar to rotten eggs. No one wanted to live in Trona. The stink permeated everything. Some even said, the metal skin of the cars.

"Come back here, you asshole. You're too smug. Tell me what you got."

I turned back and said deadpan. Words concerning Jimmie came tough. "I know who killed Jimmie Poe."

For a micro-second, his mouth sagged open before he regained control. "You've got to be shittin' me?"

"I got the killer's moniker. I just need access to the OSS computer."

Hamond quickly sat in his big chair and typed on his keyboard. "I've got access. Go with your information."

"Check for the name Wizard."

He looked up and stopped typing. "We've already been down this road. There's gotta be five hundred gang members named Wizard. Predominantly Hispanic gang members. Grimes has already checked it out. Nada. Zip. That's the best you got?"

"No. Cross reference it with DOH."

Hamond smiled and added in the additional information for the search. He sat back and stared at the screen with a stunned expression.

"What?" I asked. "Who is it?"

"First tell me how you got to it? How you've linked up DOH with this mess?"

"Come on, don't do this."

"Do what?"

"You're gonna give it to Grimes and freeze me out. Do it after you're the one who gave me the assignment in the first place. You were even specific in my marching orders."

"I also told you to go easy. And what did you do? You went right out and screwed the pooch. That's what you did. Not in any small way, either. Did it right out in the open in front of God and everyone. In my wildest dreams, I couldn't have...never mind. Now give. How do you know it's DOH? We knew about the Wizard tattoo but not about DOH. That changes everything."

Through clenched teeth, I asked. "What's his name?"

Hamond stared, hesitated a long moment. "You and I both know what you'll do if I give you the name."

"It's what you wanted, wasn't it? The nuclear option. It's why you called me in and went against orders from the top who wanted to exclude me from the investigation."

He said nothing.

"You don't give me the name. It'll take twenty-thirty minutes to call up a gang guy and get it from him."

Hamond thought about that. "Jessie Wannamaker. He has a house in Phelan, not five miles from where you found Poe. You're right. This is probably the guy. It fits the tattoo and the location."

I stood to leave.

"What are you gonna do?"

"I'm gonna talk to Wannamaker."

"Dave, he's DOH. He'll have a whole house full of motorcycle thug assholes. Tell me how you got to this guy. We'll call in Grimes and get a game plan together. We'll go at these guys hard, I promise you. But we still need to take this guy down the right way. Wait, let me run him CNI and NCIC." His fingers again worked the computer, the keys clacking. He suddenly sat back in his chair, disappointed.

"What?" I asked.

"Jessie Wannamaker died more than two years ago, a 187 at the Sundowner Bar in Cajon Pass. The Jimmie Poe killing just got cleared, exceptional means."

Chapter Fifty-Two

I sat in Captain Hamond's office, stunned. The death of DOH's Wizard wasn't fair. Jessie Wannamaker killed Jimmie Poe, and then later, he too was killed in a knife fight in a bar. In no way could that be considered poetic justice. Wizard didn't deserve to die in a bar. He needed to live out a rotten, horrible little life in Pelican Bay's Supermax. That equated to one hour of sunlight per day (only if he was a good boy) and total exclusion from any human contact. That was the big one. People need to be around other people, or something in them dies. The will to live gets snuffed out.

They only get to see four concrete walls, hard plastic, and steel bars twenty-three hours out of every day. In Supermax, the prison personnel use modified hard plastic laundry carts to move the inmates around. They slide the cart up to the hard door. The inmate slips in; they close the cart locking the inmate in. They then wheel him wherever he needs to go within the prison environs. Keeping him from harming other inmates and prison personnel. Treating them like dirty, smelly laundry.

Brutal on the psyche. The liberal thinkers call it cruel and unusual punishment. The surviving victims call it fair. The guards call it being able to go home at night. I guessed I was now one of those surviving victims and found Jessie Wannamaker's disposition fell far short of fair.

Hamond said, "We still need to know how you got to DOH. How you linked them to Poe. I'm guessing it came from whatever you were doing last night out on Hickory. That also changes things." He stood. "I need to brief the executive staff. If they let me work a little of my verbal magic without being too fed up with your antics, I might be able to cover for you. This is good work, Dave. You saved the department a lot of man hours and the county huge court time costs."

"Yeah, that's my job, saving the county money." I stood.

Hamond stopped in front of me. "Write your sup on this, brief Grimes, and then take two weeks off until all of this crap has time to settle down. Lie low. I mean it. That's an order."

Two weeks off. I could use the time to find Dad. But not even that idea could fill the huge hole created from the lack of closure. A hole large enough to cause an ache in my chest.

Half of Jimmie Poe's body had been washed away, her bleached white pelvic girdle left out, exposed to the sun. The other half gnawed on by domestic dogs. Then there was the chamois and the bone-rattling around in my trunk. Sweet Jesus. How in the world could I accept a computer's data return as a disposition for that kind of situation? One so personal.

At least I could write a supplemental report and leave out the part about Jimmie being an outlaw motorcycle gang groupie who only joined the department to be a double agent. I could at least protect her reputation. I wouldn't be the only one who'd figure out that part. But like me, they'd let it die a quiet death rather than stir up the newshounds into a feeding frenzy.

Poe had two bullets in the back of her head.

What had she been thinking seconds before the first one was fired? Had she been thinking about a life wasted. About whether it was going to hurt? Was she afraid to die?

Of course, she was afraid to die.

Was she thinking about me?

There it was again, the self-centered, egocentric crap.

I wanted to kick something in Hamond's office. He'd already walked by me and out past Debra Ann, headed to executive staff country across the hall. I pulled back to kick the wall and stopped. I'd only break a foot.

I did what Hamond ordered. I asked Debra Ann to page Grimes, 911, to return to the office. I'd brief him on what I discovered. He'd then shut down the entire operation, call off the dogs. Then I'd write up the sup…and what then? If I took time off, I'd go crazy for sure.

I could run down Sloppy Joe for the murder warrant. He had another house up in the high desert that I could knock. Yeah, I could do that.

* * *

Two hours later, I'd briefed Grimes and had written the sup. I was careful to compare the dates of death. The date when Jimmie Poe left her note and abandoned her job and the date Wizard was killed. There was a three-day span in between where Wizard did what the DOH was best at, ruining the world for others. In and of itself, in my mind, that wasn't enough to clear the case of "exceptional means." Wizard more than likely did it, but I needed more.

I pulled the autopsy report on Jimmie and found a note from the pathologist that confirmed Jennifer Fitzpatrick's statement about her sister, what Jimmie had told her: *"Left glutinous maximus muscle has a recent irregular shaped scar, possibly made from a laser."*

The removed tattoo: *"Property of DOH."* That about clenched it. If Wizard was still alive, the circumstantial case would be enough to take to a jury and get a conviction. Most times with murder, circumstantial was as close as you got.

I pulled the homicide report that chronicled Wizard's untimely demise and found the case ended as a twofer. Two for the price of one. A rival motorcycle gang member was arrested and convicted of a smoking-knife type murder. The deputies arrived on scene with the suspect still present. With blood on his clothes, the knife on the ground. He also made a spontaneous, unsolicited statement: "I killed him, the chickenshit bastard. He deserved it. And I'd do it again, too. The guy spit in my beer." Later in court, he tried to get the statement suppressed due to the amount of alcohol in his blood that "impaired his good sense." Didn't work. The jury probably didn't believe he had enough good sense to be impaired. He was now working off a sentence of twenty-five to life in the Q. Out in twelve and a half. *If* he kept his nose clean.

Jennifer Fitzpatrick needed to be told about her sister's killer. I owed her that much. I wandered out to my detective car and once again headed up the Cajon Pass to the high desert.

Chapter Fifty-Three

y mood continued to sour as I navigated Cajon Pass and then the side streets south of Bear Valley, where I finally turned south on Hickory. The street looked entirely different in daylight and took on an almost normal Andy of Mayberry appearance. Odd how darkness can shroud an area with an evil intent.

I stopped at the last stop sign on southbound Hickory. Close enough to see biker thugs standing in the yard in front of Leo Archuletta's house. There to commiserate the loss of commerce the recovered stolens represented. Someone had dragged a fifty-gallon drum around to the front and lit a fire. Orange flames licked at the sky, and black smoke roiled into the air. All of them had beers in their hand, some even drank from 40-ounce, Old English 800 bottles. Malt liquor with a lot of knock-you-on-your-ass kick.

A throng of Harley Davidson bikes sat at the roadway edge, again dispelling the hometown USA atmosphere and dropping that evil vibe over the entire block.

As I drove closer, I picked out Leo himself holding court amongst his peers of black knights. He'd bailed out of jail, of course. The justice system in place to protect the innocent and wrongly incarcerated also did the same for the worst society could offer. A malignancy that apparently could not be excised without killing the host.

But that wasn't what further soured my mood. Across the street, standing in the yard, stood Big Babe talking with Jennifer Poe. I should've driven on but was obligated to Jimmie to protect her sister. Or was it a pang of jealousy salted with a bit of dislike. Okay, something stronger than dislike.

I pulled up and parked in front of Jennifer's house. Big Babe stopped mid-sentence to scowl. The MC group across the street grew more obstreperous. One threw a beer bottle that hit the telephone pole by the detective car. Broken glass and foam rained down. The air filled with the scent of fermented hops.

Out of the house, next door stepped Walter with his trusty shotgun loaded with buckshot. He sat in a lawn chair facing the barrel fire and the drunken thug uglies. I got on the radio and asked for the watch commander at Hesperia station to go to channel three. I briefed him on the situation and asked for a marked patrol unit to sit on the street, at least for a couple of hours. Hickory, now a powder keg.

I got out, took off my suit coat, and tossed it in the car. The sheriff's star clipped to my belt and .357 in plain view, so later in court, they couldn't say they didn't know I was a cop. I took the walkway up to Big Babe and Jennifer.

"You got balls showing your rat-face around here."

Jennifer reached out and put a gentle hand on Big Babe's arm. "Tito, be nice."

I ignored Big Babe for fear of what might happen. He had two or three inches on my six foot and outweighed me by forty pounds. I wouldn't play fair, and if he pushed it, I'd shoot him in the leg point blank. I tried to imagine what that would feel like for me pulling the trigger. Whether it would relieve some of the pressure behind my eyes rising to a peak. "Mrs. Fitzpatrick, would it be possible to talk to you in private?"

"Hell no, she's not gonna talk to no rat-bastard like you."

"Hush. Tito, please don't use language like that around me. Let's go into the house, detective."

"What do you have that this punk wants?"

I couldn't tell him even if I wanted to. If I said I was there to investigate the death of Jimmie Poe he'd figure out Jennifer's game. Then I remembered Jimmie's status with the gang. Remembered that, in all likelihood, the piece of shit standing before me probably knew Jimmie in the carnal sense. He and his entire group of outlaw thugs knew her that way. They were the entire reason for Jimmie's death.

Rage boiled over. I opened my mouth to say the words that would light off the fight when a car came roaring down Hickory. A sheriff's marked patrol car from Hesperia station. Another one came seconds behind it.

Big Babe pulled back to slug me. I trapped his arm, swung him around in a bar-arm, and kicked his legs out from under him. We slammed to the ground, me on top. He grunted hard, all the air knocked out of him.

Two deps ran up and pounced on his back as he struggled to get away. We got him cuffed and stood up. I didn't recognize the two deps but appreciated them a great deal.

Jennifer had fled the sudden violence. She'd gone into the house, did it without so much as a whisper of sound. The thug uglies across the street yelled and threw bottles that clumped to the ground around us. Some shattered. One of the deputy's reached for his lapel mic to call for backup. I stopped him.

"It's over. We don't need any more drama. Could you book this guy for PC 243? I'll be along to fill out the probable cause declaration."

Big Babe continued to make an ass of himself, struggling and calling all of us names, his face bloated red in his rage.

"No need." The dep said, "I saw what happened. I can write it for you."

"Thanks." That wasn't the response I expected. I expected a cold shoulder after what I'd done the night before, to one of our own. To a Sheriff's captain, no less.

The two deps took the struggling Big Babe to the cop car. I said, "He's already out on bail, so also book him on that section for committing a crime while out on bail."

"I got it, and hey, thanks."

"Thanks?"

"Yeah, Cordoba's a major dickwad. You'll never have to buy the drinks, least not up here in this desert."

"Thanks."

"Not a problem. How long you going to be out here? We'll keep a presence until you're done."

CHAPTER FIFTY-THREE

"Twenty minutes, and thanks again. I do appreciate the help."

The one let go of Big Babe with one hand and waved as they escorted him away.

I turned, walked to the door, and knocked.

Jennifer didn't answer. She didn't want to talk, not to me. I ruined everything for her, including her attempt to infiltrate the DOH through Big Babe.

I opened the door and stuck my head in. "Hello? I'm coming in."

I stepped in and closed the door. A coffee mug soared past my head, bounced off the wall without breaking, fell to the floor, and shattered. A good shot. She'd thrown it based on the sounds I made.

I eased over to the other side of the room, keeping my breath low, inaudible. She came and stood at the back of a living room chair and spoke to where I used to be. "What are you doing back here? Haven't you done enough?"

I said nothing and moved up behind her. Her ragged breathing covered my movements. I placed my hand on her shoulder. She didn't hesitate and swung. I caught her arm and pinned both arms against her body.

I said, "I don't want you associating with the DOH anymore."

"You have no right to tell me what to do."

I let her go, moved around, and sat on the couch. "I know I don't. I came here to tell you we know who killed Jimmie."

Her hand reached out, feeling for the chair, found it, and sat. "Tell me."

Chapter Fifty-Four

I sat in Jennifer Fitzpatrick's small living room, watching her facial reactions flush red. All her well-laid plans were ruined. Six months' work gone. She'd gone all-in. She'd done her research on the DOH, found the best place to set her trap, then sold her house in Upland and moved to the high desert, Hesperia. She struck up a relationship with the DOH, in particular Big Babe. She put her life on the line.

All to have me come in and overturn her apple cart.

"Tell me!" She again demanded.

"Like I told you last night, your sister had a tattoo of a Wizard on the small of her back. 'Wizard' is a moniker for Jessie Wannamaker."

Her mouth sagged open, and her eyes widened. She tried to stand and couldn't. Her hand slipped off the armrest. "But Wannamaker's dead. He died two years ago. Wait, you mean that—"

"That's right. How do you know about Wannamaker?"

"Tito told me, of course. I haven't been sitting on my hands for the last two years. I've developed quite a bit of intelligence on the gang. If you're saying he did it, that he killed my sister, then all of this is for naught."

Now she sounded a little like a sad wannabe cop groupie with the double-O Seven syndrome, the thrill of the hunt snatched from her grasp.

I said, "Wannamaker was killed in a knife fight two years ago in a bar. Three days after your sister disappeared. Sometime in that three-day window, he killed Jimmie and buried her in the desert not too far from his house. Not far from the gang's clubhouse."

Her chin rose up, "Wait. Three days after she disappeared?"

"That's right, I personally checked the dates."

"When did Judith leave the department the first day she didn't show up for her shift? When did she leave the note?"

"On the third of May. Wannamaker took the shiv to the chest on the sixth, three days later."

"No, I don't believe it. She came by my house on the third of May. I know because she picked me up and drove me to a routine doctor's appointment. She said she had to go to work later that day. We talked. She sounded so happy. She said that the whole mess with internal affairs was over, that she was in the clear. She was going to call you and ask you out to dinner."

The only way Jimmie could be confident about the IA investigation was if she heard from a source that the department couldn't prove their case against her. They couldn't prove that what she'd written—what I'd written— on the booking app for Nico Sumter had anything to do with his death. Which was possible. I got up and went over to the phone on the kitchen wall.

"What are you doing?"

"Checking on something."

I dialed Hamond's direct line. He picked up, "Homicide, Captain Hamond."

"Captain, I need you to check something for me."

"Dave? What are you doing? You're taking two weeks off, remember? Or was I just dreaming that part of our conversation?"

I ignored his question. "Only someone with your kind of juice can get the information I need."

He said nothing, doing a slow burn.

He finally said, "Leave it alone, Dave. The case has been cleared, exceptional means."

"I want it locked up tight. Don't you want it locked up tight?"

More silence. "What do you need?"

"Thanks, Captain, you won't regret this."

"There is no way in hell I won't regret this but go ahead."

"Could you please walk over to IA and pull—"

"Son of a bitch, Dave. Are you kidding me?"

261

"I just need to know if the investigation against Poe had been cleared due to lack of cause."

"I do this, you'll let it drop? Let it go to sleep like it's supposed to, now that we know who did the killing?"

"Yes, of course. Why wouldn't I? I'm just dotting the i's and crossing the—"

"You're an asshole."

"Put me on hold. I'll wait while you check."

The phone clicked, and music came on.

Three minutes later, he came back. "You're right. The case was in the crapper. They couldn't prove the motive or the intent. Now, what does this have to do with—"

"Had IA notified Poe yet?"

"Hold on." Click. The music again.

Only this time for one minute. He came back on. "How did you know she wasn't notified?"

I closed my eyes and put my head against the wall. Jimmie had somehow found out she was off the hook. Which meant the note she left was a total sham. The note now became part of her murder. Someone other than Jimmie had written it. A forgery.

"Captain?"

"No, Dave. Son of a bitch. Don't do this. Don't you dare do this."

"I have information that Poe knew the case was a no-go. That means—"

"Yeah, shit. I know what it means. It means you just couldn't leave it alone. Could you?"

"You want the same thing I want. You want the right—"

"Shut up. Just shut up a minute and let me think. Not two hours ago, I briefed the executive staff that this thing was all wrapped up. Now you're making an ass out of me. Your bullshit is once again bleeding over onto the rest of us."

I let him continue his rant and turned around. Jennifer stood close, listening to the conversation. How long had she been there? She could move like a cat. How much of the captain's side had she heard? She smelled wonderful. Her brown hair gleamed. Her eyes were—

CHAPTER FIFTY-FOUR

"Okay," Hamond said, "Here it is. We are labeling this one code purple."

Code purple didn't exist. It was something he just pulled outta the left side of his ass.

He continued. "You, and you alone, will follow this very weak lead until you run up against a wall. If you find something, fine. I'll go back to the executive staff hat in hand and ask for forgiveness. If you don't, then we very quietly let it die just the way we have it now. Angina, Dave. You're giving me angina." He slammed down the receiver.

I hung up. Jennifer stepped away. I kinda liked her standing close.

I was an idiot. An attraction to a witness involved in a murder investigation equaled bad juju on too many levels.

She said, "What are we going to do now?"

"We? You're out of it as of right now. No more dabbling in murder and mayhem for you."

"So, you're saying you got this?"

"Yes, and I promise to keep you appraised. Right now, you should work on getting packed up and moving back down the hill away from DOH where it's safe. Can you get your old job back?"

"Just hold on, cowboy. I'm not moving one inch until you put this thing to bed. If you don't in the next, say, twenty-four hours, then I'm back in. I was making headway before you stuck your big bazoo into my life. Just horned right in. I would've gotten to the bottom of it on my own. I was almost there."

"Is that right? Run this out for me. What was going to happen when you did figure it out. When someone like Big Babe told you what actually happened? Were you going to throw him to the ground and handcuff him for conspiracy and then go after Jessie Wannamaker?"

"Now you're being ridiculous."

She turned to walk away. I reached down and with two fingers, took hold of her two fingers. She froze and slowly turned back to face me.

I lowered my voice, which came out with a little rasp, "I love your moxie, your need to find out who killed your sister. But take it from someone who knows, your involvement was going to have only one outcome and—"

"And what?"

"You're too nice to end up that way."

The silence between us started to manifest in a way that, like before with Jimmie, scared the hell outta me. I stepped back. "I'm sorry. If I only have twenty-four hours to solve this thing I need to get on the road."

She listened to my retreating footsteps until I reached the door. She said, "What are you going to do?"

"What you said a few minutes ago about Jimmie knowing the IA case no longer having any merit? That's what's going to solve the case. That means *you* solved the case."

Her hand flew to her chest, over her heart. Tears filled her brown eyes. It was the stupidest thing in the world, but I never wanted to kiss someone more. I was a fool for thinking I could. We hadn't known each other long enough. I hadn't earned it.

Her other hand slowly rose, extended out in front. A silent request.

I muttered. "Ah, ta hell with it." I hurried back to her. Took her in my arms and kissed her. With no thought at all that I might've misread the signs.

She didn't resist and gave herself to the kiss.

All that pressure behind my eyes, all the stress fell, dissipated the same as a morning mist when the sun hits it.

Chapter Fifty-Five

I tried to pull away from Jennifer Poe, extract myself from the tangle, her body, and mine. Kissing her was wrong on so many levels. The biggest one fell under the violation of department policy about cavorting with a witness, victim, or…even suspect. To cavort wasn't exactly the term used in the written mandate, but it fit far better than "thou shalt not fraternize."

The definition of cavort: *to apply oneself enthusiastically to sexual or disreputable pursuits.* That's exactly what I had in mind right in the middle of that wonderfully hot kiss. I couldn't help it, the desire an undeniable force.

That's why I forced myself to break from the embrace. Only she wouldn't let go. She held on tight, ran her fingers up into the hair at the back of my head. Her body hot to the touch.

Maybe I wasn't trying hard enough to break away.

On another one of those oh-so-bad levels: This was Jimmie Poe's sister, for crying out loud. How wrong was it to cavort when I should've been out chasing down her killer?

She leaned up on her toes and hushed a hot breath into my ear.

I stood on the edge of disaster. I fought the urge to pick her up and carry her to the couch to continue what I should never have started.

I gently pushed her away. "Wait. Please stop. I can't. Not right now. I need to finish this first."

She turned her back to me, her arm around her waist as she bent slightly, her other hand covering her face as if ashamed.

I came up behind her and put my hands on her shoulders. "Please don't do that."

She tried to tug away. She turned back to face me, her eyes big and brown and wet. Beautiful. The memory of the kiss and holding her in my arms demanding that I do it again. Was I only interested in her because she reminded me so much of Jimmie? Reminded me of those wonderous three kisses that night under Trigger? Reminded me that I had pushed Jimmie away and now here was a second chance to right that wrong that had dogged my thoughts for the last three years?

She said. "Then you better get after it, Cracker Jack. A woman can only wait so long." She smiled, her face wet with tears. "What are you going to do with that information?"

"The note?"

"Are you going to tell me that it's against department rules to release information in an ongoing investigation?"

"You cracked it. You have every right to know." She didn't have that right, but I didn't care anymore. "Whoever left that note is the one who killed her. And—"

She'd brought me back to reality, brought me back to thinking about the case.

She said, "What is it. You just thought of something?"

The woman had honed her intuitions to a fine point. I took her hand and led her over to sit on the couch. We automatically sat close, our knees touching. I moved away, the distraction would cloud all logical thought. And worse, judgement.

I said, "The note was found in her apartment."

"Right. I know all about that."

"I read the missing person's report and the homicide sups once homicide jumped into the investigation. The witnesses who lived around her didn't mention any DOH thugs coming to her apartment. And DOH wouldn't have for fear of exposing—" I stopped myself from saying, "exposing their double agent." I hadn't told Jennifer about her sister's complicity in a felonious conspiracy to leak law enforcement information to the Disciples of Hate.

"Exposing what?"

"Ah…I mean…Listen, you can't see these guys. They are despicable in

266

every respect. It makes them very visible. They have long, dirty hair, tattoos, heavy boots, chains hanging from their jackets and pants. Someone would've seen one of these guys if they came to her apartment."

"I understand. That makes sense."

"And—" I stood to get further away from her orbit. Without doing it on purpose, I was still thinking about our kiss still present on my lips. I walked around the small living room area. "...And that note is now part of the instrumentality of the murder. It does not in any way fit the DOH's MO. Not when it comes to their common method of murder and mayhem. They always, always make a statement. They make it loud and messy." I snapped my fingers. "Son of a bitch."

"What?"

The investigation just shifted again. I sat down in the chair to think it through. Jennifer waited, let me have the time.

It was someone Jimmie knew, someone close enough to know about the IA investigation in order to write the note. But not close enough to know that the department IA dogs had been called off. They'd used the note as a reason for Jimmie to disappear and be deemed a missing person. That person would also have to know all about the DOH. Know enough to bury her out by their clubhouse. And at the same time close enough to Jessie Wannamaker's house to throw off suspicion. That couldn't have been a coincidence. There were no coincidences, not working homicide. Was that enough to throw Jimmie's murder back onto the DOH?

No way, not with the note and the location of the body dump. DOH was not that sophisticated. And whoever did it had to have access to Jimmie's apartment.

So, who fit that criteria?

It had to be someone close to Jimmie. It had to be. Someone who knew enough to throw the murder off onto the DOH.

I turned to Jennifer. "Hey, talk to me. Tell me about Jimmie's friends. Who did she talk about? Who did she—"

Talking it through made another coin drop in my memory. I snapped my fingers again.

"What? I'm not sure I know of any of her friends."

"One night, I dropped Jimmie off at a friend's house out in Baldy Mesa. It was too late, with too much alcohol involved, to drive down the hill. I think it was in Baldy Mesa. A double-wide mobile home. Do you—"

"Valerie. Judith talked about staying with a woman. When Judith was first assigned in the desert and before she got an apartment of her own, she stayed with Valerie. When I asked if I could meet Valerie, Judith said, "Naw, she's not the kind of person I'd bring around." I remember it because I'd thought at the time that if Valerie wasn't that kind of person, why was my sister hanging around her in the first place?"

"That's good. That's really good. Did Jimmie say anything else about Valerie? Anything at all?"

"No. Can't you remember where you dropped Judith off that night? Can't you try and drive it again. Recreate it. I'll go with you." The excitement in her words rose. Tantalizing. Sparking desire, yet again.

"I'd love to take you with me but what if I come across something that needs to be checked? I'd have to leave you in the car. Taking you along would expose you to the wrong element." I came over and kissed her forehead. "Stay by the phone I'll call you with whatever I find."

I opened the door to leave.

She half-whispered. "That's not fair, Cracker Jack. That's not fair."

Chapter Fifty-Six

I wandered out to the detective's car on the street, too caught up in conjuring the memory of that night. The one underneath Roy Roger's rearing horse, Trigger. Jimmie's long, deep kisses, in the moonlight, the way she felt in my arms. And then wrongly comparing it to what just happened with Jennifer.

The kisses with Jennifer, not seconds ago, similar in every respect including the overwhelming desire to spend more time with her. I'd screwed that up with Jimmie and didn't intend on making that same mistake.

A marked Hesperia patrol car sat across the street. One house south of the biker gang get-together.

I got in my car, still thinking about the past. How I drove Jimmie to her friend's house that night, the directions she gave. Pulling up street names from her words. The memory seriously marred from her sitting next to me. And me doing nothing about it. Me being afraid to take that giant step. Afraid of commitment. What a fool.

I came out of my funk to the sound of a closing door. Jennifer, in a nice dress with stylish military boots and a sweater, came out using her white cane with the red tip.

"Now what?" I said to no one.

Simultaneously, Walter with his shotgun came out of his front door, got into his sand-blown Jeep Grand Wagoneer, backed up, stopped in the street, and hurried over to Jennifer. He helped her to the passenger side.

"Ah, what the hell." I got out. "What's going on?"

She rolled down her window. "Did you say something, detective?"

"What are you doing?" I spoke around her to Walter who'd returned to the driver's seat. "Walter, what's going on?"

He shrugged, "She said she wants me to drive her to Baldy Mesa. Said we're gonna be looking for a double-wide mobile home on a little hill with an elevated spit of land that goes out to it. Shouldn't be too hard to find. Before the big crowd moved into the high desert, I used to go out that way a lot to get firewood."

I said, "Jennifer, how did you know the description of the mobile home?"

She smiled. "I guess I just remembered it. Come on, Walter, let's go, we're burning daylight." She let out a little chuckle at her joke.

This wasn't good. I put my forehead against the support post on the jeep. Trying to think. "Walter, this is not a good idea. Going out there will lead to nothing but trouble. I'm asking you please not to do this. To let me handle it."

"Dave, I guess I'm a sucker for a pretty face. I'm gonna do whatever Jen asks me to do. Sorry, Buddy." He started the Jeep.

I yanked open the back door to the jeep and got in. I tapped her on the shoulder, "We are going to talk about this as soon as this is all over."

She smirked, "I would expect nothing less."

Walter looked up. I caught his eye in the review and clocked his jealousy. "Backup to my cop car. I need to get a few things."

He did as I asked, and two minutes later, we headed for Baldy Mesa, the little voice in my head screaming that this was a bad idea.

* * *

Two hours later, Walter had me thoroughly turned around and lost in Baldy Mesa's arroyos, hillocks, and rolling foothills. We'd first tried back-tracking using my memory of what Jimmie had told me that moon-drenched night and fell short of the goal.

Walter too often took us cross country rather than using the roads. The jeep's occupants bouncing all over the interior until I'd had enough. But kept on, afraid of appearing too much like a weak sister in front of Jen. She

2

had to have been having a worse time of it not being able to see.

Walter suddenly stopped. The dust cloud caught up and engulfed our vehicle, settling on the paint and glass, blending us into a desert sand dune. That's what the desert did, it reached up and took control of all those who would invade, pollute, and attempt to reside in a place humans didn't belong.

The dust cleared, but the view remained obscured through the windows. The quiet and total lack of movement didn't matter, my body kept going, the same as your legs did when stepping onto shore after a long stint at sea.

"There. What do you think, Dave? That look about right to you? That's the last one of those kinds of hills that I can think of."

He only said that the last three times we stopped. I couldn't see out the windows and got out.

We still sat about three hundred yards from the little hill. Just like the others he bird-dogged for us, this one also had a double-wide mobile home.

"To tell you the truth, Walt, I don't know. Like I said it was dark that night."

"Look there, it's got that little spit of land that goes out to the hill jus' like you said."

"Could be." I bent over to stretch my bound-up back when Walt's door closed. I jumped back in just as he took off. He almost left me behind. He did it on purpose.

Instead of driving around the hill on flat terrain to find the public access to the property, Walt shifted into four-wheel drive, drove the three hundred yards across the desert floor to the base of the hill, and then straight up the side. I reached up and held onto Jen's shoulders. "Hold on, Walt's trying to kill us. Walt?"

Jen patted my hand and laughed. "Walt knows what he's doing."

"Hey there, Dave, you need to take a breath, or Jen's gonna think you're some kind of sissy boy."

The jeep rocked from side to side going over dips and bumps while climbing almost straight up. At least it seemed like it was straight up. A tree trunk wasn't as steep.

We crested the top and bounced to a stop right in front of the mobile home's front door. This one had the right kind of wooden stoop, only now more weathered. The yellow light bulb over the door almost cinched it for me. But in the bright daylight, it still looked different.

A grungy man in a raggedy black heavy metal tee shirt, denim pants, and barefoot stepped out on the stoop, holding a pistol down by his side. He hadn't shaved or taken a bath in who knew how long.

"Git the hell off my property, now, or I'm gonna shoot your sorry ass."

I said, "Stay in the jeep." I got out holding up my sheriff's badge. "Sheriff's department. I just want to ask you a couple of questions."

He flipped the gun back into the mobile home, did it with just his wrist as if trying to hide his movement. "I got nothin' ta say to no stinkin' law dawg." He backed up ready to flee inside and close the door.

"Wait. Just wait a minute, would you? I promise I don't care if you're wanted or what you got going on inside your home."

He hesitated. "You got a warrant?"

"I don't need a warrant to talk. And all I wanna do is talk." I came around the front of the jeep with my hands raised. "My name's Dave Beckett. Come on down here, and just let me ask you a couple of questions."

Jen got out with her red-tipped white cane. "Mister, my name is Jennifer. He's telling the truth. We just want to ask you a couple of questions about my sister."

"I told you to stay in the car."

She whispered as she walked past, using her cane as guide, "You're not the boss of me, Cracker Jack."

This had to be the way Hamond felt when I did exactly opposite of what he told me to do.

"You got a blind woman along with you? What the hell's that all about?"

Jen said, "My sister was murdered, and we're looking for the killer."

I cringed. When interviewing a subject, you never gave away your hand until you absolutely had to. Now the guy on the porch had too much information to use to dodge around my questions.

The man said. "Well, I didn't kill no one if that's what this is all about."

I stepped alongside Jen, got ahead of her, and stopped. "Look, you don't want me to do this the hard way. I can come back with your probation officer if you like. Then, we'll conduct a Bravo Search terms search. You think you could survive that?"

"How do you know I'm on probation?"

"I don't go anywhere without researching everyone who lives at the location."

Jen poked my back with her cane and whispered. "You're bluffing. That's dangerous, what if he's not on probation?"

I didn't turn around and swiped at her cane still stuck in my back. "Hush."

The man on the porch looked inside and then back out as he weighed his options. "Okay, you get two questions." He came down the porch.

Chapter Fifty-Seven

The man came down the rickety wooden porch steps. He meandered over to an empty wood spool that once held wire and sat. The yard area was cluttered with spools of every size. There were also two fifty-five-gallon drums with their tops cut off and fire-blackened. He put one dirty foot up on his knee. As if he now sat on the stage of one of those talk shows where no one had all their front teeth. A show where they had black-shirted bouncers standing by, ready to break up the fistfights when someone claimed to have had carnal relations with the other's girlfriend.

I walked over to him and stood to the side, so the sun wouldn't shine in my eyes. I wanted to read his expressions when he lied. He shifted to face me.

"What's your name?"

He shot me a quick smile, showing off a meth-mouth filled with yellow and black teeth and unhealthy gums. "That gonna be one of your two questions? You sure you wanna waste it on a name?"

I took a step closer. "We're no longer playing any stupid games. Now you're out in the open where I can put my hands on you. Look around. You have everything I need to make a case for theft and stolen property. You're stealing wire from the phone and electric companies and burning off the rubber sheaths. Then you sell off the copper. You're gonna answer all my questions or find yourself sitting in the Victorville jail. Pick your poison."

He lost his smile and abruptly brought his foot down off his knee as if getting ready to bolt. Behind me a shotgun racked. The sound struck fear in those who understood what it meant. I didn't have to turn and look. Walter had pulled out his gauge.

"What's your name?"

"Hector Collins and I don't live here."

"You're lying. I'm not in the mood to play the name-game. I don't really care what your name is. Do you live here or not?"

He hesitated and then nodded after he had a chance to think about it.

"Who else lives here with you?"

"Does Valer—"

"Jennifer, please don't say anything." I turned back to Hector. "Do you live here with anyone else?"

"I share the rent with a couple of guys. Why?"

"Guys, no women?"

"No. Why?"

"How long have you lived here?"

"Six-seven months."

Jennifer and Walter got back in the Jeep, getting ready to go.

"Who do you rent from?"

Hector squirmed a little.

I said, "I don't care if you have a rental agreement. I don't even care if you're squatting. I just need to know if a woman lived here three years ago."

Jenifer got back out of the Jeep and returned closer this time, five feet away.

"I tolt ya, I've only lived here for six or seven months so how would I know?"

"Street talk. You know what's going on. You talk to people."

Jennifer said. "I'll give you fifty dollars."

Hector's head whipped around to look at her. "Lemme see the green."

She reached into a slip type pocket in her dress and extracted a wad. She pulled off the red rubber band and thumbed passed three hundred in twenties until she came to a fifty. She peeled it off and held it out.

Hector started to jump up. I kicked him in the chest, knocking over the spool he'd been sitting on. I didn't want him anywhere near Jennifer. The kick came out of instinct and nothing more.

Jennifer still held out the bill. "What's going on? What's happening?"

Hector coughed and choked and writhed on the ground, making a little dirt angel.

When I didn't answer, she said. "You're a brutal man, Dave. I didn't think that before, but I do now."

I walked over, grabbed Hector by his tee shirt, and yanked him to his feet, tearing the shirt half off. "Tell me."

He held up his hand. "Okay…Okay. I got a paper. Someone stuck to our door. An eviction. Says we gotta get out. Says the marshals will be coming to kick our ass out in thirty days. I'll get it. Just don't kick me again. Ya about kicked a lung out."

I followed him up the two steps. He stopped at the top. "You can't come in."

"I'm not gonna let you arm yourself. I told you, I don't care if you have a full-blown meth lab in there. I work homicide."

"The paper's right inside the door on the floor where I tore it off and threw it down. I'll jus' reach inside and get it."

I took out my .357 and held it down by my leg. "Slowly, you understand."

"Dave?" Jennifer said.

Hector said, "What the hell's the matter with you? You some kinda Wyatt Earp?"

"Get the paper."

"All right. Take it easy." He reached in. His hand came back out with a paper, one with official writing. I'd seen similar admonishments a thousand times working the street. It was like he said, it was an eviction notice. He handed it to me. I holstered my gun, took the paper and took hold of his arm, escorting him down the steps and back to the stool where he sat.

Jennifer took a couple of steps, offering the fifty. "I'm sorry about all this."

She wasn't cynical enough and too vulnerable to live across the street from Leo Archuletta.

Hector scurried over, his eyes locked on me, and grabbed the money. He retreated back to his spool and sat. The kick taught him a lesson.

I uncrumpled the paper and read the top part, all boilerplate until I got to

276

the bottom.

Owners:
Val Verde Property Management Inc.
14943 Bear Valley Road
Hesperia Calif. 92345

I walked over to the Jeep, helped Jennifer get in. I got in the back and closed the door. I'd worked patrol in Hesperia and knew the hundred blocks by rote. I told Walter to take us to Bear Valley and Cottonwood. He said nothing. Put the jeep in gear and took off. This time using the public access.

Chapter Fifty-Eight

I n the jeep, Jennifer asked. "What'd you find out? What was on the paper?"

Walter jockeyed the steering wheel over the washboard road until we finally hit the asphalt, and smooth sailing. I wasn't sure how he could see through all the fine dust that had settled on the windshield.

"Just another lead that's taking us somewhere else. Hector had an eviction notice from a management company. We're going to check with the management company's records to see who was living in the mobile the night I dropped Jimmie off. Hopefully, it'll be someone named Valerie."

"You think the management company will just give up the records without a court order or something like that?"

"No, you're right, it could get sticky. We might have to wait for a subpoena to be issued."

Only it didn't work like in the movies when the good guys just pulled a court order out of thin air. To get a subpoena I had to go through a district attorney, and the DA had to have an open case to assign the subpoena to. I wasn't officially working a case. If the management company played hardball, we'd be left without any options.

It would take us twenty-five or thirty minutes to get back to Hesperia. Walt drove like a crazy man off-road, but on the pavement, he was a ninety-year-old woman who only drove on Sundays to pick up her weekly cigarettes and Schlitz malt liquor beer.

I stared out the window, thinking about Jennifer and what would happen after the investigation ended. And it *was* going to end. They usually ended abruptly without warning. I now had a firm hold on the thread that would eventually unravel the entire sweater. I'd been there before and recognized the feeling. The scent of the prey growing fresh.

Then my thoughts shifted to our rag-tag trio, two of which were just along for the ride. It was okay to have them while searching for a house, but now I would need at least the appearance of professionalism to talk the management company out of their records. The odds weren't good that the next contact would be successful.

We popped out at the Summit. Walter navigated the jeep onto the 15 freeway north and got off at Bear Valley Road. He headed east.

I could almost picture the strip center in my head, even the offices. I just couldn't conjure up an image of Val Verde Management Company.

The strip center came into view, and the anxiety started to rise. In the past, I'd been able to talk my way around some of the most obstinate "keepers of the record," and hoped I could do it again.

Walter took his foot off the accelerator. The jeep slowed. He looked in the rearview. "Dave, we got company."

I turned around. Out the dusty back window, a Sheriff's marked patrol car from the county station was pulling us over using its rotating red lights.

"Walt, don't stop here. We're almost there. It's right there on the right. See it? Pull in the parking lot."

"The cop's not gonna like it. They get angry when you don't pull over when they hit you with the lights."

Jennifer reached over and put her hand on his arm without saying anything, her head still turned, facing the open window, taking in the warm desert air. Her eyes seeing nothing at all, missing out on the empty blue sky and desolate desertscape.

The cop bumped the siren when we didn't pull right over.

"It's okay." I said, "Almost there."

Walter stuck his arm out the window and pointed so the cop would know he intended to stop just down the road a piece.

"You two stay in the car. This time I mean it. You don't listen to me this time, you'll get me into trouble for sure."

Walter pulled up and stopped. He nosed the Jeep close to the big plate glass window of Val Verde Property Management company. The window had a multitude of 8x11 ads for property for sale. On the inside, plainly visible, three women sat at four desks, one desk empty.

I got out of the jeep and looked back at the patrol car, hoping I knew the deputy. I let out a sigh of relief when Seven Sam Three got out. He'd pulled up behind the jeep, blocking any chance of escape.

"Beckett, what the hell? You just can't stay out of trouble, can you?"

I held out my hands. "What I'd do this time, Sarge? I'm just driving around minding my own business."

"Apparently you're not. Cordova put out a stop and detain on you. He's down at HQ and heading up here code-three. What'd you do this time?"

"Nothing. The guy we talked to in Baldy Mesa must've had more balls than I gave him credit for. He must've called in and complained, and dispatch called Seven Charlie."

"Then, for sure, you're in a bind. He's got you, like you had him when you stopped him for a duce." Oscar shrugged. "I thought he'd wait until things cooled down a little before he made a play to get even. Now it'll look too much like stomping a whistle-blower. I guess he doesn't care about the optics. He just wants a piece of your ass."

"I haven't done anything."

"That's exactly what he was telling the board of deputy chiefs about his drunk driving arrest. You never should've poked that bear. What are you doing ridin' around in an old Jeep Wagoneer doing follow-ups with these two?"

I lied. "I needed to get in some out-of-the-way places, and Walter here volunteered to help."

"And the woman?"

I squirmed a little.

"Dave? Who's the woman?

"She's Jimmie Poe's sister, Jennifer Fitzpatrick."

"Ah, for cripes sake. Are you kidding me?"

"Yeah, I know. I couldn't shake either one of them without causing a huge problem. So I brought 'em along."

He shook his head and pointed to the window. "Whatta ya doing here at this place?"

"I'm trying to run down a renter, a woman who knew Jimmie."

"The Jimmie Poe killing's all wrapped up. We got the word from downtown. They told us you solved the thing, and the killer got himself killed all on his own. You're telling me that's not the case?"

Hamond had admonished me to tread lightly and not to overturn the apple cart. Yet again. Hamond preferred that the Poe homicide remained closed.

"I was just trying to make the case a little stronger, so I can sleep at night."

He had his thumbs hooked in his gun belt and chuckled. "You know I'd like to see into that messed up brain of yours just for a couple of seconds. Your worldview must really be...ah, unique. It's got to be like some kind of acid trip. Brain cells misfiring all over the place. Airplanes dropping out of the sky, devasting earthquakes. And filled with nothing but people who kick dogs."

I started to go inside, not real pleased with his description of me. I liked and respected the man too much.

He reached out and took hold of my arm. "Whattaya doing?"

"Cordova isn't here yet. I thought I'd go in and get the information I came for."

He let go. "You're not gonna stir up some giant shit storm, are you?"

"Of course not. I just want to ask who lived in a particular mobile home on a particular date. Is that okay, papa? Come with me. I can use the uniform as a little extra motivation."

He followed me in the door.

Chapter Fifty-Nine

The bell on the door to Val Verde Property Management jingled as we entered the cool air-conditioned office. The three women had been watching us through the window, probably wondering what the heck was going on.

I took in each woman in turn looking for the manager and spotted the desk deepest inside with the monument that read, "Valerie Greene, Manager."

I headed over to that desk and slowed when my eyes locked on hers.

I knew this woman.

She wore a plain, unremarkable pastel dress. Her hair was in an up-do that had been in style a decade or two ago. What caught me up short and put me on alert was her body language: stiff, ready to flee as if guilty of something. She stood when we walked in. Her hand hung down to her side next to the open desk drawer. But it was the anger and vehemence in her expression that caused me to stop completely.

And then, all on its own, her face popped up in my memory.

"Ah, shit."

Behind me, Oscar said, "Dave, talk to me, what's going on?" He moved to the side and stayed back three feet in a good flanking position to cover.

I brought my left hand up while my right slowly made its way to the .357 on my hip. "Now, just take it easy, Valerie."

Again, from behind. "Dave?"

"Sarge, this is Captain Cordova's wife."

"*God damnit*, Dave. Back out of here now. Don't do this. You tricked me into this."

He thought that if I couldn't go after Cordova himself, that his wife would be the next best target of my misguided revenge. And that I hadn't told him my plan. He didn't know I had no idea she'd be there or, more importantly, the part she played in the whole mess.

I had not known her name the night before when she picked up her drunk husband after I arrested him. I had also not put her face to the woman on the stoop to the mobile home the night I dropped Jimmie off. But now I had. No doubt about it.

And she was acting guilty as hell.

"You!" She finally spit out.

She yanked a Colt .38 from the desk drawer and fired.

I gave the order to my hand to draw my gun. But it wouldn't comply. At least not quick enough to save my ass. The first bullet stung my right ear lobe. The second clipped the top of my right shoulder and spun me around. Good thing. The third one would've taken me in the right upper chest.

As I fell to the floor, the other two women in the office screamed. White smoke filled the air in the tight confines. The plate glass window shattered and fell in sheets.

The gunshots continued to tear the delicate fabric of society.

Seven Sam Three stood tall in a shooter's stance and shot until his gun clicked empty.

His rounds took Valerie Greene in the torso, neck, and face. She wilted straight down. Her face bounced off the open desk drawer before she hit the floor with a wet smack.

It was all over in three seconds.

I struggled to my feet as the two women ran from the office screaming.

Oscar stood stock still, staring at the place where Valarie Greene once stood. His expression, one of shock. His gun still up and aiming down range.

Oscar Fuentes, Seven Sam Three, my good friend, took a bullet to his upper abdomen, his tan uniform shirt turning dark maroon.

I got to him and took hold of his arm. He shook me off. He slowly turned to look me in the eye. He tossed his gun which clattered to the floor.

He reached up, unpinned his badge, and tossed it as well. He turned and staggered, almost fell. I caught him.

"Outside." He said. "Get me outside."

I helped him out the door and over to the wall, where I eased him down. I put my hand on his wet wound.

With tears in my eyes, I keyed his lapel mic. "Sixty-Two Henry Eight. Shots fired. Shots fired. Seven Sam Three is down. Roll med aide. Expedite med aid. 14943 Bear Valley Road. Expedite, Expedite."

But it didn't matter. I'd seen enough death to recognize the glazed-over look in Oscar's eyes.

I slid down the wall and sat next to him. I picked up his hand and held it.

Walter got out of the jeep and cautiously came over. "Beckett, you're bleeding." He had a roll of paper towels he'd gotten from somewhere. He took off a long run, balled it up, and pressed it against my shoulder. Blood instantly soaked all the white. "Son, that was...that was—"

"Walter, stand up, turn around, and put your hands on your head. Do it right now, please."

"Why?"

"You hear all those sirens? Those cops are rolling in hot to a volatile situation. They're pumped up on adrenaline, believing one of their own is down. You don't want them to make any mistakes. Stand up, go on, do it."

He did as I asked.

"Damnedest thing I ever saw. One of them bullets went right through that winda, came right through the windshield. It's okay, though. Missed us both. Jen's okay."

From the jeep came Jen's voice. "Dave? Dave, are you okay?"

I wasn't okay. I, too, wanted to take my badge and fling it out into the street over what I had just caused.

Out on the street, cop cars slid sideways and banged up the driveway into the parking lot. Cops appeared from all sides, guns drawn. None of them yelling "Show me your hands." They saw Seven Sam Three sitting next to me. Me holding his hand. They saw all the blood. They saw my tears that wouldn't stop flowing.

Two deps ventured inside and came back out. One of them asked for an eta on med aide and, at the same time, asked for homicide to respond.

I was Homicide. Homicide *was* on scene.

A dep appeared and knelt next to me with a first aid kit. Another started to handcuff Walter, a precaution until things got sorted out. "No, don't. It's okay, he's with me."

Another car skidded to a stop out on the street, the parking lot too full for him to enter.

Captain Cordova, in a suit and tie, came running up. He didn't slow to take in the two downed deputies sitting in front of the building. He ran right on into the building.

From inside came a horrific keening like that of an animal out in the wild with his leg caught in trap and the realization that life as he knew it was over.

Chapter Sixty

Four hours later I sat on the hospital bed waiting to be discharged, my shoulder already stitched up—well, stapled anyway, and my mutilated earlobe bandaged. I couldn't tell which hurt the worst and that was with painkillers onboard. What kind of pain would tomorrow bring? The pain, in this case, helped tamp down the emotions that threatened to choke me. I no longer wanted to be a cop. And law enforcement had defined me for too many years. It had destroyed my marriage.

Captain Hamond appeared at the curtain. He came in and sat in the chair. He stared at me. A huge lump grew in my throat, and like a kid on the playground, I fought back the tears.

He finally said, "You don't have anyone, friends, family? No, I guess you wouldn't. You're Dave Beckett, the bone detective. Your job is your life." He, too, recognized the situation with just one glance.

"I'd like to think you're my friend." My words were pathetic, a weak sister's attempt to solicit the comradery, that I so desperately needed. Had to have.

He said nothing.

I asked. "How bad is it? It must be pretty bad if Homicide hasn't come to interview me yet." Homicide always interviews the crooks last. Once the crime scene has been worked and the wits and victims interviewed, all the information possible is gathered first before the suspect is given his chance to bury himself.

Now, I was the last to be interviewed.

I was the criminal in this stupid little play.

Hamond kept staring at me. Finally, he said, "You didn't fire your gun. That scene out there is one godawful mess, with witnesses out the ass. And to tell you the truth I don't know how you came out of it unscathed. I mean it looks like you did nothing wrong. My homicide guys are just giving you a break after what happened." His tone shifted lower. "Oscar was a good friend. We went through the academy together."

"I'm sorry. I had no idea that was going to happen. I still don't understand why it did."

Hamond nodded. "Do you know why his badge was tossed on the floor?"

I knew, but I would never tell. Oscar thought that he had helped me in some sort of demented vendetta. After I thought about it, though, I guessed my involvement really didn't matter. I'd been worried about being a pariah for just arresting a captain. He'd just shot and killed a captain's wife. In an instant, I had ruined his career, his legacy, his life.

Oscar had been ready for retirement, and he didn't go out in a way he'd ever have imagined. A horrific, senseless slaughter that punctuated a sterling career.

"No, I don't, captain. I don't know why he tossed it. He was in a lot of pain. Maybe he didn't know what he was doing."

Another long silence.

Then Hamond said. "Cordova copped out. Spilled his guts about the whole sordid affair."

"Why did Valerie kill her friend Jimmie Poe?"

"Somehow, Jimmie Poe found out that Valerie Greene was working for The Disciples of Hate. You had the why right, you just had the wrong who. Apparently, Valerie belonged to the DOH and had been tasked with getting close to someone high up in the sheriff's department. Back when Cordova worked narcotics, Valerie was a snitch for him. Cordova can be a cold fish, and the whole social scene with women didn't come easy for him. Once Valerie blew in his ear, he fell head over heels in love. Valerie took control of him. He gave her any information she wanted. You know, he worked homicide for a while as a sergeant before he was promoted out. When Jimmie decided she would rather be a cop than a biker's old lady, Valerie felt threatened. Cordova admitted that he deep-sixed at least two homicides linked to DOH. That's aiding and abetting after the fact. In addition to all the other operations against DOH that Cordova and Valerie informed on. They were exposed to thirty or forty years in prison. That was the motive. When you showed up with a uniform, she thought she was going to prison for the rest of her life."

Now, it all made sense.

Maybe that was why Cordova was such a dick to all his subordinates, he hated himself for what he'd become, for what he was doing to the job. He hated being a hypocrite.

Hamond stood. "You wanted the Poe murder wrapped up with a big red bow. Well, you got what you wanted." He walked over to the curtain and put his hand on it. "If you're up to it, there's someone here to see you." He slid the curtain aside and disappeared for a moment. He came back, escorting Jennifer.

"Dave?"

"I'm over here."

She followed my voice right into my arms. I buried my face in her neck and hugged her like there was no tomorrow. She kept wanting to talk. I wouldn't let her. I wasn't ready yet.

* * *

Three hours later, after the homicide interview, they wheeled me out of the hospital in a wheelchair to my waiting detective car. Jennifer was driven home by a patrol dep. I told her I would come see her the next day. She said, "Rest up first. Don't come until you're ready."

My overheated sense of paranoia heard instead, "Don't bother to come."

I sat in the car, staring at the hospital wall. I got out, opened the trunk, and retrieved a backup duty gun. Did it without a second thought. I felt naked without one. Back in the car, I sat and looked at it and, for once, saw it for what it was: a tool of destruction.

And I was nothing more than a burnt-out greyhound with thousands of more rabbits to chase. I'd lost that desire to pursue.

I started the car, backed up, and headed out of the hospital. The parking lot was almost empty at three o'clock in the morning. I wanted a drink and knew if I took one, it'd be the end of me.

I rolled the window down and took in the cool desert air on my face as guilt continued to smother me and the world.

I'd gotten Oscar killed.

I reached down, unclipped my sheriff's star from my belt, and tossed it out the window. This tired greyhound was officially retired. No more. My thoughts shifted to how I would go about hunting down Dad. Maybe talk him into opening another café, just him and me. The fledgling idea forced back the guilt and let a little air into my lungs.

I wasn't in a hurry and meandered down side streets before going to the freeway. I naturally gravitated to Hesperia to the south, where I had once worked patrol.

I popped out on Main Street, also near vacant. I turned west, headed now for the 15 freeway.

Red and blue lights in my rearview caught my eye. Two Hesperia units a mile back, coming fast, were chasing a full-sized Ford F-150 truck. The sight of them confirmed it: I was done. I didn't get that hard pang to jump in and help, to join in the chase.

I was through for sure.

I pulled over at Cottonwood and waited for them to pass as the law dictated.

The Ford truck came on fast but braked a little to make sure the intersection at Cottonwood was clear. In that split-second, as the truck rolled through the intersection, I got a glimpse of the driver.

Joseph Jamison.

Jo Jo Jamison.

Sloppy Joe.

"Oh, hell no." I reached down, clicked on the police radio, and then the unit's siren and red light. I fell in behind the two patrol cars.

As I did, I tried to remember exactly where I'd thrown my badge out the window. I'd be doing a lot of walking along the road once the sun came up.

A Note from the Author

The incident with the drunk driver and the Highway patrol chasing him right by me when I was driving home is true. What happened subsequently was changed to serve the story. The pursuit of the 300Z on Ranchero Road and then the tracking of the suspects across the desert is also true. Seeing that car full of mud and the suspects nowhere around was shocking.

The main plot thread about the rape suspect has been modified to fit the story. I did arrest that rape suspect at his front door based on his spontaneous statement. He went to prison for a long time.

The landlord/tenant dispute happened pretty much the way I wrote it with some minor tweaks. The talk with the shrink afterward I tried to write exactly the way I remembered it.

The interview with the bank clerk happened the way I wrote it, but I could not break her from her story and the suspect was not under the bed. This one was wishful thinking. I knew what had happened, knew she was the suspect and they got away with it.

The murder suicide with the three deputies did happen. I put it in as backstory because I knew two of the victims, one was a good friend. I just could not write the scene. My wife and I received a phone call at 3 am telling us what happened. They didn't want us to hear it from some other source.

The stolen car at the gas station with Danny Dyer (not his real name) watching while he drank a cup of Joe happened exactly the way it's written. As did the arrest in the conversation with Danny Dyer about sitting across the street from a mortuary and observing a different gas station. Then the fight afterward.

A good friend who was involved in the landlord tenant shootout did, tragically, commit suicide.

291

Growing up I was estranged from my father and didn't get to really know him until much later in life.

Way back when, I did have someone's stomach pumped on his birthday and it made case law on search and seizure.

When I was working narcotics, my team did hit a house and we did wait for the owner/suspect to come home. Dopers continued to come to the door to buy dope. We set them on the living room floor and put in *Scarface*, the movie with Al Pacino. We also bought them all cheeseburgers and milkshakes. In the end the suspect heard on the street what was happening, and he did call his house and ask us what we were doing there.

And finally, my team was tasked with tracking down a homicide suspect and in reading the case file I found the chamois story. It happened pretty close to the way I wrote it.

The victim was identified through the tattoo on the chamois. The interesting thing about this true-life story was the suspect was a woman. And after tracking her for days me and my team finally found her in a house, two miles from where I lived with my family. It's a small world.

Acknowledgements

Most of all, I would like to thank Harriette Sackler, a great editor who all too often puts up with this temperamental author. Thank you, Harriette, I owe you.

And a big thank you to Shawn Simmons, I have never met a more dedicated, hard-working editor. Great job, Shawn.

About the Author

During his career in law enforcement, best-selling author David Putnam has worked in narcotics, violent crimes, criminal intelligence, hostage rescue, SWAT, and internal affairs, to name just a few. He is the recipient of many awards and commendations for heroism. *A Lonesome Blood-Red Sun* is the second novel in the Dave Beckett, Bone Detective series. Putnam is also the author of the very popular Bruno Johnson series. *The Sinister* is the ninth novel in the best-selling Bruno Johnson Crime Series, following *The Disposables, The Replacements, The Squandered, The Vanquished, The Innocents, The Reckless, The Heartless,* and *The Ruthless.* Putnam lives in the Los Angeles area with his wife, Mary.

SOCIAL MEDIA HANDLES: twitter.com/DavePutnam
   Facebook.com/DavidPutnamBooks
   Instagram.com DavidPutnamBooks
   www.Goodreads.com/davidputnam

AUTHOR WEBSITE:
   www.davidputnambooks.com

EMAIL:
   David@DavidPutnamBooks.com

Also by David Putnam

With Level Best Books:

A Fearsome Moonlight Black

With Oceanview Publisher:

The Disposables

The Replacements

The Squandered

The Vanquished

The Innocents

The Reckless

The Heartless

The Ruthless

The Sinister

The Scorned (coming 2023)

The Diabolical (coming 2024)

Printed in the USA
CPSIA information can be obtained
at www.ICGtesting.com
LVHW091059250124
769598LV00004B/133